Coastal Lights Legacy – Book One

REBEL LIGHT

Marilyn Turk

Marilyn Turk

ISBN-13: 978-1-946939-75-3
ISBN-10: 1-946939-75-7

PRAISE FOR REBEL LIGHT

"*Rebel Light* by Marilyn Turk is an absolutely delightful yet compelling read. If you like Civil War stories, romance, and heart-pounding action, you will love this book!" --- **Kathi Macias**, award-winning author of more than 50 books, including *Red Ink*, Golden Scrolls Novel of the Year.

"Rare is the novel that explores deep issues such as life on the Civil War home front, slavery, racism, and finding true love through the lives of compelling characters. Marilyn Turk achieves this and more in *Rebel Light*, a story that touches your conscience and your heart." --- **Henry McLaughlin**, award-winning author of *Journey to Riverbend*.

"*Rebel Light* is a sprawling look into a turbulent past that slowly ratchets up the tension and romance in a way sure to delight fans of sweet historical fiction. The setting is deftly drawn, putting one firmly into Civil War era Florida with eye-opening clarity. I like a book that transports me to another time and place, and this fit the bill. Well done, Ms. Turk!"--- **Linore Rose Burkard**, Award-winning author of Regency breakout novels for the CBA.

DEDICATION

To my husband Chuck, who endured my ramblings about historical facts and fictional characters with a fine line dividing the two, and who joined me in my quest to learn more about the history of the Florida panhandle.

I'd also like to dedicate this book to Cecil Murphey, whose encouragement enabled me to write it.

Chapter One

February 1861
Gulf of Mexico

Footsteps pounded overhead, jerking Kate awake.

Where was she?

Muffled men's voices grew louder when a loud thump above accompanied a burst of light into the area where she lay.

She sat up, her eyes gradually identifying shapes through a haze of dancing specks of dust. Wooden crates stacked upon each other, barrels and large sacks beside them - she was in the hold of her father's ship. Now she remembered.

She hid there the night before.

Her throat tickled from the musty air as she untwisted herself from the cramped position where she'd slept on the floor wedged behind crates. Rolling her shoulders to ease the ache in her neck, she stood to stretch her long legs that begged to straighten. Placing one hand against the rough planked walls, she tried to find her balance in the rocking ship. A mixture of odors from the crates and stale sea water in the hold soured her stomach, and she strained to inhale some of the fresh air coming in through the newly-open hatch above.

"I'll get it. It's in one of them barrels down there," a man called out, as he came down the ladder into the hold.

Kate ducked back down behind a stack of crates. She wasn't ready to face her father yet. Not before she'd prepared an explanation for why she was there. It was a last-minute decision to go to the docks and hide onboard her father's ship, instead of traveling north to Alabama with Aunt Elizabeth and the household servants as they evacuated Pensacola. She hadn't really meant to lie, telling her aunt she would ride with her friend Sarah's family, even though Sarah knew nothing about it. But she had to do it. Her world was coming apart as she watched families leave their homes, scatter and separate in all directions due to threats of war. She had to stay with her father, or when would she see him again? Surely he would understand why she was so afraid to say goodbye this time.

Her eyes watered and her nose tickled. Oh, dear, no. Too late she realized she was next to a crate of chickens, those creatures that always made here sneeze. Kate's heart raced, and she held her breath while she listened to the sailor whistle as he moved boxes around. *Please don't come over here.* She pinched her nose to stifle the oncoming sneeze.

Time crawled as she waited for the man to leave. She held her lace handkerchief tightly over her mouth. But her efforts were useless.

"Achoo!" Kate sucked in her breath.

"Who goes there?" the man called out.

For a moment, all she heard were chickens cackling and waves splashing against the boat. Kate waited as long as she could, trying not to sniff. She didn't hear him anymore. He must have gone back up the ladder. She leaned around a crate to peer at the hatch opening.

"Ouch!" she cried out, as her head was yanked back

when someone grabbed her hair.

"Gotcha!"

Her heart pounding against her ribcage, Kate spun to face her captor. The man's mouth fell open as recognition registered. "Well, look who we have here! The Cap'n's daughter - a stowaway! The cap'n don't like stowaways, ya know. Makes 'em walk the plank," he chortled.

"Let me go!" She jerked her hair out of his hand.

"Almos' didn't see you, but when the sunlight hit that blazin' red hair o' yourn, it lit up like a candle!" The annoying, toothless deckhand laughed at his own remark.

Betrayed by her hair - that long, wavy mass of red curls she tried so desperately to control. Someday, she'd cut the culprit off.

Kate got to her feet, standing eye to eye with the man, and shot him an angry look.

"Better come on now, miss. We gotta go see the cap'n."

Kate leaned over and picked up her valise that had served as her pillow. The man gave her shoulder a little nudge toward the hatch. She whipped around, her loosened hair slapping him in the face. The startled deckhand stepped back.

"I'll thank you to take your hands off me, sir!"

"Yes, ma'am. Ain't you the feisty one? The cap'n sure is gonna be surprised! Heh, heh."

Kate moved to the ladder and climbed with one hand, the other holding her valise against her skirt to hide her ankles from the man below her.

Bright morning sunlight temporarily blinded her as she poked her head through the opening of the deck. She gulped in the fresh salt air. Then she saw the silhouette of her father at the ship's wheel. Bracing herself for the confrontation, she pulled herself up and stepped out.

~

"Katherine Mary McFarlane! Great Scott! What in heaven's name are you doing on this ship?" Captain

Andrew McFarlane stood with his hands on his hips, scowling at his daughter.

Kate reluctantly lifted her gaze, trembling at the fire in her father's coal black eyes.

She'd always thought him so handsome in his dark blue and white captain's uniform, but he didn't look attractive now. Just angry. Very angry.

"Well? What do you have to say for yourself, young lady? What are you doing on my ship?" The frosty air formed steam coming from his nostrils.

"Papa, I didn't want to go with Aunt Elizabeth. I wanted to be with you," she pleaded.

"And your aunt agreed to this request?"

"Well, no sir, not exactly. She thought I was with Sarah's family," she whispered.

"And why did she think that, Katherine?" Hearing him use her proper name was not comforting. "Did you lie to her? Did you lie to your Aunt Elizabeth?"

"I . . . I didn't mean to. I just thought . . ."

"Katherine, you know better than that. You have really done it now, lassie. Elizabeth will have a spell of angina when she discovers the truth. How insensitive of you to put your aunt in such a predicament!"

His words stung, and her eyes filled with tears.

"I'm sorry, Papa. I didn't mean to upset her. But if I had told her the truth, she would never have let me come with you."

"Nor would I. This ship is no place for a young woman. What am I supposed to do with you?"

"I can help you on the ship. I can be one of your crew." Muted chuckles came from the men standing around them, watching the encounter with amusement. She leaned in closer to her father, clasping her hands. "You've taught me how to sail and how to handle a boat."

Her father glared at his crew. "Men! This is none of your affair. Carry on with your work!" Lowering his voice, he inclined his head toward her. "Katherine. These are dangerous times with a war brewing. And you're not qualified for this type of sailing. This is not a little skiff like we sailed in the bay."

"But Papa, I must be able to do something." Tears streamed down her face as her heart squeezed in her chest. "I can't go back home. Nobody's there anymore."

"No, Kate," he said, his voice softening, "you cannot go home. None of us can. Maybe when this cursed turmoil is over, life will get back to normal again . . . but you cannot stay with me. At the moment, I don't know what to do with you, but you cannot stay on this ship!"

He spun around and addressed the tall mulatto man behind him. "John, take her to my quarters so she can make herself presentable."

Kate looked down at her rumpled blue and white gingham dress and tried to smooth it out with her hands, then pulled her shawl together to steel herself against the brisk February wind

"I'll see you at dinner, Kate." With a parting glance, her father strode away, hands clasped behind his back, muttering loudly enough for Kate to hear, "Thank God, her dear mother isn't around to see this."

Kate stood helpless as she watched him go, helpless and unwanted. She lowered her gaze and noticed the dark smudges marring the pale skin on her hands. She wiped them on her skirt, then reached up to twist her loosened hair and tuck it under, increasingly aware of how unladylike she must appear. Was she an embarrassment to her father? Her cheeks grew hot under the scrutiny of the sailors who glanced sideways at her while going about their duties.

John walked up and took her by the arm. "Come on, Miss Kate. Let's get you down to cap'n's quarters." He scanned the darkening sky. "Look like a storm comin'."

"John, what is Papa going to do?" Kate searched the Creole man's face for the usual smile, but found none.

What was that expression? Disappointment? She'd never seen him so serious. Her lips trembled. Was he upset with her too?

John studied her a moment, then shook his head. "I'll fetch you some water so's you can clean youself up fo' dinner."

Kate implored him with her eyes. "John, why doesn't Papa understand that I should be with him?"

"Miss Kate, I'se afraid you de one who don't understand. Sometimes you gots to think about people besides youself. This sho is a mess you got him into. I wouldn't want to be in his shoes right now. No suh."

Kate dropped her head and took a step in the direction of the captain's quarters.

~

"I've been thinking about where to take you, and I've arrived at the best possible conclusion." Her father pushed his dishes aside and unrolled a nautical chart.

Kate peered up at him. "Where, Papa?"

"Your great-aunt Sally's home in Apalachicola. She's family, and you should be safe with her."

"But I don't even know her!" Her fork clattered as she dropped it on her plate.

Aunt Elizabeth had said Aunt Sally was eccentric, whatever that meant. She was the widow of Kate's great uncle Duncan, her grandfather's brother, who had been a sea captain like generations of McFarlane men back in Scotland. He had died of yellow fever several years ago. His son, who was her father's age, had married and also become a sea merchant, but then he too caught the dreaded disease and died. Aunt Sally must be a very sad and lonely woman.

"You'll know her soon enough. It's about two days' journey from here."

"I wish I could stay with you, Papa."

Andrew McFarlane gazed at his daughter with

tenderness glowing in his eyes. He reached over and patted her hand. "Aye, Katie, I know these times are troubling. But my place is at sea, and yours is on land. You're a young woman now, and the sea is no place for a woman. Soon you'll marry and have a family of your own."

Marry? Whom would she marry? Despite Aunt Elizabeth's best efforts to involve her in social engagements and find potential suitors, Kate had never found anyone to her liking. No one ever measured up to her father – in stature or character. All her friends had beaus or husbands, but she wondered if she'd ever find someone to love. Aunt Elizabeth said she was too picky.

Kate sighed, twisting the napkin in her lap. Reluctantly she glanced back up at her father. "How long will I have to stay there?"

"Only the good Lord knows when this madness will end, Katie. Hopefully, it'll be soon."

"But when will I see you again?" Kate's heart wrenched as she fought back tears. "When will you come back and get me? Before my birthday?"

"Ah, Katie, how could I possibly miss your birthday? But that's still some eight months away. However, I'll move heaven and earth to be with you on your important day as I always have."

At least she could count on one thing in her life to stay the same.

Kate's father pushed his chair away from the table. "Come, Kate, let me show you something. Take a look out the window."

She joined him at his side as he pointed to the clear night sky, its sparkling stars shining against the vast blackness. "See this glorious creation, Kate? That same God who made this beautiful world will be watching over both of us. We're connected to each other because we're connected to Him. You just have to trust Him."

"I'll try, Father."

Her gaze shifted away from the window to the wall, where the glint of a brass lantern caught her attention. Pointing to it she said, "What type of lantern is that?"

Her father reached for the lantern, lifting it from the hook. "This is a signaling lantern. It belonged to my father, your Grandfather Donald. It's a 'prototype,' one of the first ever made. There were two of these crafted in New York several years ago. The other one belonged to my father's brother, Uncle Duncan."

"How does it work?"

Her father showed her a lever that made the shutter slide back and forth when moved. "There's a special lens inside that magnifies the light and allows it to be seen for miles."

"Like a lighthouse?" Kate leaned in for a closer look.

"Well, I suppose you could say it's similar. It creates a flashing pattern similar to the Morse code. If a ship is in distress at night, it could send a signal."

"Have you ever used it?"

"I only know a little of Morse code, but I have the handbook if I ever need to know more. Your Grandfather Donald and Uncle Duncan used to send signals to each other for amusement, but thankfully I've never needed to send a distress signal."

A distress signal? Right now, she felt like sending one. But to whom?

~

Later that night Kate pulled the journal from her valise. *The time is soon coming when my father and I will separate once again. I am more afraid than ever because I'll be living with someone I don't know in a place I've never been. And what will happen to Papa? He says to trust God. I want to, but why did things have to change? Why did people start talking about war and scare everybody away from their homes? I hate those Yankees for making this happen!*

~

The next evening Kate's father took her up on deck and pointed to a light flashing in the distance. "See that, Kate? That's the light from the Cape St. George lighthouse."

"Is that Apalachicola?"

"It's on the island west of it. Thank God for the lighthouses. Without them, we'd surely get lost or end up shipwrecked. We should arrive at Aunt Sally's house tomorrow morning."

Tomorrow? The splendor of the nighttime sea dimmed in Kate's eyes, as she feared her future and mourned the loss of her past.

Chapter Two

The golden glow of morning sun appeared above the horizon, warming Kate against the chilly air as she sat in the skiff being rowed toward the opposite shore. Her heart raced with fearful anticipation. What would Aunt Sally be like? Would she be difficult to please? Angry to have an unexpected guest forced on her?

The little boat passed between the white sandy beaches of two islands, one with the lighthouse on it and the other named St. Vincent's Island, according to her father.

The water changed from dark blue to turquoise as it became shallow and clear enough to see the sandy bottom below. Seagulls cried overhead, swooping close to the water while the winter wind skimmed the surface, creating foamy whitecaps.

Kate scanned the shoreline. "I don't see a town." Did Aunt Sally live on a farm?

"Aunt Sally's house is on the outskirts west of town, so we'll reach it before we get to the town itself," her father said. As they drew closer to the mainland, he pointed ahead. "There. You can see the top of her house."

Her pulse quickened with anxiety as Kate squinted against the bright reflection off the water as a widow's walk appeared, perched on a roof peeking through the tops of the trees on the shore. The house sat on a small bluff overlooking the water. Dense palmetto undergrowth along the bank hid the rest of the house, and even the rooftop disappeared from view as they neared the shore. Thick marsh and reeds reached out to one side of a small sandy beach where they landed the skiff.

Kate's father ordered the crewmen to stay with the boat as he, John, and Kate climbed out. They found their way up a narrow path that opened onto a large yard with a grand old house surrounded by massive moss-draped oak trees. In the side yard, a short man in baggy clothes hoed a garden alongside a thin, light-skinned Negro woman.

Kate's father walked over to them. "Good day. Do you know where I might find Sally McFarlane?"

The man turned around and a woman's voice said, "I'm Sally McFarlane. Who's asking?"

Kate's jaw dropped as she reconciled the man's clothing -- trousers, hat, and work gloves -- with the female face and voice. Was she Aunt Sally?

"Aunt Sally! It's Andrew, Donald's son," her father said, removing his hat as he continued toward the woman.

Aunt Sally's eyes widened. "Andrew McFarlane! Why, what on earth . . . ?"

"I'd like to introduce my daughter, Katherine Mary McFarlane. Come here, Kate."

Aunt Sally looked at Kate. "Well, my, my, if you're not the spitting image of Margaret!"

Kate had heard that before – from her father and Aunt Elizabeth. The thick, curly red hair, the pale skin, the tall, slender body were like her mother's had been.

"Let's go inside where we can sit down and you can tell me the reason for your visit," Aunt Sally said.

Kate's father motioned to John. "This here is John, Aunt Sally. He's my first mate."

John nodded to Aunt Sally as she eyed him up and

down then glanced at the Negro woman standing nearby.

"This is Bessie. Come on in, Bessie, and let's get these folks some refreshments. Why don't you make us a pot of coffee? And let's get some of those teacakes you made yesterday. We can use a little rest before we get back to work."

Kate walked beside her father as they followed Aunt Sally, but approaching hoofbeats drew their attention to the road beside the house. A man in uniform reined his horse to a halt, and Kate's heart leaped at the sight of the handsome soldier.

The young officer tipped his hat. "Good afternoon!"

Aunt Sally glanced up at him. "Hello, Clay. What brings you out here?"

He smiled cordially down at the older woman. "Mrs. McFarlane, we observed a boat coming to shore and wanted to make sure you were all right."

"Why, thank you, Clay. This is my nephew Captain Andrew McFarlane and his daughter, Katherine, from Pensacola."

The soldier touched the brim of his hat and nodded in their direction. "Lieutenant Henry Clay Harris of the Franklin Rifles." His gaze lingered on Kate, who tried to avert her eyes from staring at the man with wavy, coal black hair and square jaw – perhaps the most handsome man she had ever seen. Her face grew warmer, as if he had touched her on the cheek. She reached up to tuck an errant strand of hair behind her ear.

Captain McFarlane extended his hand as he strode toward the man on the horse. "Pleased to meet you, Lieutenant Harris. It's comforting to know your men are protecting our citizens here."

"Yes, sir, we'll defend our shores against enemy invasion." Lieutenant Harris leaned down to and shook the captain's hand. "Pensacola? How is it there? We've heard reports of fighting between the forts."

"There've been no shots fired yet, but I expect there will be any day. The federals have moved into Fort Pickens across the bay, while state troops are arriving daily to support the other forts. That's why most of the townspeople are evacuating."

"And you, sir? Are you a navy man?"

"No, sir. I'm a sea captain and will continue to conduct my trade as usual for as long as possible."

"I see. Will you be staying here long?" Lieutenant Harris glanced at Kate, who tried to unlock her stare.

"Not I, sir, but my daughter may be here awhile. She'll be much safer here than in Pensacola."

Kate's cheeks burned as the men discussed her.

He returned his attention to the captain. "Very well. I'll make sure these ladies are looked after. You can rest assured we'll keep them safe."

"Then I thank you, sir."

Lieutenant Harris tipped his cap, then turned his horse around and trotted off.

Kate gazed after the rider as her heart beat wildly. Lieutenant Clay Harris had stirred her in an unexpected way. Would he come back again? Her heart fluttered at the prospect. She inhaled a deep breath and exhaled slowly to calm herself.

In the house Aunt Sally led them past a massive grandfather's clock to the dimly lit parlor, its heavy drapes blocking the sunlight. She motioned for them to sit down, then removed the man's hat and gloves and put them on the table beside her chair.

The woman's face showed signs of wear, like the house in which she lived. Wrinkles and sun-darkened freckles were framed by gray hair pulled into a long thick braid that fell down her back when freed from the hat. She wore a too-large man's shirt as well as trousers, rolled up at the top and the bottom. Kate towered over the woman, who couldn't have been five feet tall when stretched to her full stature.

"Well, Andrew, I gather this is not a social call on your old aunt."

"No, ma'am. As you may have gathered, I need to leave Kate here with you for a while."

Aunt Sally leaned forward in her chair, resting her hands on her knees. Kate studied her unusual aunt. Who was this little woman who exuded such strength and verve?

"So I understood from your conversation with Clay."

"Yes, as I was telling him, the state of affairs in Pensacola is not pleasant. In fact, I'm afraid the city will be even more dangerous when war breaks out."

"Aye, there's been a lot of talk around here about war too. You met one of our local boys who joined up with the state guard to protect our town from a possible invasion."

Kate noted the trace of Scottish in her aunt's speech as her father continued. "What course of action follows will more than likely be determined by what the new president, Abraham Lincoln, does. It's reassuring to know you have some protection here."

"But why did you bring her here, Andrew? Doesn't she have a guardian?"

"Yes. She was supposed to go north to Alabama with Elizabeth, Margaret's sister, and stay with relatives there."

"Looks like she got lost. This isn't Alabama." Aunt Sally's eyes twinkled as she glanced at Kate.

Kate's face warmed under her aunt's gaze.

"You're right about that. She ended up on my ship, quite to my surprise. I believe she wanted to be a deckhand."

"Ha! She did, eh?" Aunt Sally eyed her great-niece with a knowing smile. "And she has changed her mind now?"

What she had thought was a good idea now sounded foolish, hearing her father and her great aunt discuss it. Kate looked away, scanning the room while her future was being discussed. She noted the dusty furniture, aging upholstery, and a man's portrait on the wall with an uncanny resemblance to her grandfather. So that was Great-Uncle Duncan.

". . . so I was hoping you could take her in for a while."

"And what am I to do with a young lady? It's been a long time since there were any young people around here, much less young women. I don't have much to offer, and we have to work hard so we can eat."

"So it's just you and your servant, Bessie? You have no men to help out around here?"

"Just me and Bessie. Joe, Bessie's brother, died about five years ago, so we've been doing everything ourselves. We used to farm all the land around us when Duncan was still alive. That's one of the reasons he wanted his house so far from town. But after he died, we reduced our garden to what Bessie and I could handle. We get by all right."

So that explained it. The house was falling apart because there were no men around to help the women. How amazing that they had survived by themselves!

"Kate can help. Put her to work. If she could be a crewman on a ship, she can earn her keep here," her father said with a wink.

Kate tried to close her gaping mouth. What could she do? She had never done anything besides sew, do needlework, or tend the roses around their house in Pensacola.

Her father motioned to John. "John will stay here to help you women. He'll be able to do work you women can't do alone. I regret he won't be with me on the ship; however, I feel you need him here more than I do now."

Kate's shoulders relaxed. It would be more like home with John's familiar face around. Yet she remembered John telling her he was looking forward to being on the ship again, something he hadn't done in several years. Her stomach wrenched with guilt, knowing it was her fault he would have to stay. As she glanced from John to her father, she realized this decision had been made before they arrived.

"Well, now, that presents a different situation. We'd certainly welcome the extra hands." Aunt Sally looked over at John, still standing by the doorway.

John nodded his agreement as he smiled warmly. Bessie lowered her gaze as she moved past him to serve the coffee.

"Well, then, Andrew, looks like we have an agreement. How long do you expect this situation to last?"

"I wish I could tell you. I'll be going south to continue my trade in Cuba where I have business associates, but a lot depends on whether there's a war or not. I did, however, promise Kate I would be back for her birthday in September. That's as far as I can predict for now." He stood and offered his hand to help Aunt Sally up.

The group walked out the back door and headed for the water.

"Are you sure you can't stay the night? You've not had much time to visit."

"I'm sorry to leave so abruptly, Aunt Sally, but I'm already behind schedule."

Kate winced, knowing she was to blame for his delay.

They all walked down to the shore to see her father off. Before climbing into the boat, he hugged Kate tightly. "I love you, Katie. You'll be all right here. John will take care of you. And I'm pleased to know there are soldiers nearby who'll keep a watch over the area as well. I pray God's protection over us all until we meet again." He reached out and clasped John's shoulder. "John, you take care of these women."

"Yes suh. I'se gonna do dat, Cap'n,"

"God go with ye!" Kate and Aunt Sally said in unison, repeating the family's age-old Scottish farewell.

Captain McFarlane got into the boat and cast off, leaving the others standing on the shore, waving goodbye.

Tears ran down Kate's face as she watched her father go away once more.

Chapter Three

"Rise and shine!" Aunt Sally's robust voice rocked Kate out of her deep slumber.

Coming into the bedroom, Aunt Sally threw open the curtains, revealing a gray pre-dawn sky.

"What time is it?" Kate groaned, straining to open her eyes.

"Time to get movin'. We've got work to do! Get yourself dressed and come on downstairs."

Kate sat up and hugged her knees as she scanned the unfamiliar room. Aunt Sally's house -- her new home, at least for now -- was so unlike her home back in Pensacola. This room bore no resemblance to her own sunny warm bedroom with bright yellow gingham curtains, matching quilt, and bright golden wallpaper. What a dreary place. The sparse furnishings, plain bare walls, and drab curtains were stark reminders of her situation, as if she'd been put in jail for her disobedience.

Kate shivered in the cold room and pulled the covers up to her chin. For once she was happy to have such long, thick hair to keep the cold air off her back. Why was it so chilly in there? Her gaze fell on the dark fireplace. Aunt Sally had said they used their wood for cooking and only lit the fireplaces when it was really cold. Surely it was cold enough for a fire now. After all, it was winter.

She continued to survey the room, noting the little table next to the bed with only a kerosene lamp sitting on it. On the opposite wall between the two windows was the washstand with a bowl and pitcher. The only hint of color came from the faded old patchwork quilt on the bed. Apparently this had once been the bedroom of Aunt Sally's son. Maybe sunlight would brighten the dull room, whenever the sun came up. Right now, though, it still seemed like evening. And felt like it too.

Kate quickly dressed, stopping before the mirror to braid her hair, coil it around, and tuck it into itself. Then she wrapped her shawl around her shoulders and hurried downstairs. When she walked into the dining room, Bessie handed her a cup of steaming coffee. Kate turned her head away from the aroma rising from the top. She'd never cared for the strong brew, but the hot cup warmed her hands.

Aunt Sally noticed that she didn't take a sip. "Aren't you going to drink that? You'll need it to get you going this morning."

"Actually, I prefer tea. Do you have any?"

"Ha! Well of course, a proper young lady would prefer tea. Problem is, we don't have any around here. I used to drink tea myself, but I've become more accustomed to coffee. In fact, I haven't had any tea since my dear Duncan brought me some from England many years ago -- even though I do believe they sell it at the mercantile. Looks like you'll have to develop a taste for coffee until we can get you some tea. It'll help warm you up."

"Thank you. I'll try it." Kate braced herself to get the hot drink down her throat. The taste of burnt wood assailed her tongue, but she was grateful for the warmth as the fluid trickled down her insides.

"Well, how about some breakfast? Bessie's got some biscuits cooking already. Why don't you take that basket over there and go out to the henhouse with her? You can help gather the eggs, and she can introduce you to her children."

Children? She hadn't seen any children, but she dared not go near a henhouse. Bessie went out the back door and paused on the porch, waiting for Kate.

"Well, go ahead. Take it." Aunt Sally thrust the basket at her.

Kate hesitated to grasp the handle, as if it were going to bite. How could she refuse?

"What's the matter? You eat eggs, don't you?"

"Yes, but ..."

"Well, what is it, girl? Haven't you ever collected eggs before? You're going to have to help out around here. Now go on with you! Go get those eggs."

"I'se can help Bessie, Miz Sally." John gave Kate a knowing glance as he walked into the house.

"Why, that's nice of you to offer, John, but I think Kate here needs to learn know how to do it."

Turning to Kate, she said, "Go ahead now. You can do this. Bessie will show you how."

Kate silently beseeched John to rescue her, but Aunt Sally had already given him a cup of coffee and started talking with him about work needed around the house. *Oh Lord. Not chickens again!*

She followed Bessie reluctantly to the henhouse. As they approached the area, the shy, soft-spoken Negro woman started talking about the chickens, becoming increasingly animated as she described each one. "We has fo' hens and one rooster. Red's his name. And dat's Pecky over dere; she always hungry. And dat's Pokey. See how she pokes her head into everythin'? Dat dere's Prissy. Look how she struts so! And dis one here's May." Kate raised her eyebrow as Bessie continued. "She born in May."

Kate smiled at Bessie's response. They really were like her children. When they reached the door to the building,

Kate stopped. She would just wait outside while Bessie went in to collect the eggs. Bessie, however, grabbed her hand as she ducked through the low doorway and pulled her in, pointing to each nest. "Put yo' hand in dere and feel fo' de eggs. I can see dere's some over in dat one. Don't be shy. Go ahead and get 'em."

Kate complied and groped around in the straw, holding her breath. One egg, two. Her head spun, her lungs ached for air, but the tiny chicken feathers floating around renewed her resolve. Eight . . . nine . . . ten. Kate burst out of the henhouse, inhaling the fresh cool air as Bessie watched wide-eyed. As Kate started back to the main house, her throat began to tickle and her eyes watered. Just as she entered the back door of the house, she let go of the sneeze that had been building.

Eggs flew in all directions as the force of the sneeze shook her whole body.

"My heavens! What on earth?" Aunt Sally stared at the mess, then at Kate.

Kate sniffed, pulling her handkerchief out of her pocket and wiping her eyes and nose. "I tried to tell you, Aunt Sally. I'm sorry, but I have an aversion to chickens."

Giving Kate an incredulous stare, Aunt Sally let out a deep sigh then bent over laughing until tears rolled down her cheeks. "Why, I never heard of such a thing! Well, let's get a rag and start cleaning this mess up. Guess we won't be having eggs this morning."

Kate's shoulders relaxed as she giggled along with her aunt. Thank God, she wouldn't be asked to get the eggs again.

After warm biscuits with honey to go along with the hot coffee, the group went outside to the garden where the sun was coming up over the horizon, sending golden rays of light through the trees and warming the air.

"Here, put this on." Aunt Sally handed Kate a calico sunbonnet. "With that fair skin, you'll burn if you get any sun on your face. And Lord knows how you'll freckle with that red hair."

Kate accepted the simple bonnet, while Aunt Sally put on the man's hat she had worn the day before. Then Aunt Sally gave Kate a hoe and some work gloves and told her to start hoeing.

She stood there, studying the implement. What was she supposed to do with it?

Seeing Kate's confused look, Aunt Sally quirked an eyebrow. "I suppose you never handled one of these before."

"No, ma'am. Our garden in Pensacola wasn't near our house, but several blocks away, with all the other gardens on Garden Street. John and some of our other servants used to go there to work it. The only garden near the house was our rose garden. Aunt Elizabeth and I tended to the roses when it wasn't too hot."

"I have some rose bushes too, on the other side of the house. You can take care of those if you'd like, but since it's winter, they're not doing anything, and you need to learn about this kind of gardening." Motioning for Kate to follow, Aunt Sally walked between the rows, pointing out the plants. "What we have here are some collards and some turnip greens." Kate noted the green leafy clumps. "Over here we have some yams." She halted, studying the ground. "Oh, bother! Looks like deer have been in the garden again."

When John eyed the hoofprints in the sandy soil and partially eaten plants, he said, "I can make a fence 'round it. You got any wood I can use fo' it?"

"Why, that would be grand, John. You have to make it pretty high though, because those deer can jump. Use the wood from that old fallen-down shed over there. Kate, come over here and I'll show you how to use that hoe. We got a load of manure from the Richardsons' place we need to work in. This soil is nothing but sand if you don't add some good manure to it."

Manure? Kate's stomach did a quick turn. Was she going to have to hold her breath all day? Fortunately, the manure was "aged" and didn't deliver the odor she expected. For the rest of the day, Kate worked with the tool, gaining some proficiency as she turned over the soil. The women toiled side by side as they tended the garden.

John dragged up boards from the shed, nailing them into place to make a fence, humming all the while. How did he have the energy to hum? Kate was tired from the unfamiliar labor. Her unskilled hands were cramping and sore, despite the work gloves she wore. She had to admit, however, that John's song, one she'd heard other servants sing in Pensacola, made the work more bearable.

As dusk approached, John hammered the last nail into the fence, enclosing the garden with a protective barrier. He straightened his body to its full height, brushed off his hands, and said with a smile of satisfaction, "Any deer can jump dat fence now can fly."

"Ha! Let's hope they can't," Aunt Sally said, wiping her hands on her pants. "And not a minute too soon, either, as it'll be dark shortly. These winter days don't last long."

Bessie fixed a simple dinner of greens with bits of cured ham and cornbread. She served the meal to Kate and Aunt Sally in the dining room before joining John out in the kitchen building some twenty feet away from the main house. After dinner, the sound of a harmonica came from that direction, as John played his favorite instrument.

"Looks like Bessie's glad to have some company," Aunt Sally said.

"They do seem to get along well, don't they?" Kate dried off the last plate her aunt handed her after rinsing it at the porch sink. Gathering the stack of clean dishes, she carried them inside while Aunt Sally held the door. "How long has Bessie been with you?"

Placing the dishes back in the cupboard, she followed

her aunt to the parlor and sat down in one of the upholstered chairs across from her aunt. It was barely warmer inside the house, without a fire in the fireplace. Kate picked up the crocheted afghan lying across the back of the chair and covered her lap, tucking her hands underneath for warmth.

"A long time," Aunt Sally said, finally answering Kate's question. "Duncan bought her and her brother from a man who had a bad reputation for mistreating his slaves. Bessie was scarcely fifteen years old at the time, and scared half to death when she came here. She's been with me some twenty years now."

"Is she still a slave?"

Aunt Sally shook her head. "Heavens, no. After Duncan died, I gave Bessie her freedom. She could've left if she'd wanted to, but she stayed."

"Same is true for John. My grandfather bought him in Louisiana when he was about nine, then my father freed him after my grandfather died. He's been with us since before I was born. He's always been part of our family, although Aunt Elizabeth would hate to hear me say that about a Negro. He never married. Did Bessie?"

"No. She had her eye on one of Mr. Orman's slaves, but he ended up with another woman on the Owl Creek plantation upriver."

"She's rather pretty. And very light-skinned." Aunt Sally's own sun-darkened hands weren't any lighter than the colored woman's.

"You know what that means, of course. Her daddy was probably the man who owned her mama." Aunt Sally nodded her head as she gave Kate a sideways glance.

"And he sold her?" Kate's mouth dropped open. Who would do such a thing? She'd heard about how slaves were treated on some plantations, but living in the city, she never saw any evidence of it.

"And she's better off now that he did."

"I suppose you're right." Kate shuddered at the implication. "Well, thank God, she ended up with you, Aunt Sally."

"It's been only the two of us for the past five years. We look after each other."

Warmth flooded Kate as Aunt Sally's comment reminded her of her own friendship with her best friend, Sarah. With the age difference, Bessie could be more like a daughter to the older woman. What a unique relationship the two of them had.

"I was wondering if you ever eat any of the chickens," Kate asked. "Bessie's so fond of them, it seems she'd be distraught if one had to be killed."

"Oh yes, we eat chicken. We let some of the eggs hatch into bitties and grow up into chickens that we'll eat."

"So, does Bessie name those?"

Aunt Sally's eyes twinkled. "Yes. She calls them 'dinner.'"

The woman's sense of humor was disarming. Kate couldn't help but smile, followed by a yawn.

"If you'll excuse me, please, I think I'll turn in."

"Go right ahead. You worked pretty hard today. You'll get used to it."

Used to it? She doubted that would ever happen.

Up in her room, Kate poured some water from the pitcher into the basin on the washstand and proceeded to rinse her face. The reflection from the small mirror gave her a start. Who was this person looking back at her? Aunt Elizabeth would not have approved the hint of freckles threatening to break through Kate's pale skin. The cool water was like salve to her throbbing hands, blistered despite the heavy work gloves she'd worn. She dabbed her face with the towel, then undressed, her sore fingers fumbling to unbutton her blouse. Every inch of her body ached. Working like a servant was an experience she'd never been prepared for.

She crawled into bed and pulled the quilt over her weary body, her head sinking into the feather pillow. She missed her home, her friend Sarah, and especially, her father. Maybe she should have gone with the others to Alabama. Now here she was in a strange place with people she didn't know, working like a field hand. Tears gathered in her eyes. How would she ever survive until her father returned to take her away from this place?

Who would be her friend in this strange place, so remote from the town? The face of Lieutenant Henry Clay Harris stole into her mind, bringing with it the same tingles she'd felt during their first encounter. Warmth spread throughout her body, an unfamiliar sensation and reaction. No man had ever had that effect on her before. Could he be a friend, or perhaps more?

As her eyelids collapsed shut, a tiny kernel of hope planted itself in her mind.

Chapter Four

So much work to do. Each day the women worked in the garden, hoeing and planting seeds for the spring vegetables, while John began making repairs to the house. There were shutters to re-hang, trees to trim back, and porch railings to mend. Kate finally got some respite when Aunt Sally relieved her from hoeing after seeing the blisters on her hands, giving her some ointment to put on them. Still she helped plant seeds, bending and squatting until her body ached all over, complaining about the hard labor she subjected it to. When would she ever get used to it? Every night, she collapsed into bed, too tired to dwell on missing home.

One morning the sound of pounding feet drew their attention to a group of soldiers approaching, led by a familiar-faced officer on horseback.

"Good morning, Mrs. McFarlane." The young lieutenant tipped his cap to the older woman.

"Good morning, Clay . . . that is, Lieutenant Harris."

"How are you all doing out here? Is everything all right? "

"Aye. Everything's just fine. I'm enjoying the extra help I have now."

The young man nodded and turned his attention to the

rest of the group, fixing his eyes on Kate, who smiled and tried to avert her gaze. Sitting straight and tall in the saddle, his demeanor reminded her of the knights of medieval times she had read about in books. "Miss McFarlane? I hope your great-aunt isn't working you too hard."

Was it getting warmer outside or was it the heat rushing to her face while her stomach did flips? The tall, fine-looking lieutenant with his rich brunette hair and penetrating gray eyes had a smile that unsettled her. Did he find her attractive? The thought gave her a thrill, until she realized her position. Standing in the garden working like a common servant. Her cheeks burned. If she'd known he was coming, she would have been more presentable—not dirty and sweaty like a field hand. She reached up to her hair to tuck in any wayward strands. Then she acknowledged him with a slight curtsy and nod. "I'm fine, thank you."

Lieutenant Harris glanced at John. "Too bad you ladies have to sully your lovely hands with such labor."

When his gaze returned to her, Kate forced her focus onto the trees behind him to avoid staring at his handsome face. If she could only run inside and freshen up.

"A little work never hurt anybody. Like the Good Book says, you have to work if you want to eat. And I like to eat!" Aunt Sally emphasized her statement with hands on hips and a firm nod of her head.

Lieutenant Harris threw his head back and laughed, as did the other men with him -- except for one. This man neither laughed nor smiled. In fact, the thin, gaunt-faced fellow, whose stance was more of a slouch, glowered at everyone else. The glare he gave his commanding officer radiated contempt and disrespect. As Kate studied the man's odd behavior, he glanced her way, raking her over with his eyes in a most inappropriate way. A shiver ran down her back, and she wished for her shawl to shield herself from his penetrating stare.

"Mrs. McFarlane, you always find a way to amuse me. We'll be leaving you now. You let me know if you need our help." The lieutenant tipped his hat again to Aunt Sally and Kate as he ordered his men to leave.

"I certainly will. And be sure to give my regards to your parents."

Kate eyed her aunt curiously after the men left. "You know his parents?"

"Of course." Aunt Sally motioned for Kate to follow as she walked over to the water pump. "His father, Henry Harris, owns the mercantile downtown, and is pretty well set. I've known the boy all his life. He's been up north going to a university. Came home a few months ago and joined the Guard when he heard Florida was thinking about seceding. Right nice-looking lad, isn't he?"

Her aunt stepped aside from rinsing off her hands, and Kate took her turn.

"Oh, I really didn't notice."

"Dear, don't pretend you weren't admiring what a handsome man he is. He certainly noticed you."

"Why, what do you mean?" Kate walked up to the porch alongside her aunt, where they propped their tools against the house then took their seats in the wicker rocking chairs. Kate sighed with relief as she plopped down.

"Oh, don't be so smug, Kate. I saw that little spark between you two. I'd be surprised if he doesn't come calling, but next time without his men."

Kate experienced a little twinge of excitement, but then remembered the unpleasant man with the disrespectful expressions.

"Aunt Sally, who was that other man with the lieutenant -- the one who seemed angry?"

"Oh, that was Eugene Blackmon. He always looks angry and doesn't like anyone. Bad blood. His family has a sordid history and he's just like them, from what I hear. Too bad the Guard let his kind join. I wouldn't want him in my company, if I could help it."

"What do you mean, 'bad blood'?"

"Well, his daddy's a drunk, mean as a snake, like his granddaddy was, and I hear he beats his poor wife. Heard none of them is honest and would just as soon steal from you or shoot you, if they so desire. There's even been talk that some of that bunch started the warehouse fires we had two years ago." Aunt Sally's rocking chair kept a steady rhythm as she spoke.

"Why haven't they been arrested?"

"Oh, they have been. Several times, for fighting and such. But nobody could ever prove they started the fires, or else they were afraid to, so the skunks get out and go back to their ruthless ways."

"He made me feel quite uncomfortable. I didn't like the way he looked at me … but at least he's on our side and not our enemy's."

"I guess you're right about that, although I find it hard to believe Eugene would be loyal to anyone but himself. His kind resents anybody who's perceived as better than he is, like the Harrises. They blame people who have done well as the reason they're poor. Ignorant way of thinking, but it justifies his lowly life in his mind." Aunt Sally shook her head. "You'd do wise to keep your distance from him. On the other hand, Henry Jr., 'Clay,' is a fine young man, and hopefully can keep Eugene reined in. Speaking of Clay, he sure did cut a fine figure in that uniform, didn't he? I always did like a man in uniform. When my dear Duncan wore his dress uniform, it thrilled me so it made me tremble." The chair stopped rocking as Aunt Sally's eyes took on a faraway gaze.

Kate smiled, blushing at the thought. She liked men in uniform as well, especially her father. And now Lieutenant Henry Clay Harris, who gave the uniform a whole new perspective. However, not even a uniform could help a man like Eugene Blackmon.

Chapter Five

Kate cradled the hot cup of coffee between her cold hands, content to inhale the aroma and feel the warmth while she and Aunt Sally sat on the veranda, observing their new morning ritual. Aunt Sally took a sip of her coffee, the steam rising from the surface. Bells tolled from the direction of town.

"Are those church bells?" Kate turned her head to listen.

"Aye, that's the bells at Trinity Church."

"I didn't realize today was Sunday." Had she been here only a week? "What time are church services? I should start getting ready."

"I don't plan on going. Been some time since I darkened the doors there."

Not go to church? She and Aunt Elizabeth had always gone to services at Old Christ Church in Pensacola. She thought everyone went to church on Sunday. At least everyone back home did, even though some people acted like they went more for the purpose of being seen than for worship. She recalled ladies and gentlemen dressed up in their finest clothes, nodding to each other as they strolled through town on their way to church.

"Then what do you do on Sunday? You don't work in the garden, do you?"

"Heavens, no. I do believe the good Lord wants us to have a day of rest. So I go fishing. God knows where to find me."

"You do what?"

"I go fishing. That's the most restful thing you can do."

"You like to fish?" Kate had never known a woman who went fishing. But then, Aunt Sally was unlike any woman she had ever known.

"Sure do. In fact, Bessie and I both like to fish. Would you like to go with us?"

Still trying to understand Aunt Sally's revelation, Kate slowly shook her head.

"I believe I'll just stay here and work on my embroidery, if you don't mind."

"Suit yourself. Now, if you'll excuse me, I'm going to get our fishing poles and dig some worms."

Kate stared after the woman as she headed to the barn. Why didn't she go to church? She wanted to ask, but assumed Aunt Sally would have given her reasons if she'd wanted to. Certainly Aunt Sally believed in God, yet not attending church was unthinkable for the faithful. Was every person in town gathering at the church in response to the bells Kate heard earlier? It didn't feel right not to be going to church on Sunday. She'd welcome the familiarity of being inside a church right now, keeping a normal tradition and feeling God's presence.

Yet there was nothing normal about her current life. Did God even knew where she was now? But she couldn't go to town by herself, much less, without an escort. She didn't even know where the church was, or the town either, for that matter. It must be down the road that ended at Aunt Sally's house, but how far? So far, the only place she had seen was Aunt Sally's, and the only other people she had encountered were the soldiers.

Soldiers. An image of Lieutenant Harris's handsome face invaded her mind, quickening her heart rate. Was he going to church today? Was he a God-fearing man? She hoped so.

After she retrieved the embroidery work from her valise and went back outside on the veranda, she watched Aunt Sally and Bessie as they headed down to the water. John, following behind the women, turned around and waved to her as a big grin spread across his face.

"We be back later, Miss Kate. You just rest up while we catches us some dinner."

John seemed happier than she'd seen him in a long time. Why, he acted like he was delighted to be here. Seeing how well the group of fishermen fit together made her more lonely. Why did she always feel like an outsider? She missed her friend Sarah. If only they could talk! Poor Sarah. Her fiancé, Lark Hamilton, had joined the Union side, and her father had reacted by cancelling their wedding plans. Kate could only imagine how she felt.

After a while she got bored with the embroidery, the task made more difficult with fingers stiff and sore from gardening. Perhaps she'd write in her journal if her fingers allowed. But first she needed to stretch her legs. Laying her handwork aside, she stood and began walking around the grounds of the house. Neglected roses by the front porch displayed barren brown branches in their winter dormancy. What color were their blooms? She'd ask Aunt Sally where she kept the pruning shears, and trim them in preparation for spring blossoms.

As she continued her stroll in the yard, she studied the old home. How grand it must have been at one time -- a masterpiece even, as was evident by the carved gingerbread latticework, shutters, broad porches, and cupola, crowned by the widow's walk. Years of neglect and weather had taken its toll on the structure, however, creating the aura of a sad old queen.

The dwelling was large, with a veranda on three sides of the first floor. On the front of the house, a second-floor balcony was accessed by the upstairs bedrooms. The rear of the house faced the water, taking full advantage of the ocean breezes. Tall windows downstairs would probably be open during the warmer months so wind could blow through and cool the interior. The front and back doors opened onto the central hallway, which would also allow for nice circulation during the summer.

Gazing up, Kate noticed the widow's walk sitting atop the house. She had forgotten all about it since seeing it the first day they arrived. How did one get to it? This would be a good time to find out.

Kate pushed aside guilt for being nosy and entered the house, then climbed the stairs to the second-floor landing. Scanning the area for a way to go farther up, she spied a door at the opposite end of the stairwell. She rounded the stairs to the door, then tentatively grabbed the knob, expecting to find the door locked. Although the doorknob was tight, as she twisted harder it loosened and turned, then gave way when she pushed. A narrow set of stairs rose before her, barely visible in the darkened opening.

Gathering her long skirt in one hand, she groped her way up the tight staircase, fending off cobwebs long undisturbed. At the top, Kate found herself in an attic filled with dusty relics of a forgotten past. Maybe someday she'd inspect those, but today her goal was to find the opening to the widow's walk.

When her eyes became accustomed to the dim light, she gazed around the room. A short ladder led to a door in the roof. She struggled to push an old sea chest out of the way. Her long skirt would make ascending the ladder difficult and she needed her hands free, so she pulled the skirt up above her boots and tucked the extra material into her waistband. Her height shortened the distance from the floor to the top in the small room, and she was able to reach the rusty latch once she stepped on the second rung. With some effort she unlatched it and pushed the door open. Like the hatch on her father's ship, the hinged panel fell backward onto the roof.

A burst of cool air and bright light rushed in as the outside world invaded the room. Kate pulled herself up through the opening to a sitting position, and then stood to find herself high above the ground on the widow's walk. The view was breathtaking and marvelous, allowing her to see above the treetops and get a panoramic view of her surroundings. The cool winter breeze refreshed and invigorated her. As she scanned the horizon, she could see the shimmering water of the sound, the islands, the lighthouse, and even the deep-blue waters of the Gulf of Mexico beyond. To her left, in the direction of the town, a couple of steeples poked through the treetops. So that's where the churches were. On the opposite side of the house lay a large marshy area bordering Aunt Sally's property, where an osprey sat in the top of a dead tree.

Hearing voices and laughter coming to her from a distance, Kate looked down to the water of the sound and saw a skiff with three people seated onboard. She shielded her eyes with her hand against the glare of the brilliant winter sun, and recognized Aunt Sally and John with their hats on and Bessie with her bright red headscarf between them, their fishing poles hanging out on either side. A twinge of pain stung her heart, remembering her isolation. Of course, she'd been asked to join them, but refused. Was she alone because it was her decision, or was it her destiny?

Eyes misting over, she spun away from the sight and toward the front of the house. Her hand flew to her mouth as she gasped at the scene before her. Probably no more than half a mile from the house was the military camp. People milled about a number of tents -- men in uniforms as well as women and children who had accompanied them. Was that where Lieutenant Harris was? She squinted to find a familiar face, but couldn't recognize anyone from that distance. But what if they could see her? How embarrassing that would be!

Yet the wonder of being above everything else thrilled her. Was this how God saw the world, looking down from heaven, able to see everything at once? She twirled around in a circle, arms outstretched and head lifted to the clear blue sky as her spirit soared. How wonderful it was to be out here above it all, temporarily freeing her from the mundane world below. What a special privilege it was to share this place with God and the birds of the air. This would be her church, her place to meet God alone and privately. Her heart swelled in worship of the Creator. *Thank You, God, for giving me this time alone with You, even though I'm not in Your house.*

She brushed some leaves and small branches off the walk, evidence that no one else had been up there in a long time. Why didn't Aunt Sally ever come here, instead of depriving herself of the joy it held? Perhaps she once did. Maybe the woman had difficulty climbing the ladder at her age. Or could it be the name that discouraged her? Widow's walks were intended for a sea captain's wife to watch for her husband's return, but Aunt Sally's husband was dead, so maybe she had nothing and no one to look for anymore. How sad. What must it feel like to have no one to watch for? At least Kate had her father.

As her thoughts returned to her father, her gaze drifted back to the lighthouse. What a comfort to know it would guide him back to her. She was thankful for the protection it represented and grateful for the lighthouse keepers who maintained them. Maybe someday John could row her over to the island so she could meet them and thank them in person. Did they know the Palmer family who lived at the Pensacola lighthouse?

Movement from below interrupted her thoughts.

Glancing down at the copse of trees near the edge of the

property by the water, her breath caught. Someone was there. A figure stood near one of the trees and appeared to be watching the house. Chills raced through her as she froze in place. She was alone. Who was he, and what was he doing there? If he had seen the others leave, he knew she was alone. Had he seen her on the roof? Her heart pounded against her ribcage as she tried to think of what to do. Perhaps she could step back and shield herself behind the branch of one of the huge oak trees that stood beside the house.

The sound of approaching voices signaled the return of the fishermen. Kate lifted her gaze to the water, then back to the shadowy figure. It was gone. She exhaled deeply, welcoming the sight of familiar faces as they stepped back into the yard. Hurrying back inside, she closed the hatch behind her, skimmed down the ladder, and ran downstairs to the second-floor landing just in time to hear Aunt Sally's voice call out to her.

"Katherine, are you upstairs? Come on down and get ready for supper. We're going to eat well tonight!"

And eat well they did. Bessie made some hushpuppies and fried the fish they'd caught that day. The three fishermen laughed and told stories about each other's skill, or lack thereof, while they sat outside on the back porch.

"Miz Sally, good thing dat big ole fish got hisself loose or it would've pulled you clean out of de boat! It was bigger than you is!" John was especially jovial, acting like a schoolboy coming in from recess. He stretched his hands apart to show Kate the size of the fish.

"I would've managed, even if you had to hold my feet to keep me from going in after him. He would have been worth the trouble!" The vision of the little woman being pulled into the water by a fish made them all laugh until tears ran down their faces. Kate couldn't remember when she'd laughed so much.

After dinner Kate went out to the barn to see John.

There was so much to tell him about what she had seen from the widow's walk. She wanted to ask him to row her to the island someday, but more importantly, she needed to tell him about the man lurking nearby. However, when she opened the barn door, there sat John and Bessie, laughing and talking with each other. Kate's face warmed. Thinking she'd intruded, she tried to step back outside without being noticed. Too late. John looked up and saw her.

"Miss Kate, you need somethin'?"

"I, well, no, nothing important. I was thinking about Father's return and had a few questions for you. But it can wait. I didn't mean to interrupt you."

"No harm done. Have a seat over dere." He pointed to an old stump.

Bessie rose from the old milking stool she'd been sitting on. "I needs to get to bed anyhow. Here, take my seat, Miss Kate."

Bessie made her way to the door, and as she turned to say goodnight, the glow on her face reflected the light in John's eyes. The attraction between them was tangible, and Kate marveled at how quickly their relationship had developed. She'd seen that look before on Sarah's face when she talked about her fiancé Lark. But she had never seen John act that way. Why, John must be fifty years old, and Bessie near thirty-five, based on what Aunt Sally had said. But the attraction was there, without a doubt.

A niggling feeling irritated her conscience. Not that she was jealous of them. Of course she was happy for John. But she feared losing his friendship. He'd crewed on her grandfather's ship as a boy, but as long as she remembered, he lived over the stable at their home in Pensacola. Ever since she was a child, she had visited him there, enthralled by his stories about growing up in the swamps of Louisiana. Kate had always confided in John without fear of judgment, although he occasionally quoted a Bible verse to make a point. He probably knew her better than anyone;

as he said, he'd "know'd her since befo' she was born."
Tears welled up in her eyes at the thought of giving up their
companionship.

"What's wrong, Miss Kate? Did somethin' happen?"

Brushing away the moisture, Kate recovered her
composure and plopped down on the vacated stool. Soon
they were talking again like always, as if picking up a
conversation never ended. John told Kate about the day's
outing, encouraging her to join them next time.

"John, how far do you think it is to the lighthouse?"

"A few miles. Why you needs to know?"

"I'd like to go there and meet the keepers. Could you
row me over someday?

"Sho, when we has enough time. Best to go when de
tides goin' out, so's we can move mo' fast. Den we has to
come back when de tide's comin' in. Has you asked Miz
Sally if you can go?"

"Not yet. But surely she'll let us. Perhaps someday
when we don't have a lot of work to do here."

"I'se likes to see dat day come. We's been workin'
mighty hard since we done got here. "

Kate nodded then remembered something else she'd
seen from the widow's walk. "John, did you know the army
camp isn't very far from here?"

"I didn't thinks so. I heard dem marchin' and even
smelled de wood fires. How you knows where it is? You
didn't go out walkin' by you'self, did you? Your papa
would skin me alive if he thought I let you do dat."

"Why, no, of course not! I heard noises while I was
outside and just assumed they were close."

"Uh huh." John didn't sound convinced. He sat back
and crossed his arms, with one eyebrow raised.

"Well, I guess I'll be heading off to bed." Kate stood
and brushed off her skirt.

"Miss Kate, hold on a minute. You forgettin' to tell me
somethin'?

She never could keep a secret from him.

"Did I mention that I went up on the widow's walk today?"

"Dat right? No, ma'am, you didn't say nuthin' about dat. How you get up dere?"

Words spun out of Kate's mouth as she told him about her adventure, her excitement building as she demonstrated the panorama with her hands.

John put his hands forward as if to stop her. "Slow down dere and take a breath." A broad, toothy smile spread over his face as he listened to her descriptions of the surrounding area.

"Oh, John, it's the most wonderful place! I felt like a bird, flying above the earth. I can't wait to go back up there."

"Does Miz Sally know you was up dere?"

"Not yet. But I'll tell her. I promise."

"Maybe you should ask her if she minds you goin' up dere. You best be careful too. It's awful high. We wouldn't want you blowin' off in a strong wind."

Kate smiled at his protective chiding. "I'll be careful. And I'll ask Aunt Sally if it's all right. I'm sure she wouldn't be opposed to the idea."

"Well, you be sho. Dis her house, you know." John stood and stretched his arms out to either side. "Guess we best be turnin' in. Tomorrow we gots to get up and work."

More work. She wished there was another day of rest. Kate nodded. "Good night, John."

"Good night, Miss Kate."

Kate went back to the house and up the stairs to prepare for bed. As she lay down, scenes from her visit to the widow's walk ran through her mind. Her heart began to race when the image of someone watching the house interrupted her pleasant memories. In her excitement, she'd forgotten to tell John about the stranger.

Chapter Six

"We're going to town today," Aunt Sally announced as they cleared away the breakfast dishes. "I need to order some food and supplies at the mercantile. Kate, you get to see what Apalachicola is like. Bessie and John are coming with us."

No work today? Kate was so relieved to have another day of rest that she could hardly contain her excitement. She bounded up the stairs to her room to make herself presentable. Would she see Lieutenant Harris? She twisted her long curls and pinned them up, placing her bonnet atop the hair to hold it in place, then changed into the blue-and-white gingham dress, the dress she didn't work in. Grabbing her reticule and shawl, she raced down the stairs to join the others. As she and Aunt Sally began what turned out to be a mile-long walk to town, John and Bessie stayed some distance behind, seeming to prefer to keep to themselves while they talked on the way.

Trudging along the sandy road bordered by tall pine trees with dense spikey palmetto underneath, they tried to walk where wagon wheels had packed down the thick sand to keep it from filling their shoes. They had gone half a mile before they saw another house.

"That's the Richardson place." Aunt Sally nodded in the direction of the property where cows grazed in an adjacent field. "We trade them eggs for milk, since our cow died. Mr. Richardson has a smokehouse too, and the best ham and sausage around."

After they passed the house, Kate saw the spire of a church steeple peeking out through the treetops.

"Aunt Sally, that church up ahead . . . is that the one whose bells we heard yesterday?"

"Aye, that's Trinity Church."

"Is that the church you attended?"

"Yes, that's where my family worshipped."

"Might I ask why you no longer attend?"

"Yes, you may. After my dear husband and son died, I wore the black mourning dress for a long time, as I grieved for them so deeply. When I returned to church looking for comfort, all I got was pity. I could hear people talk about me, pointing me out as that poor, pitiful woman who'd lost her men."

Aunt Sally shook her head and continued. "It made me feel worse to hear their comments. I couldn't even pay attention to the sermon because of the discomfort I felt from all the stares and whispers. I finally decided I couldn't abide it anymore, and I'd just have to meet God somewhere besides church. I don't believe He really minds."

"Oh, I see." Kate's heart ached for her aunt. "It's a shame you were treated that way."

"Aye, and then when I quit attending, they had even more to talk about. Guess they thought the poor woman had lost her religion. Well, I might have, if I'd continued to wallow in self-pity. But one day, I sensed the Lord say to me, 'That's enough, Sally. You need to get busy and get on with life.'" Aunt Sally pointed her finger as if giving orders. "My servants needed me to run the household, and I had to buck up and do it. Then, when I quit wearing dresses and started wearing britches, the town gossips knew I'd lost my religion and my mind too!" She laughed out loud.

"So you do believe in God, then?"

"Well, of course I do! Anybody who doesn't is just plain foolish."

They continued on in silence while Kate digested what Aunt Sally said. So that explained why the woman didn't go to church. But what about the men's clothing? She hadn't changed to a skirt, even for going to town.

She finally mustered up the courage to ask. "So why did you quit wearing a skirt and start wearing men's britches?"

"Just more practical, that's all. A skirt gets in your way when you're working outside, if you haven't noticed. Those big skirts that are so popular now are particularly cumbersome. Why, the gals can barely get through the doorways these days, especially with a hoop on. I'm not trying to attract any suitors at my age, so I'm wearing what I can work in, which happens to be my husband's old clothes. In a way, I guess wearing them makes me feel a little closer to him. But never mind, that's foolish talk."

The sounds of the town reached Kate's ears and ended the conversation as they reached the main thoroughfare. Steamboat whistles rang out over the din of business in the downtown streets, which were full of wagons, people, and bales of cotton. The four of them wove their way through the activity, trying not to get run over by drays loaded with merchandise. At the end of the street where the waterfront began, rows of three-story red brick warehouses stretched along the water's edge.

Ferry boats and steamers lined up along the river, unloading or loading their goods, puffing and blowing through their tall smokestacks. Cotton was stacked beside the docks and piled so high on the boats, the smokestacks were barely visible. As the group turned and walked down Main Street toward where it ended at the water, vessels of all sizes could be seen passing each other as they ferried freight to the larger ships waiting in deeper waters outside the entrance to the bay. The ringing of auction bells sounded alongside the call of auctioneers.

"I didn't realize Apalachicola was such a busy town." Kate dodged a young courier running down the sidewalk.

"Oh, yes, the town starts getting busy in the fall when the cotton begins coming from Georgia and Alabama. Have you ever seen so much cotton? The steamships bring it down river and unload it here. Then the lighters, the smaller boats, take it to those large ships waiting out in the deep water, and then those ships take it up across the ocean to Europe for their mills."

They stopped on a street corner as Kate observed all the activity.

Aunt Sally continued. "We ship a lot of cotton to New England too, but now that Florida's seceded, that might stop. The town's population grows a hundredfold when the season is in full-swing, with men coming from places like Columbus, Georgia, and other cities up north to work here. They're either bachelors or they leave their families up north. By June, the season's over, and they go back home."

"Why don't they stay and move their families down here?"

"Too hot. Plus they're afraid of swamp fever, which tends to appear during the summer. A few of them have homes in town, but they're pretty plain, since the wives aren't here to fix them up. The rest of them stay in one of the hotels or boarding houses."

As they passed a doorway, Kate pointed to a sign hanging outside. "French Consulate?"

"Ah, yes, we get a lot of folks from Europe who come here to buy cotton."

The bell jingled on the door as Kate and Aunt Sally entered the mercantile, bordered by the tailor shop on one side and the butcher shop on the other. Bessie and John waited outside on the sidewalk. When Kate stepped inside, a myriad of smells, including leather and coffee, assaulted her senses. The shelves were lined with jars, boxes of various sizes, and stacks of goods, while barrels and crates filled the aisle.

"Good morning, Mrs. McFarlane." The portly shopkeeper behind the counter greeted them cordially. "I see you have a companion with you today."

"Good morning to you, Mr. Harris. This is my great-niece, Katherine McFarlane, from Pensacola. She will be staying with me awhile."

The perky little blonde standing next to the gentleman looked up from her tablet, pencil suspended in the air as her eyes widened with interest. Coming from behind the counter, she practically danced over to Kate.

"Hello, I'm Cora. I couldn't wait to meet you. I've heard so much about you!"

The petite girl's bright blue eyes glowed with excitement as her blonde ringlets, tied by a cheerful pink ribbon, bounced in affirmation. Her wide smile was contagious, and Kate found herself smiling in return.

"About me?"

"Yes, of course. Clay Harris is my brother. You know, *Lieutenant* Harris," she said with emphasis on the lieutenant. "I think you made quite an impression on him."

Kate's heart skipped a beat as blood rushed to her face. The girl's brother was Lieutenant Harris? What could he possibly have said about her? More than likely commented about her height. Most people did.

Before Kate could respond to Cora's comment about Clay, the attractive blonde began rattling off questions so quickly that Kate blinked in surprise and wondered when the girl would take a breath. "I haven't seen you at church. Will you be attending Trinity or one of the other churches? How long will you be here? What's the news from Pensacola? Did you see any Union troops? Isn't it just terrible what they're doing to us?"

"Cora, dear, let the young lady have a chance to answer one question at a time. Please excuse my daughter, Miss McFarlane. She's quite a talker, I'm afraid. Cora, maybe you two can get together at another time to talk. Let them take care of their business now." The man frowned at his daughter, motioning with his head for her to get back behind the counter.

Kate spied some bolts of fabric nearby and reached out to examine them.

"Of course, Papa. I'm sorry." Cora turned back to Kate. "I didn't mean to bother you. Would you like to come to church with us next Sunday? We can pick you up in the carriage, can't we, Papa?"

"Well, yes, of course we can, Cora, if she'd like to come; that is, if her aunt doesn't mind." Turning to Aunt Sally, he said, "Mrs. McFarlane, we can take you as well."

"Katherine may go with you if she wishes, and I thank you for your offer, but I won't be accompanying her. Your family will be escort enough for her."

All eyes turned to Kate for her answer. Still trying to take it all in, she glanced from one to the other.

"Why, yes, that would be nice," she said at last.

"Oh, that's grand! I can't wait to introduce you to my friends." Cora bubbled with excitement. "I'm sure Clay will be pleased as well."

Would he? Kate hoped his sister was right.

"That's settled, then," the shopkeeper announced with a note of finality. "We'll come to collect you next Sunday morning. Now, Mrs. McFarlane, do you want your usual order?"

"Aye, plus a few other things. Do you have any tea? My niece here has a taste for it."

"Yes, ma'am. Just came in on one of the British ships. Mrs. Harris is very fond of it too. Will that be all?"

"I need two pairs of work gloves and some nails."

"I heard you had a new man. Glad to hear you have

someone to help you take care of that big place."

Aunt Sally harrumphed.

"Here you are." Mr. Harris handed a sack to each of them. "I'll send the rest of your usual order by a drayman."

The women turned to leave the store, while Cora called behind them, "See you on Sunday!"

Outside the store, both women sighed relief, then laughed together.

"Cora certainly is a talkative girl, isn't she?" Kate giggled behind her gloved hand.

"She could talk the bark off a tree."

"I can't believe Lieutenant Harris talked about me.'"

"Of course he'd talk about the pretty new girl in town. I'm sure everyone else has heard about you by now as well, what with his daddy being the main town merchant and his sister being Cora."

Kate blushed. Pretty? "But what on earth did he have to say about me? We've barely met."

"Kate, don't sell yourself short. An attractive girl like you is certain to draw attention in town, not only from the young men but also from jealous girls who'll see you as competition."

"That's just nonsense. What would I be competing for?"

"Well, if you remember, Lieutenant Henry Clay Harris is a right handsome young man, and many a girl would like to capture his attention."

Kate tucked a lock of hair behind her ear. What had he told Cora? She hoped she'd made a favorable impression, despite the circumstances of their meeting. Would he indeed be pleased about Cora inviting Kate to join them on Sunday?

The women proceeded to the butcher shop where Aunt Kate bought some salt pork and a roast. A few soldiers stood on the sidewalks while others walked down the street. Kate scanned the scene to see if Lieutenant Harris was among them. Sensing someone looking at her, she turned and was dismayed to discover Eugene Blackmon standing across the street, his eyes fixed on her. When he caught her looking back at him, he winked and grinned as if she were familiar. Kate shuddered and spun back around, pretending to look in a shop window and regretting ever looking in his direction.

John moved behind her, blocking the view between Blackmon and Kate. She relaxed her shoulders, feeling safer with the shield of his strong presence.

"Thank you, John. That man frightens me."

"I knows, Miss Kate. I'se keepin' my eye on him. He de kind what always looks like he up to somethin', and it ain't no good. Don't you worry, though. I'se gonna make sho he don't come too close to you."

Aunt Sally had continued walking and missed the whole incident. When she realized Kate was still behind her, she stopped and turned back.

"Is there something in that store you want?"

"No, ma'am. I was just admiring the fine bonnets they carry."

"Do you have a bonnet to wear Sunday?"

Kate shook her head. "I only brought this everyday bonnet, since I didn't have room for many things in my valise. I didn't think I would need a better one at sea."

"Then we better get you a nice one for Sundays. You can't wear that calico one you've been wearing in the garden, either, and I'm sure you want to look your best when Clay Harris and his family come to fetch you for church."

The two women went inside where Kate chose a nice straw hat with a wide brim. She reached into her reticule, thankful for the money her father had given her. The hat was a practical choice and one she could change by adding various ribbons, flowers, or feathers. She looked longingly at a new readymade dress on display, examining the details.

She could create something similar if she had the right materials. Perhaps she could alter one of the two dresses she had brought with her. She did need a hoop, though, since she hadn't brought one on the ship. A Sunday dress wouldn't fit properly without one.

"Do you sell crinolines?" Kate asked the saleswoman as she took the hat.

"Yes, we do. Right over here."

After purchasing a hoop, Kate and Aunt Sally left the store and spent the next couple of hours visiting other merchants in town. Aunt Sally bought a new blade for the scythe so John could clear out some of the underbrush in the yard, as well as some boards to use for mending the henhouse and the barn. Kate looked over her shoulder occasionally to see if the dreadful Eugene Blackmon was nearby. She didn't care to see that man again

"You have some nice hotels here," she commented to her aunt.

"Yes, with all the out-of-town businessmen, they stay full during the season. Of course, most of the town soirees are held in their ballrooms too. Perhaps you'll be invited to one."

An image of herself entering a hotel ballroom on the arm of Lieutenant Clay Harris floated through her mind.

"The café over there has good food." Aunt Sally nodded toward the opposite corner of the street. "Are you hungry, Kate?"

"Oh, yes, I would enjoy some refreshment."

Kate turned to John and Bessie. As if in response to her unspoken question, John smiled. Taking Bessie's hand, he started down the street toward the waterfront.

"Me and Bessie brought us somethin' to eat. We goin' over to dat clump of trees down dere, rest our feet, and watch de boats. We'll meet up with you ladies back here after we all finish eatin'."

~

White lace curtains fluttered on the windows of the modest dining room where Kate and Aunt Sally sat at a table, enjoying the breeze. Other ladies in the dining room glanced their way and whispered while Kate shifted uncomfortably in her chair, sensing she and her aunt were the topic of their conversation. Even though her aunt dressed in an unconventional way, sparking curiosity, how unfair and rude for the woman to be the object of derision.

Her face grew hotter as her irritation increased, and she fanned herself briskly with the menu as if she could blow away the gossip. Even the waitress gave Aunt Sally the once-over when she arrived to take their order. Kate straightened her back, sitting tall in her chair, and lifted her chin in defiance.

"Ladies. Mrs. McFarlane." The waitress turned to Kate. "What may I get you today?"

Aunt Sally spoke up. "Good day, Mary. This is my great-niece Katherine from Pensacola. I think I'll have your special. What would you like, Kate?"

Kate smiled. "I'm pleased to meet you, Mary. Yes, I believe I'll have your special too."

As the waitress turned away from the table, Kate leaned over and whispered to her aunt. "Aunt Sally, I feel like the ladies at the other tables are talking about us."

"They probably are. Of course, since you're the new girl in town, that's understandable. But they're probably talking about me too, since they usually are when I come to town."

"Doesn't that bother you?"

"Oh, it once did, but now it's water off a duck's back. I just let it roll on off. I guess they have nothing better to do but spend their time talking about somebody else. Of course, I usually come in early and take care of my business before they even have a chance to see me. I can't remember when I've spent this much time in town. But I wanted to show you around. Besides, it's a special treat to have lunch in town with my great-niece."

Kate smiled and shook her head, admiring the older woman for her spunk. Aunt Sally was half the size of Aunt Elizabeth, but twice as strong. What irony. Where did she get that strength? She hoped some of it would rub off on her someday.

A few of the ladies nodded at them as they passed their table, and some stopped to inquire after Aunt Sally's health and to meet Kate. They were all fashionably dressed. Kate arranged her hands in her lap as if she could cover her own dress, which looked rather plain compared to theirs. She would never have gone to town in Pensacola in such poor style.

"It seems many of the ladies here dress very well."

"They attempt to follow the latest fashion. Are you worried about not having a nice dress for Sunday?"

"I'm afraid so. I had several nice dresses in Pensacola but couldn't bring my trunk with me on the ship. This one and the one I've been wearing in the garden are the only dresses I have here. But maybe I can make some alterations to this one so it'll be more attractive."

"I can help you with that. I have a few nice dresses I don't wear anymore, and even though you're much taller than I, we can use one of the bodices, add a few details, like ribbons and lace, and make it very stylish. I'm sure we can add some fabric to the skirts and give them a border to make them longer. I'll get them out of the wardrobe when we get home, and you can decide which ones you'd like to have."

What type of old dresses would Aunt Sally have? Certainly nothing fashionable; however, Kate was willing to make the effort and see what she could create with what was available. One of the few things she could do well was sew, and she enjoyed being creative. On Sunday she hoped to make a better impression on Lieutenant Clay Harris than she had before.

Chapter Seven

On Sunday morning Kate gathered the shawl around her shoulders against the crisp, cool air as she waited for the Harris family to arrive and take her to church. She was pleased with the dress she and Aunt Sally had designed using parts of the older woman's wardrobe, accentuated with a lace collar and rows of dark green velvet ribbon, which matched the ribbon on her new bonnet. Her thick amber hair, now in control and partially covered by the bonnet, was parted down the middle, braided, and pulled back into a bun at the nape of her neck in the latest style. It had taken all three women – Kate, Aunt Sally, and Bessie – to achieve that feat. The grin on his face indicated that Lieutenant Harris was pleased with Kate's appearance as well.

"Good morning, Miss McFarlane. You look especially lovely today." The young lieutenant hopped down from the carriage, eager to assist her. The warmth of his hands on her waist radiated through the fabric of Kate's dress as he helped her up. She climbed onto the seat and sat next to Cora, who beamed with pleasure and gushed with praise.

"Miss Mc-- Do you mind if I call you Katherine? You do look pretty today! Is that a new dress? That lovely shade of green is especially flattering with your red hair. Plus it matches your green eyes."

"Thank you, Cora. I like your dress too. And yes, please call me Katherine." The petite blonde wore a pink satin flounced dress with a matching jacket. Her blonde ringlets were partially covered with a spoon bonnet, tied under her chin with pink ribbon. "Where is the rest of your family?" Kate asked. Aunt Sally had told her the Harris family had several children.

"Oh, Sam has to make two trips to collect the whole family. After he deposits us at church, he'll go back to our house and get Father, Mother, and my little brother and sister." She nodded in the direction of the Negro driver handling the reins. Clay turned his head to the man and snapped his fingers in the air.

"Let's get going, Sam! We don't want to be late for church."

Kate watched the Negro's jaw tighten as he nodded and clicked the reins to start the horse moving. Kate's stomach tensed at Clay's condescending attitude, but she brushed the uncomfortable feeling aside and addressed Cora.

"How many sisters and brothers do you have?"

"There are five of us altogether. Clay is the oldest, then my sister Emily, who's married and lives in Columbus, Georgia. Then there's me, my brother William, who's ten, and my sister Rebecca, who's six."

"Does your married sister have any children?"

"Not yet. We're hoping there'll be one on the way soon, though."

Sitting across from them, Clay remained silent, unable to get a word into the conversation between the two young ladies. His intense gaze filled Kate's stomach with butterflies, and she fidgeted with the folds of her skirt. Whenever she glanced his way, he flashed her an engaging smile, further unsettling her.

They arrived at Trinity Church, and he assisted the two

women out of the carriage. "Let me introduce you to our friends," he said, taking Kate on one arm and Cora on the other, as they ascended the stone steps of the church.

The building faced the bay; its tall portico, supported by two massive white columns, reminded Kate of Greek temples in pictures she'd seen. Most of the women huddled together to stay out of the brisk February wind, while the men stood at the bottom of the steps, allowing room for the women and their hooped skirts. Clay greeted each person and presented Kate to them.

She was introduced to Mr. and Mrs. William Porter first. Clay noted that Mr. Porter was of the Apalachicola Land Company and was also the Belgian consul in town. Next she was introduced to Cosam Bartlett, editor of *The Apalachicola Gazette*, which Clay proudly stated as Florida's first daily newspaper. She also met bank directors, the Mansion House Hotel proprietor, and the port collector. Kate's head swam as she tried to remember each person's name. Clay then took her over to an aristocratic-looking couple, whom he introduced as Mr. and Mrs. David Raney. Mr. Raney was a cotton merchant who also served as mayor. His wife was president of the women's guild at the church.

"You must come join us for tea sometime," Mrs. Raney said. "The other ladies in the guild would love to meet you. We're sewing banners for our men to carry into battle. Won't you join us?"

Before Kate had a chance to answer, they were joined by Clay's mother and father and his younger brother and sister.

"Miss McFarlane, so happy to see you again," said the senior Mr. Harris. "This is my wife, Nell, and our two younger children, William and Rebecca." The little boy, who looked remarkably like Clay, gave a quick bow while his younger sister curtsied shyly.

Nell Harris, short and blonde like Cora but rotund like

her husband, smiled warmly and clasped Kate's gloved hands in her own. "So very nice to meet you, dear. I do hope you enjoy your stay in our fair city. Cora has told me so much about you. Perhaps the two of you can spend some time together -- that is, if your aunt agrees."

Kate smiled at the warm invitation as Clay pushed open the heavy oak church doors and held them for the others to enter. "Let's get you ladies inside out of the cold. I believe the service is about to begin."

Mr. Harris proceeded down the right aisle to the fourth row and opened the door to the Harris family pew. His wife slid across while the younger children jockeyed for position on the bench until Mr. Harris moved the boy to his side and Mrs. Harris lifted the young girl to her lap, making room for Cora, Kate, and Clay.

Most of the pews were reserved for certain families, as Clay explained. "When the church was founded, the pews were rented to help cover the cost of the new building. A few years ago, some people complained that the practice wasn't hospitable to newcomers, so the custom was abandoned. However the families of the founding members still sit in the original pews they rented. Your great uncle Duncan was a founding member."

"Really? Did he rent a pew?"

"Yes he did, but when your aunt quit coming to church, she gave her pew to a new family. It's that one over there." Clay nodded toward a young family seated across the aisle on the third pew.

Kate noted the location then looked around. Although she had seen several Negroes enter the church by a side door, she didn't see them seated inside.

"Where did the Negroes go?" she whispered to Cora by her side.

"Up in the balcony. That's where the slaves sit."

Kate glanced up behind her and saw a row of Negroes seated in the balcony. Would John and Bessie sit there, even though they were no longer slaves?

The sound of the Erben Pipe Organ interrupted her thoughts as the small choir began to lead the congregation in song. "Love divine, all loves excelling, joy of heaven to earth come down."

The Reverend William Saunders delivered the sermon. While listening, Kate admired the rich wood paneling of the church. Clay had told her it was white pine, cut in New York, then shipped in sections down the east coast where it was assembled in Apalachicola.

She tried to focus on the pastor's words, but couldn't help scanning the congregation. There were a few other uniformed men, but none looked as handsome as Clay Harris in comparison. Doubtless the other young women present envied her position as his guest, if she had correctly read their expressions.

After the service, the parishioners bid each other good day. Kate had received several invitations to visit other families by the time they departed from the church. Mrs. Harris implored her to have Sunday dinner with their family.

"Thank you for your offer, but perhaps another time." Kate wanted to accept, but felt it improper to do so without first requesting permission from her aunt.

"Next week, then," Mrs. Harris said.

Kate smiled and nodded. "If Aunt Sally doesn't mind, I'd love to."

Mr. Harris extended an elbow to his wife. "It's warmed up nicely, dear. Let's walk the few blocks home and not wait for the carriage. Shall we?"

Nell Harris's broad smile answered him as they nodded their goodbyes to Kate and began strolling away from the church, the younger children in tow.

The ride back to Aunt Sally's was lively with conversation as Cora commented on practically every woman's attire at church. "Did you see that hideous hat

Ada Richardson was wearing? She looked like a rooster. Oh, and did you notice the colossal brooch Mrs. Miller had on? It must have cost a fortune. I heard it was made to look like an exact replica of one of Queen Victoria's brooches. She doesn't look like a queen to me."

Cora giggled with amusement at her own comments. Kate's ears rang from the constant chatter. The girl could be amusing, but she certainly liked to gossip.

Clay chided his sister. "Now, Cora, it isn't polite to speak of people that way. Miss McFarlane must be astonished by your remarks."

"Yes, dear brother. I'm sure tongues are wagging about our Katherine now. Did you see the way the other girls stared at her? They were quite jealous that she was your guest."

"*Our* guest, Cora. You're exaggerating, as usual."

Had they forgotten she was present, speaking of her as if she weren't? She glanced from one to the other, not knowing how to interject a comment to remind them.

"Well, I know *one* young lady for certain who was unhappy to see Katherine with you." Cora smiled and nodded her head assertively.

At her comment, Clay shot his sister a menacing look that temporarily silenced the talkative sibling. His gaze returned to Kate, as did his magnetic smile. "Please forgive my sister for her foolish talk. I hope you won't think her too rude. Did you like Trinity?"

Kate's cheeks warmed as she returned the smile. The banter had been entertaining at least, although she didn't care to be drawn into a conversation about the parishioners. "I found your church to be very beautiful. I especially liked the organ and how the walls resounded with its music. Of course, I enjoyed meeting the other church members as well. It was very nice of you to invite me to come with you."

"You may come with us every Sunday if you wish."

Cora's eyes twinkled as she smiled at Kate. "I really hope you will. Next time perhaps you can join us for lunch."

"Thank you. And yes, your mother invited me to join you next week. That would be nice. I'll speak to Aunt Sally before I give you a commitment, if you don't mind."

When they returned to Aunt Sally's, Clay jumped down and helped Kate out of the carriage. She said goodbye to Cora then turned to the house. Clay walked alongside her to the door, where he faced her with that smile that melted her insides. "I enjoyed having you with us today. I do hope we can make this a habit."

He tipped his hat then left as she stood there speechless. She could only manage a little wave of her hand as they rode off.

When she entered the house, Aunt Sally had lunch waiting in the dining room.

Kate removed her hat and hung it on the hall tree, then slipped off her shawl and placed it over the back of her chair in the dining room before sitting down.

"So, how did you like the church?" Aunt Sally asked.

"Oh, I think it's beautiful. The wood is lovely, and the organ music was wonderful."

"We do have a fine organ; that's true. And what was the sermon about? Did you enjoy Reverend Saunders' message?"

"Yes, I did. He preached about brotherly love and quoted the passage from John that says we should love one another."

"That's a good one for them to hear. I wonder how many of them actually took it to heart."

Kate remembered the way Cora gossiped on the way home and found it difficult to reconcile her conversation with the sermon. An attitude of love was definitely missing. She doubted Cora realized the harm with such talk. Maybe someday they could discuss it, if they became better friends.

"Aunt Sally, Clay told me your family once had its own pew at church."

"Aye, yes. That we did. Back when the church was built, they needed money, so they rented pews. I believe that was our banker's idea. We wanted a church building, so those of us who could, paid for one. I turned ours over to a new family when I quit attending."

"I see." So Clay's story was correct. The other members must have been surprised when Aunt Sally relinquished her family's pew and her ties to the church's history.

"So who did you meet?" Aunt Sally continued. "I'm certain many of our town's more prominent citizens were there, as always."

Kate listed the names of the members she had met -- those she could remember -- while Aunt Sally nodded.

"The town faithful. Some things never change."

"So you know everybody there?" Kate was surprised her aunt had ever associated with the town gentry.

"I know the people you mentioned. They've been members since we built the church. Don't know the newer families, though. And did you enjoy your time with the Harrises?"

"They were very nice and invited me to have lunch with them. I declined, of course, because I hadn't spoken with you about it."

"That's very thoughtful of you, and of course you may, any time you wish. You need to spend time with the folks in town."

"But I hate leaving you to eat alone."

The older woman laughed. "My dear, I've been alone a long time, and I've gotten used to it. Besides, Bessie and John are here if I want company."

Her statement reminded Kate of the slave gallery at church. "I noticed there's a slave gallery in the church. Do you think Bessie and John would want to sit there?"

"You can ask them. Bessie's been staying home with me on Sundays, but she might want to go with John."

After lunch the older woman said she was going to rest a while, since it was too windy for fishing. Kate decided it was a good opportunity to talk with John and headed to the barn, pulling her shawl tightly around her against the brisk wind coming off the water. She expected to find Bessie with John again. But John was alone, working on a tool and whistling one of his familiar tunes.

"Good afternoon, Miss Kate. You lookin' fo' somethin'?"

"Well, no. I mean, yes. I'm looking for you. Where's Bessie?"

"Bessie's workin' on a pot o' stew fo' tonight's supper. We needs somethin' hot to take de chill off our bones. Feel like it gettin' colder."

It certainly was chilly in the drafty old barn. Kate shivered. "Aren't you cold in here, John? How do you stay warm?"

"I keeps my shirt buttoned up and puts on a blanket when I gets real cold. It's not too bad, though. Better'n bein' outside. Sometimes I visits Bessie in de kitchen house too. It's real warm in dere, with de cook-fire goin' in de fireplace."

John's place above the stables back home had been more comfortable and had its own fireplace to keep him warm in the winter. Now he slept in a hayloft. Even so, the man never complained about his circumstances, and somehow, always managed to be in good spirits.

"So, Miss Kate, how you likes dat Trinity Church?"

"It was very nice. You'd love the organ music. The inside of the church reminds me of Christ Church back home, but it has much more wood paneling. And John, they have a slave gallery so the Negroes can worship too. Would you be interested in going next Sunday?"

"I sees if Bessie wants to go with me. Dat would be real

nice, bein' in church. Was de preachin' good?"

"Yes, I thought so. The reverend spoke about loving one another."

"Dat's right. 'Love one another. Dat's what Jesus tole his disciples dat night He done washed dere feet. Dey was so surprised when He done dat! Acted like He was dere slave, He did."

"Yes, you're right. You know the Bible so well. Have you memorized the entire book?"

"Ha! Don't know it all, but my gran maman back in Barataria done read it to us ev'ry day. I heard dem stories so much, dey burned in my mind. Guess dat's why I remember it, even now, all dese years pass."

"You were blessed to have a God-fearing grandmother that raised you." Much like her Aunt Elizabeth had raised her when her own mother died.

"Dat's right. I thanks de good Lawd ev'ry day fo' her and what she taught me. It hep'd me get through lots o' hard times."

"Like when the government captured the camp and sold you as a slave, even though you were only a young boy?" Kate was familiar with John's past, even though Aunt Elizabeth said John "stretched" the truth about being the son of a pirate. But John never lied, so Kate believed everything he told her.

"Dat's right. De good Lawd saw to it dat a godly man, yo' grandpa, was de one what bought me. He was a good man and taught me mos' everythin' I know about sailin' and horses. Den, when he passed, your papa give me my freedom. Yes, suh, de good Lawd was lookin' out fo' me."

Kate shook her head. She couldn't understand how he could say that. "But John, you lost everything – your family, your home . . . ."

"Dat's a fact, but I gots a new home and a new family. And I gots you."

Kate lowered his gaze, not knowing what to say but

thankful for the man's protective tenderness towards her. She studied her hands and wrapped them in the edge of her shawl.

John broke the awkward silence. "So you comes here to talk about me? Or you wants to talk about your new beau?"

"My beau! I'd hardly call him that. I only went with his family to church."

"Now, now, Miss Kate. I seen dat sparkle in you eyes when you looks at him or when his name is said, and how yo' cheeks get pink. I ain't seen you with dat look before. Tell me de truth now, you likes him, don't you?"

"Of course I like him. He's quite charming, a real gentleman." Warmth rushed to Kate's face and spread throughout her body. "However, I believe it's far too soon to call him a beau."

"Well it's a good thing he be a God-fearin' man. Dat's a blessin', fo' sho."

A God-fearing man? He must be, since he took her to church, even though they hadn't discussed anything spiritual.

"They've offered to take me to church every Sunday. While I appreciate being their guest, I still feel uneasy about leaving Aunt Sally at home. They offered to take her as well, but she declined. She's a difficult woman to understand. She gave me her reasons, yet I can't believe she's stayed away from church so long."

"Well, I'se sho Miz Sally gots her reasons fo' not goin'. Dat woman, she knows her mine."

"That's for certain. I wish I were as sure of myself."

"Someday you gonna be. It take time to figure out what you believe and what God wants you to do."

"And you know that, John? You know what God wants you to do? How can you be so sure?"

"Miss Kate, you just has too many choices. Maybe it's been a blessin' dat I ain't had so many. But I knows what I believe, and I knows where God want me to be."

"And where is that, John?"

"Right here, lookin' after you, Aunt Sally, and Bessie. I gots me three good women to look after, and I'm thankful fo' de privilege."

Did God want Kate to be there too? She hadn't considered that possibility. After all, it hadn't been in her plans. What reason would God have for her to be there? And did Clay Harris have anything to do with God's plan for her?

Chapter Eight

A blustery freezing rain greeted the household the next morning, putting aside any plans to work outdoors. John got the fire started in the parlor's fireplace, and Bessie lit the oil lamps throughout the house. After the chickens were fed and the eggs gathered, Bessie served Kate and Aunt Sally a breakfast of biscuits and jam, eggs, and coffee. As Bessie placed the food on the dining room table, Aunt Sally glanced up with a raised eyebrow. "Bessie, did you and John have your breakfast yet?"

"No, ma'am, we's gonna eat out in de kitchen house when I gets finished serving you and Miss Kate."

"That's nonsense! It's foolish for you and John to have to eat out there and traipse back and forth in this weather to wait on us."

Bessie's eyes widened in surprise. "But, Miz Sally, dat's what we always does."

"Well, it's time we put a stop to that. Don't know why I never thought about it before. Y'all get your plates and sit right here in the dining room with us."

Kate's mouth fell open, mirroring Bessie's look.

"But, Miz Sally, we's fine with eatin' out in de kitchen. We been doin' it all 'long."

"Well, that doesn't make it right, does it? No, there's room at this table for all of us." The older woman banged down her cup, coffee splashing out. "Go get John, and you two come in here."

Kate didn't know what to say. What would Clay Harris think about Aunt Sally's suggestion? She doubted he would approve.

John and Bessie brought their food and sat down with them. At first the atmosphere was a bit uncomfortable, but John changed it as he turned to Aunt Sally, seated at the head of the table. "Thank you, Miz Sally. Does you mind if I thanks de good Lawd fo' our food?"

"Please do, John. That would be quite appropriate."

John bowed his head and everyone else followed suit. "Dear Lawd, we thanks you fo' givin' us dis warm, dry place to come in out of de storm. We thanks you fo' dis good woman who is so givin' and kind, like you tole us to be. Bless dis here food, Lawd, to make us strong. Amen."

After breakfast, Aunt Sally suggested they all go into the parlor as the sound of rain and sleet hitting the windows reinforced their plans to stay inside. When the group gathered near the warm fireplace, John scanned the room, his eyes resting on the large Bible sitting atop a small table. "Miz Sally, why don' you read de Bible to us? Been a long time since I heard a Bible read."

"I wish I could, John. But I haven't been able to see the print in that book for years, unfortunately. I'm afraid that old Bible has just been gathering dust."

John glanced over at Kate. "Why don't you read it, Miss Kate? I bet you can see dose letters."

Aunt Sally's face lit up. "Well, that's a grand idea, John! Kate, would you mind? That would be a most pleasant way to spend a dreary day inside. Duncan loved God's Word. He used to say, 'the key to God's light is in His Word.'"

Kate smiled and nodded, while John handed her the

heavy book, which she placed in her lap. She ran her fingers along the embossed leather cover, reminded of the Bible back home and the times when they gathered to hear her father read from it. "Aunt Sally, this is a beautiful old Bible. Where did you get it?"

"Duncan brought that one from Scotland. It's been in his family for years."

"Truly? We had one like it back home. I believe it was my grandfather's."

"Sure you're right about that. Since Duncan and your grandfather Donald were twins, there had to be two of everything so they were both treated equally. Their father even bought two of these Bibles so when his sons got married, they each received one."

No wonder the Bible looked the same. The raised letters were like her grandfather's Bible, but the cover seemed thicker. "Where should I start reading?"

"Psalms. That's my favorite book."

Kate turned to the middle of the Bible, then read from Psalms for the next hour, while the others listened, sometimes nodding or John saying, "Um hum, dat's right." A sense of family knit the odd group together while they shared God's Word.

Kate's throat was getting dry, so she stopped reading. "Could we have some tea?"

"Sounds good to me!" Aunt Sally slapped her hands down on her pants. "We can hang the teapot over the fire in here to heat the water."

They all stood and stretched, while Bessie went to get the teapot and Kate accompanied her to retrieve the cups and tray. John fetched more wood off the back porch to add to the fire. When they returned to the parlor, Aunt Sally showed them a box she had taken off the bookshelf.

With a wink, she scanned their faces and said, "I've got a grand idea for a way to spend time." She carefully opened the carved wooden box and revealed its contents.

"Dominoes!" Kate clapped her hands. "I haven't played with dominoes since I was a little girl." A cozy memory of sitting around a table, playing the game with her mother and father, filled her with warmth.

John cocked his head and eyed the ivory game pieces suspiciously. "I don't know much about playin' games."

Bessie grabbed his arm. "Come on, I knows, and I can show you. Miz Sally, she done taught me how."

They went into the dining room, where Aunt Sally spread the pieces out on the table and explained the game. Time passed quickly as the four of them matched up their dominoes. Kate couldn't remember when she'd had so much fun. When John's stomach started growling loudly, they all laughed, then looked at the grandfather clock in the corner.

"It must be dinnertime," Aunt Sally announced.

Bessie rose quickly from the table. "Dat stew should be good and done. I'll go fetch it and check on my babies while I'm out."

John rose too. "I needs to stretch my legs some after sittin' so long. I'll he'p you, Bessie."

The rain had let up, though it was still cold and wet as Bessie put her shawl around her shoulders and started out the door to the kitchen. John grabbed his hat and coat and followed her.

A few minutes later, the two of them came back empty-handed.

Bessie wrung her hands on her apron. She glanced up at John, who spoke to Aunt Sally in a serious tone.

"De stew's gone, Miz Sally."

"Gone? Where'd it go?"

"Don't know, but look like somebody done took it – pot and all."

The woman's mouth dropped open. "Why, who on earth…?"

John shook his head. "No tellin', Miz Sally, but dere's

muddy tracks in de kitchen house. I should've gone to check on it befo'. I would've caught dat thief!"

Bessie eyed him warily. "And what if he'd attacked you? Lawd, Miz Sally, who would do such a thing as stealin' someone else's food?"

Aunt Sally looked down and sighed. "Somebody real hungry, I guess. They must not be from around here, though, or they would've known they could just ask me."

Kate shivered with uneasiness as she faced Aunt Sally. "Not from around here? Why would a stranger be so far from town?"

Their eyes opened wide with understanding as if the answer struck them at once.

"De soldier camp. It ain't far from here. Must be some hungry soldier," John said.

"Well, I would think most soldiers would have better manners than to steal someone's food," Kate declared, hands on her hips.

Aunt Sally shook her head, placing her hand on Kate's arm. "Seems like it all right, Kate. But not all soldiers have manners."

Kate gasped and placed her hand over her mouth as the image of an ill-mannered soldier came to mind. "Not Eugene Blackmon!"

"Could be. He's that unscrupulous. But we don't know for sure it was him. Unfortunately there might be some other rascals out there too." Aunt Sally stretched out her arms to the side. "Well, we better keep an eye on things from now on. We'll just have to eat something else tonight. Thank God, we have other food."

John cleared his throat to speak. "Miz Sally, don't you worry. I won't let nobody sneak in again. No, ma'am."

~

The next day dawned cold and grey but not raining, so Aunt Sally and Kate were able to get out of the house. They met Bessie and John on the back porch bringing breakfast from the kitchen house.

"Let's not abandon our Bible reading after we eat," Aunt Sally said. "When I still had my family here, we always gathered each morning for a bit of God's Word. There's no reason why we can't revive the practice."

John smiled at the older woman with warmth in his deep brown eyes. "I thanks you, Miz Sally. I feels like I'se goin' to church. Dis cold weather's turned out to be a blessin', after all."

Church. Kate's heart skipped a beat at the memory of Clay Harris taking her to church. Had he and his men been in their camp during the nasty cold weather? It was hard to picture him camped out in a tent, deprived of all the comforts of home. Had he thought about her anymore? He appeared to like her, but it was Cora who had invited her to go with them, not he. Maybe he was just being polite. Maybe there was someone else he was more attracted to. And what was that silent message he and Cora had exchanged after the service when she remarked about someone who wasn't happy Kate was with them? Which one of the attractive young ladies had her sights set on him?

When Clay rode up on his horse later that day, some of her questions were answered. They were all outside, assessing the condition of the garden and barn since the week's storm. Clay dismounted, removed his cap, and nodded to the ladies, holding his cap over his heart. "Good morning, ladies, Mrs. Sally and Miss McFarlane. It's nice to see sunshine again, isn't it?"

"Certainly is, Clay . . . I mean, Lieutenant Harris . . . oh, whoever you are!" The older woman's confusion made everyone smile.

"I need to speak to your niece, if you don't mind."

The basket Kate was carrying nearly slipped out of her hands. She reached up to make sure her hair was still secured and tucked a wayward wisp behind her ear.

"That will be quite all right. You two can talk over

there on the veranda."

Clay escorted Kate to the porch and motioned for her to sit in one of the wicker chairs. Standing in front of her, he straightened his jacket as he eyed his reflection in the window. He cleared his throat.

"I wanted to talk to you about our Cotton Ball. Every year we hold a celebration at the end of the cotton season and award a prize to the planter with the best crop. It's a grand affair – the biggest in our fair city - and is held at the Orman house the third Saturday evening in April, when the weather's warmer. Miss McFarlane, it would be my honor if you would allow me to be your escort to the ball."

Kate lost her capacity to speak. For a few moments she could only stare up at the finely-chiseled face in front of her. Her throat began to dry, and she forced herself to swallow.

"Are you all right? Can I get you some water?"

Kate nodded then waited while he fetched a cup of water from the pump. As she sipped it, a thousand thoughts raced through her head, and she contemplated what it would be like to accompany him to the ball. Realizing he was waiting for an answer, she managed to smile and say, "Why yes, that would be lovely. I didn't know about your ball."

"Excellent! I'm very pleased you've accepted my offer. Yes, it's quite a gala. All the prominent people in town and the surrounding area for miles around, even some of the foremost plantation owners from upriver, will be there. The Orman house is the largest in the city, and Mr. and Mrs. Orman are excellent hosts. You'll have a most enjoyable time. I will personally see to that myself."

Kate couldn't stop the warmth from invading her face. It was difficult to look him in those gray eyes for fear he could see right through her and know the effect he had.

"I'm looking forward to it, and I'm grateful for your offer. Let's ask Aunt Sally, though, for her permission."

Kate's attention shifted to a figure behind Clay, lingering in the shadows of the woods. Turning in the direction of her gaze, Clay stiffened as he recognized the man.

"Mr. Blackmon, what are you doing here? Have you left your post?" Clay scowled at the man, who sauntered over in a very unmilitary style. "What is your explanation for this intrusion?"

The man gave a limp salute to the lieutenant, then straightened as best he could and glared back at the officer.

"Sir, the captain asked me to go fetch you. He didn't tell me what fer; he jes said, 'Go get Lieutenant Harris.' I didn't ask no questions. I just went."

Kate's stomach lurched at the dribble of brown liquid running down the man's chin, explaining the lump in his jaw.

"Go tell the captain I will return shortly. I am not finished with my business here yet."

"Yes, sir." Before he turned to leave, however he sneered at the lieutenant and gave Kate a knowing look. Then, glancing at John over in the garden, he shot a menacing glare as he turned away.

As soon as he was out of sight, Kate let out the breath she didn't realize she'd been holding. The man was abominable. Why did he always seem so rude and malicious?

"Please forgive Mr. Blackmon's impudence. He has no manners. I'm trying to train him to be a soldier, but teaching him manners is a lost cause." Clay turned to look in the direction the man had gone. "His kind is such low-class I would prefer not to have him in my company, yet we must take all the men we can get for our militia. I will have words with him later." He turned back to face her, his frown disappearing. "Let's forget this intrusion and resume our conversation. It seems we were about to ask your aunt's permission for you to attend the ball."

As it turned out, Aunt Sally was delighted to give her approval to Kate and Clay. "How exciting! I remember attending the Cotton Ball with Duncan many years ago. It was always such a wonderful gala."

Kate struggled to imagine the little woman she had only seen in men's clothing going to a festivity such as a ball. Much had changed in the widow's life since her husband had passed. Yet it was difficult to pity someone with so much pluck.

"Mrs. McFarlane, will you be going with us as a chaperone?"

"I don't think I would fit into such a setting anymore, but I'll consider it for Katherine's sake."

"I hope you'll give it serious consideration." He tipped his hat to them. "Well, ladies, if you'll excuse me, I must return to my duties. I'm looking forward to the celebration and, hopefully, will be able to escort both of you." He turned to face Kate again. "May we take you to church again this Sunday?"

Kate looked at her aunt for permission. Aunt Sally gave it with a nod.

"Yes, I would very much like to go to church with your family again this week. Thank you."

When he was out of sight, Kate turned to her aunt in utter astonishment. "Aunt Sally! Who would have thought he would ask me to such a gala event? Oh my, whatever will I wear? Will you truly consider being my chaperone?"

The woman laughed out loud. "Slow down, girl. Catch your breath. Of course I can believe it. The man's no fool. If he didn't ask you, someone else might, and he couldn't let that happen, now could he?"

"But I don't know anyone else."

"Kate, you have gotten the attention of many people in town. Don't think the other young men haven't noticed you."

"But I have nothing to wear to a ball. I must go into

town and purchase some material to make a gown."

"It's over a month away, so you should have plenty of time to get your dress ready. We'll go to town tomorrow and see what we can find. We can order some material if we need to. It can get here by riverboat in a few days from up north."

The rest of the day went by in a blur, as Kate couldn't quit thinking about the ball, the invitation, and Clay Harris. She couldn't remember the last time she had been so excited about going to a party. But going with Clay would be so special, like a princess with her Prince Charming. She saw herself on his arm while the other young women yearned to be in her shoes. She imagined dancing with him, being swept off her feet in his strong arms, gazing up at his handsome face. And then they would dance away together.... But wait; she would not let her imagination go that far.

As she lay in bed that night, trying to still the visions running through her mind, she basked in the glow of the invitation that held such promise. What an exciting turn of events! The promise of spring was just around the corner, and nearly everything in her life was changing for the better. Well, almost everything, with the exception of that awful Eugene Blackmon, whose presence certainly could spoil an otherwise pleasant atmosphere.

Chapter Nine

"Katherine!" Cora almost tripped over the hem of her skirt as she rushed to meet Kate coming through the mercantile door. "Aren't you excited about the ball? I can't wait to show off my new ball gown. It's the latest style! Come, and I'll show you the picture in the magazine."

It came as no surprise that Cora already knew Clay had invited her to the ball. Of course, he was her brother, but she seemed to know everything about everybody.

"I take it your brother told you he invited me and I accepted."

"He did, although I had to work on him to pry that information loose." She leaned a bit closer and lowered her voice. "I'm so glad he asked you and not someone else."

Someone else? Who else had he considered inviting? Kate shook the misgivings from her mind. "Who's going to be your escort, Cora?"

"Jacob Miller! His father is James Miller, the bank president. I don't think you've met him. He's quite good-looking and so entertaining; he always makes me laugh."

Cora needed someone to make her laugh? She had a perpetual smile. It would be interesting to meet Jacob Miller and see what type of fellow had invited Cora to the ball. "I look forward to meeting him."

"Oh, you'll like him, I'm certain. So have you decided what you're going to wear?"

"No, actually, I was hoping you could help me with that."

"I'd love to! We have some copies of *Godey's Lady's Book*, with all the newest fashions. Have a seat over there and we can look through them."

The next couple of hours went quickly as Kate and Cora poured over copies of the ladies' magazine. Some of the styles seemed too elaborate for Kate's more simple taste, yet those were the ones Cora liked the best. Finally, she settled on a style that suited her.

Next came the decision about which fabric to use. Kate's hair color posed a dilemma as they considered colors that would look best. Although the new colors of mauve and magenta were enticing, the girls didn't think those shades would be complimentary. The choice came down to either a pale blue or deep green. When Kate saw a sample of gorgeous forest green silk, she knew that was the right fabric, and Cora emphatically agreed. The fabric was expensive, but Kate decided the special occasion was worth the extra cost.

"Oh, Katherine, you'll be so lovely in that color! We'll order it today and it should be here on the next boat down the river from Atlanta. That should give you plenty of time to complete it for the ball."

In addition to the silk, Kate chose some lovely lace and ribbon for the dress's trim as well as her hair. Kate left the store satisfied with her selections and joined Bessie, who waited outside on the bench.

"Bessie, I'm very sorry I took so long. The time quite got away from me. You must be hungry."

"No, ma'am. I don't mine waitin'. I enjoys watchin' people. I likes to study dem. You can tell lots about folks by watchin' dem."

"You can? Like what?"

"Well, you see dat man a-hurryin' over dere? He late fo' some important meetin', and tryin' to think of what to tell de other folks when he gets dere about why he so late. He pro'bly gonna say he held up by some business, but truth is, he fo'got about de time because he been daydreamin' about some woman."

"Why, how do you know that, Bessie?"

"Oh, I don't knows fo' sho. But I likes makin' up stories about people I sees. It's right amusin'. And you never knows if I might be right." Bessie tittered, nodding at Kate.

What an charming imagination the woman had.

"Don't worry about me bein' hungry, neither. I brought a couple of biscuits from dis mornin' wrapped in a cloth here in my pocket. Brought you one too, if you wants it. I gots a tin cup here fo' some water when we pass a pump." Bessie patted the pocket of her apron.

"Well, thank you, Bessie. That was very thoughtful. Perhaps we can get a jar of tea from the café instead."

The two women walked over to the café, where Kate went in and purchased a jar of tea to take with them. As she waited for the waitress to return with the tea, she noticed a table in the corner where three young ladies were having a grand time together, giggling and whispering. Their glances in her direction hinted that she was the topic of their conversation. She recognized two of them from church. The third one was unfamiliar, but stood out noticeably.

Trying not to stare, Kate observed that the young woman with olive skin and coal-black hair was strikingly lovely. She wore a fashionable day suit, with its gray jacket and skirt trimmed with black velvet ribbon, and a perky black velvet hat with an ostrich feather atop her lovely face. She had an air of superiority, as if she held a place of honor not attained by anyone else in her presence.

When she caught Kate looking at her, she smiled coyly

and nodded, her eyes conveying a knowing look. Kate smiled briefly, gave a quick nod then glanced away.

The waitress returned with Kate's order and noticed Kate's unease. Glancing sidelong at the women, she leaned toward Kate. "Look at Miss Fancy Pants over there. She thinks she's better than everybody else."

Kate couldn't resist asking about the intriguing woman. "Who is she?"

"That, my dear, is the Marquesa Maria Isabel de la Vega. Isn't that a mouthful? She's visiting here for the season with her father, the Spanish consulate."

"Oh. I didn't realize there was a Spanish consulate here."

"We have several European consuls here. They all want our cotton."

"I see." Aunt Sally had mentioned that too. She studied the jar of tea in her hands. "Well, thank you for the tea. Good afternoon."

Kate took her purchase and joined Bessie outside, who frowned when she eyed Kate's expression.

"Miss Kate, you all right? Is somethin' de matter?"

"No, I'm fine. I just saw a rather interesting woman inside."

Bessie laughed and nodded. "I bet you seen de Mar-kay-sa, dat Spanish woman." Bessie stumbled across the unusual name. "She somethin', ain't she? Heard some of de other folks talkin' about her."

"Hmm. Is that so? I wasn't introduced to her, but I noticed her inside. She carries herself quite proudly, doesn't she?"

At that remark, Bessie burst out laughing again, and Kate had to smile herself, despite a little twinge of guilt about her snide remark.

As they walked along the sandy road back to Aunt Sally's, they talked about Kate's ball before the conversation turned to John. Bessie had lots of questions to ask Kate about him, and Kate was more than happy to talk about her lifelong companion. It was no longer a secret that Bessie cared for John, and he appeared to reciprocate the feeling. Now that Kate had Clay Harris in her life, she was no longer jealous about John and Bessie's relationship.

They had just passed the Richardson house when Eugene Blackmon stepped out onto the road in front of them.

The women gasped at the unexpected encounter, stopping abruptly.

Blackmon eyed Kate with the evil stare he was so prone to. "Why, look who's here. What's a purty thing like you doing out here all by yourself, Miss McFarlane?" He hissed the word "Miss," as he put his hands on his hips and planted his feet firmly apart, blocking their way.

"I am not alone, as you can plainly see, sir." Kate tried to sound civil, despite her loathing for the man. "If you'll let us pass, please, we need to get back to the house."

"Kind of smart, ain't you? I don't see your Negro man around here. Cain't believe he let you out of his sight." He turned his head to the side and spit a wad of tobacco on the ground.

Kate shuddered but tried to appear calm. Oh, how she wished John were near! And where was Clay? Wasn't this man supposed to be on duty somewhere? *Please, God, let someone else come along.* But few people traveled past the outskirts of the city on this road. Maybe there *was* something she could do.

"Actually, sir, John is coming to meet us. I expect him any moment." Her heart squeezed at the purposeful deception. *Lord, forgive me for lying. I just wish my words were true!*

They were still half a mile from home, but Bessie took her cue. "I think I sees him comin' now."

"Yes, I believe you're right. John! Over here, John! Here we are!" Kate waved her hand vigorously overhead as if she saw John approaching.

When Eugene turned around to look, the women grabbed their skirts and ran past him as fast as they could.

"Think you can outsmart me? I'll show you!" Eugene took up chase behind them.

Kate's long legs outran Bessie's, leaving the woman behind. A piercing scream rang in Kate's ears. She skidded to a stop and looked back. Eugene held Bessie, his arm wrapped around her neck.

"Let her go!" Kate demanded.

"How 'bout a trade? It ain't her I'm interested in no way."

Kate trembled with anger at the scoundrel, who pulled Bessie's arms behind her in a tight grip.

"I'll report you to your superiors, sir, if you harm her."

"You think Lieutenant Harris cares about this Negro woman? You don't know him very well, do you?"

Kate winced at the infuriating remark.

A shot rang out, hitting the tree limb just above Blackmon's head. He jumped and let go of Bessie, who ran toward Kate. They turned to see John walking up, holding Aunt Sally's rifle.

"John!" both women called out and rushed to his side.

"Afternoon, ladies. I was just comin' to meet you and thought I'd do some squirrel-huntin' on de way. Saw one up dere on dat branch, but looks like I done missed him."

Blackmon glared at them, then leaned over and grabbed his cap that had fallen on the ground. He hit it against his pants to get the dust off then snarled at them. "You better watch yourself, all of you. I'm gonna remember this. You ain't gettin' away with it, neither." Turning to leave, he spat on the ground then stalked off.

Kate breathed a sigh of release. "John, thank God, you came along! I don't know what would've happened if you hadn't. How did you happen to show up just in time to rescue us from that man?"

"Well, you know, I thinks de Lawd nudged me and say, 'John, why don't you get Miz Sally's rifle and go squirrel-huntin' right now?' I hadn't been thinkin' about doin' dat today, but sometimes de Lawd puts thoughts in yo' head at just de right time. So I don't argue with Him. If dere's one thing I'se learned in my life, it's don't argue with de Lawd. If He say do somethin', you just go ahead and does it. Good thing I listened."

John put an arm around each of the women's shoulders as they made their way back home. Bessie's soft sniffles twisted Kate's heart, and she blamed herself for the woman's distress. If she hadn't been with Kate, Blackmon wouldn't have grabbed her. If Kate hadn't outrun her, he would have grabbed Kate instead. No scenario was desirable. She was so thankful John was always there to look out for her. But it was time to report the evil man to Clay. She'd tell him about it on Sunday.

As they approached the house, Kate recovered some composure. "What should we tell Aunt Sally? I worry that our encounter with that Blackmon fellow will upset her."

The group stopped as John rubbed his chin to contemplate his answer. "Maybe we don't need to tell her everythin' dat happened. We's just gonna tell her we met up with him on de road, but I was dere, so she won't worry."

Kate considered John's suggestion. They wouldn't be lying—just leaving out a little bit of the truth. She nodded. "All right. I believe that's the right thing to do."

When they got home, Bessie, still shaken by the incident, headed to the kitchen house, and John followed to console her. Kate took a deep breath and mustered up her enthusiasm about the ball before she went inside to tell Aunt Sally about her dress.

~

When Sunday arrived Clay and Cora came for Kate as before. Clear blue skies heralded a beautiful March day, and Kate didn't want to spoil it with talk about Eugene Blackmon.

Cora's smile dazzled as she greeted Kate. "Katherine, there's a picnic after church today. Everyone in town is going. Will you go with us?"

Kate looked at Clay, who nodded and said, "It's a fine day for the outing. Please join us."

Glancing over at Aunt Sally standing on the veranda, Kate said, "Aunt Sally, would you mind if I go?"

The older woman shook her head. "Not at all. You young folks enjoy yourselves. It should be a nice day for a picnic."

After the service they left Trinity Church and joined other families on the beach along the bay, laying out blankets and quilts to sit on. Baskets full of fried chicken, coleslaw, biscuits, and jam were passed around, along with cups of lemonade. Kate helped the other ladies hand out the refreshments, including slices of pound cake for dessert.

Kate and Clay admired the scene as they sat on a quilt. The early spring weather was beginning to warm, and everyone was in good spirits, enjoying the delicious food and peaceful view of the water. A few leisure boats glided past in the bay, their sails full of March wind.

"Do you like to sail?" Kate asked Clay, lifting her face to inhale the salty air, harboring a desire to be on the water again.

"Never particularly cared for it. I don't enjoy being jostled about by the waves."

Kate raised an eyebrow as she studied Clay. He sat with one arm resting across his bent knee, staring at the water. How could he not enjoy it? These waves were mild compared to what she had experienced on her father's ship. She sighed and turned back to the bay. A hint of disappointment dampened her spirits.

However, they lifted again as the sound of water lapping the shore mingled with seagulls screeching overhead, begging for morsels of bread to be thrown to them. Children ran through the edge of the sandy water barefoot, squealing in delight as the cold water kissed their feet. Mullet fish leaped through the air, and a family of dolphins frolicked nearby, producing shouts of joy from the onlookers.

"Ever wonder why those fish jump out of the water?" Clay's younger brother asked as he stopped his running around long enough to get a drink. He pointed at the mullet.

"I think it's to attract female fish." Clay spoke to the child, while smiling at Kate.

"John says they do it to lay their eggs," Kate commented.

"John? Who is this John fellow? Someone I should be concerned about?" Clay winked at Kate as he asked.

"John is our freed man, the one my father left with me. He's quite knowledgeable about fish and things related to the water."

"Is he now? You spend time talking with this Negro?"

"Why, I've known John my whole life. Of course we've talked quite a bit."

"My dear, you must be careful about being too friendly with those people. It's not something ladies should do. Others might frown upon such habits." Clay patted her hand as he spoke, reminding her of a parent speaking to a child.

Kate tilted her head and studied him, not knowing how to respond.

Were the clouds getting darker, or were his comments shadowing her otherwise pleasant day? The setting, the food, and the company – all had seemed perfect just moments before. Her affection for the town was growing, along with her sense of belonging to the community. If only her father could share the experience with her. But would he approve of Clay? The dashing, debonair officer seemed popular with everybody.

Yet his remarks bothered her. Clay didn't understand what John meant to her, but she didn't think she could explain it to him either. And she didn't care at all for his patronizing tone. Nevertheless, she had no desire to debate the matter with him and spoil the day. There would be another time to discuss this, when they got to know each other better.

Chapter Ten

"Mr. Harris asked me to deliver this package here," the drayman said, his wagon loaded with supplies for several households.

As Kate eagerly reached for the parcel containing her dress material, he added, "I have a letter too." The man squinted as he studied the writing on the envelope. "For Miss Katherine McFarlane in care of Mrs. Sally McFarlane."

"I'm Katherine McFarlane." She took the letter bearing a Mobile, Alabama, address. Recognizing her father's handwriting, Kate couldn't wait to open the letter.

She paid the drayman for the delivery and settled into a large wicker chair on the veranda.

Dearest Katie, I hope this missive finds you well. I have been busy re-establishing my contacts in other ports since I left you. Now that several southern states have seceded from the Union, my customers in Europe are faced with a dilemma over their allegiances. In case of a conflict, they may have to take sides, a notion they disdain. In any event, I hope to continue trading with them as before, unless the conflict extends to the seas. For now, I have moved my base to Mobile. I have made contact with a Mr. Semmes, who assures me these waters will remain safe for shipping.

Meanwhile, I have notified your Aunt Elizabeth in Greenville of your whereabouts. Needless to say, she had been quite overcome with anxiety about your absence. I have assured her of your safety and relieved her of her anguish and guilt.

She sends her love and asks me to tell you that your friend Sarah is well and missing your company. Perhaps someday you two can reunite. She would enjoy receiving a note from you.

I trust you and John have provided assistance to Aunt Sally with the household duties. Please give John my regards, and Aunt Sally my love.

I will send you another missive when I can. I still intend to keep my promise to see you on your birthday in September.

Until then,

All my love,

Your devoted father

Tears streamed down Kate's cheeks. How she missed him! If only she could go to Mobile to visit him. But that prospect wasn't possible. She missed Sarah too. It would be so nice to tell her about Clay and her life in Apalachicola. Did Sarah like it in Greenville? Had she heard from Lark? Perhaps Kate could write her a letter later that day.

Lost in her reverie, she didn't hear Aunt Sally approaching.

"Kate, dear, what's wrong? Was there something amiss with your fabric?"

Her fabric! She had completely forgotten the package on her lap.

"Oh, I haven't even opened it yet. I received a letter from my father and have been reading it."

"Is he well? Does he send bad news?"

Realizing she was referring to the tears, Kate wiped her face with the back of her hand and mustered a smile.

"Oh, no. Everything's fine." She returned the letter to the envelope and slipped it into her skirt pocket. "He just told me he's now working out of the port at Mobile. He stills plans to be back here for my birthday."

"I know you miss him, dear. It must be reassuring to get a letter from him. I remember how much it meant when I received a letter from Duncan when he was away at sea. I treasured them so much, and I kept them all. They're stored in a box in the attic to this day."

Her aunt's comment reminded Kate about her visit to the rooftop. Perhaps another visit to the widow's walk would lift her spirits. But she'd have to ask permission next time, and right now they needed to work on her dress.

Aunt Sally pointed to the package. "Well, let's look at this material you've bought. I can't wait to get started on that dress of yours."

~

The next few weeks flew by, as Kate and Aunt Sally worked on her gown for the ball -- when they weren't working in the garden. There was a lot of planting to do, now that spring was upon them. Rows of beans, peas, squash, and tomatoes were planted, as well as watermelon and strawberries. The sandy soil was easy to dig, but they had to add mud from the nearby marsh and more manure from the neighbor's barn for the plants to prosper. Anticipating the tasty harvest motivated them, and Kate enjoyed the camaraderie they'd developed as they laughed and talked while working side by side, often entertained by John's singing.

After lunch each day, Kate and Aunt Sally retreated to the house, where they constructed the ball gown. Surprisingly, Aunt Sally was a good seamstress and knew how to make the dress look exactly like the picture in *Godey's*. Kate wanted it to be perfect.

Then, one afternoon while they were working on the dress, they heard John yell, "Fire!"

Kate and Aunt Sally dropped their work and rushed outside to see the barn was in flames. John and Bessie frantically tried to beat the fire out with old horse blankets to keep it from spreading to the dry grass nearby.

Aunt Sally assessed the situation and turned to Kate. "Quick! Grab that bucket and go down to the beach and fill it up with water. I'll get some from the pump."

Kate obeyed. Hiking her skirt with one hand, she grabbed the wooden bucket. The smell of smoke followed her as she raced to the water's edge, trying to maintain her balance while she scrambled down the path. Quickly she dipped the bucket into the cool water then started up the hill, water sloshing onto her skirt. Her heart pounded. She must hurry.

Suddenly an arm encircled her, jerking her backwards into the undergrowth. She lost her footing as a dirty hand clamped over her mouth, stifling the scream that tried to escape. Kate twisted one way, then the other, as she struggled to free herself. She couldn't see the face of her captor, but recognized the stench of breath and grimy fingers. Blackmon! Had he purposely started the fire to get her away from everyone else? Although she was as tall as he was, her strength was no match for his and there was no help in sight or hearing. *Dear God, please help me!*

As if summoned, an object dropped down from the tree branch and hung directly in front of them. Blackmon yelled in terror as an oak snake hissed close to his face. No longer interested in Kate, Blackmon stumbled backwards, frantically groping for his gun, while Kate took the opportunity to tear herself free. Running up the hill to the house, she reached the yard in time to see the smoking ruins of the barn. The fire was out, but the barn was lost. John, Bessie, and Aunt Sally stood nearby, surveying the damage.

"Kate, where have you been? Where is the bucket of water I sent you for?" Eyeing Kate's dress, Aunt Sally's forehead creased and her tone sounded concerned. "Did you fall? Your dress is torn."

What should she say? How could Kate tell her about Blackmon's attack when her aunt's barn had just been destroyed? Kate didn't want to further upset her with the truth, so she went along with Aunt Sally's perception, once again ignoring the sting of conviction in her heart.

"Yes, I fell, Aunt Sally. I'm so sorry I wasn't any help."

One look at John told her he didn't believe her. She could tell he somehow knew she was holding back, covering up facts that she felt best left unrevealed at this particular time. She promised herself she would tell him the entire story later.

"We still need some water on this smoking wood to make sure the fire doesn't rekindle itself," Aunt Sally announced. "I wonder how it got started. We didn't have any lightning, did we?"

"No, ma'am. Didn't see no lightnin'. It's real curious." While John spoke, he studied Kate's face, his expression revealing suspicions about what had happened. "I gets some mo' water. Dat bucket must be down de trail where you dropped it, Miss Kate."

Kate wanted to warn him not to go back there and run into Blackmon. Her pleading look must have given away her concern. He responded with a knowing smile. "I'se sho de danger is past now de fire's out. I'se gonna watch my step goin' down dat trail so I don't fall too."

Aunt Sally nodded. "We need to clear that path out some more so we all don't fall. Some of those tree roots can trip you up, and we don't want anybody falling and breaking something."

"Yes, ma'am. I gets to work on dat soon's we clear up dis here mess."

"Well, it'll have to cool off before we can do that." Aunt Sally shook her head and turned back to the house. "Come on, Kate. We'll have to mend your dress and sew that sleeve back on where it tore."

Bessie went to pump more water from the well, while Kate and Aunt Sally trudged back inside.

Dinner that evening was a solemn affair.

"John, you can sleep here on the porch now that the barn is gone. I hope you didn't lose anything valuable." Aunt Sally's compassion was genuine in her concern for the man.

"No, ma'am. Never had nothin' worth somethin'. Nothin' but de people I cares about. Still gots my harmonica too!" John grinned as he pulled the instrument out of his pocket and held it up so the others could see.

Kate stared at him in amazement. He had lost what little he had, yet he still found reason to be happy. How did he do that?

After Aunt Sally retired to bed, Kate went outside to the porch. John and Bessie were sitting on the wicker settee, talking quietly.

"Evenin', Miss Kate." The couple looked up and smiled a welcome. "Have a seat," John said.

Kate sat down in a chair opposite them. "I need to tell you the truth about what happened today." She recounted the events, while John's brow furrowed and Bessie twisted a handkerchief in her lap.

"I was afraid o' somethin' like dat." John shook his head. "Dat fella up to no good. He tole us we'd be sorry we messed wit' him."

"Messed with him? Why, that abhorrent man started all this trouble himself!"

"Sho 'nuff. But folks like him never thinks nothin' dere fault. He's set his eyes on you, Miss Kate, and he thinks I's in his way. Dis fire done shows he stoop to anythin' to get what he want. It high time you tell dat lieutenant o' yours about him, and Miz Sally too. Cain't keep dis from her no mo'. It won't he'p none. Guess you gonna have to tell her you fibbed about dat fall." He lifted an eyebrow. "Den you can ask de good Lawd fo forgiveness about lyin'.'"

Kate let her gaze drop to her lap, regretting her lie to Aunt Sally. She knew the Bible said lying was wrong, but she'd done it to protect her aunt...hadn't she? She sighed and nodded her head. "I suppose you're right, John. We've got to take measures to protect ourselves against that evil man."

It was Bessie's turn to speak. "Praise de Lawd for dat snake! Why, it could've fallen on you too!"

"I wish I seen de look on his face when dat snake drop down in front o' him!" John chuckled.

"I certainly didn't take time to turn around and look," Kate said, "but I bet it was a sight to behold. Never thought I'd be thankful for a snake, but I am. God answered my prayer, just in time."

Soon they were all laughing as they pictured Eugene Blackmon grabbing for his gun while the snake dangled in his face.

The next morning they told Aunt Sally the truth about their encounters with Blackmon. She scowled and shook her head as she heard the stories of his malicious actions.

"I knew that man was a sorry character, but I didn't know he'd been bothering you. Frankly, I'm a bit upset with all of you for keeping this from me." Looking at Kate, she said, "Young lady, your father left you under my charge. I need to know if there are any dangers around here. You must promise me you'll tell me the truth from now on. The *whole* truth. Is that understood?"

Kate nodded. "Yes, ma'am. I'm sorry. I promise."

Then with hands on her hips, Aunt Sally glared at John. "John, you know better than to keep things from me, don't you?"

John dropped his head and said, "Yes, ma'am. I knows better. I's real sorry."

"I know you are. We all live here together, and we should have no secrets from each other. We must be able to trust each other. Promise me none of you will avoid telling me the truth from now on. And we have to protect each other, but we can only do that if we all know the entire truth. I intend to have words with Clay and his superior about this. Now is there anything else I should know?" The diminutive woman looked from one to the other, silently daring them to keep something else from her.

Clearing his throat John took Bessie's hand, and with his eyes fixed on Aunt Sally, spoke up. "Well, ma'am, Bessie and me, we wants to tell you somethin', and I guess now's as good a time as ever."

Kate was surprised by John's statement and worried about the next one. Were he and Bessie going to leave them to get away from the harassment? After all, they were both free and could go wherever they wished. Maybe they wanted to go up North where she'd heard Negroes were treated better. What would she do if he left?

"What is it, John? Come on, out with it," Aunt Sally insisted.

"Bessie and me, we wants to jump de broom . . . you know, get married. Dis trouble we been havin' has made us know we don't want to stay apart no mo', and we wants to be hitched up de proper way."

Aunt Sally laughed out loud and stretched her arms out full-length as she tried to put them around John and Bessie both. Kate breathed a sigh of relief.

"That's wonderful news! I wondered when you two would confess your feelings for each other. So when do you plan to get married?"

"Soon's we can." Tenderness flowed from John as he gazed down at Bessie, who beamed her smile at him in return.

"Where will you get married?" Kate asked.

"Well, I don't thinks de preacher will marry us folk in de church, but I'm hopin' he might come out here to de house, if you don't mine, Miz Sally."

"Mind? Why of course you'll get married here! The azaleas are blooming, and the yard is right pretty for a wedding. It'll be lovely."

"And I can help. I'll make punch and cookies," Kate's excitement bubbled inside her.

John viewed her with his warm, dark eyes shining. "Dat would be right nice of you, Miss Kate. Right nice."

"Well, now it seems we have two festive occasions to prepare for – a wedding and a ball! My life certainly has become more exciting since you two arrived." Aunt Sally's eyes sparkled with delight.

"And now we have two dresses to get ready," Kate said. The others turned to face her. "That's right. We need to help Bessie get her dress ready for the wedding."

Aunt Sally nodded in agreement.

"But, Miz Sally, I only has dis one dress." Bessie looked down at her faded muslin frock with its frayed, worn edges.

"It's high time you had a new one, Bessie, especially for your wedding. Kate and I can help you with it. I have some material I haven't used, which will do just fine. We better get started right away." Aunt Sally turned on her heel and marched down the hall, waving a finger in the air. "But first thing tomorrow, I'm going to pay a visit to Lieutenant Clay Harris and maybe even the captain at that camp and demand something be done about Eugene Blackmon. Then I think it's time I make a visit to the rectory and reacquaint myself with Rev. Saunders."

Chapter Eleven

Sally McFarlane was a woman of her word. First thing the next morning, she strode over to the army camp a half-mile northwest of the house. Kate accompanied her, as did John and Bessie, not wanting to leave anyone home alone. As they approached the scene littered with tents and soldiers, Aunt Sally addressed the first soldier she met.

"Young man, can you please direct me to Lieutenant Harris's tent?"

The man appeared startled by the woman's direct manner. "Yes, ma'am. This way."

Kate kept her eyes averted and head slightly bowed to avoid the stares of the men in the camp. Although some of the married ladies from town often brought food to the officers, it was still an uncomfortable place for a young, unmarried woman to be. She wanted to see Clay, but not under these circumstances.

"Ladies!" Clay jumped to his feet and adjusted his frockcoat as he stepped out from under the tent's canopy to greet them. "What brings you to this place?" His eyes were wide with surprise as he surveyed the group.

"Clay . . . that is, Lieutenant Harris, I demand that you control the behavior of one of your men." Aunt Sally got right to the point, dismissing pleasantries.

Clay's smile vanished as his expression darkened.

Aunt Sally continued by detailing the harassing events Eugene Blackmon had engineered. Kate watched Clay as he listened. She was amazed by how aristocratic he appeared in his uniform, which was more tailored than those the rest of the soldiers wore. Even in humble surroundings, he conveyed an air of superiority.

Clay listened to Aunt Sally, occasionally rubbing his chin in thought. "Mr. Blackmon will not be a problem for you ladies anymore. I know just what to do with him. Please accept my apologies. I was not aware of his vile behavior. If he ever comes near you again, I will have him punished."

"I'll expect you to do just that," Aunt Sally affirmed with a brisk nod of her head.

Bidding him good day the group left the camp, while Kate resisted the urge to glance over her shoulder. She could feel him watching her as they walked away. What was he thinking about their visit? Would it affect the way he acted toward her? She hoped not.

Next they walked to the rectory to see Reverend Saunders. Met at the door by his wife, the ladies were invited in, leaving John and Bessie standing on the front porch. Aunt Sally turned to them with a reassuring smile.

"We'll be back shortly, and I'll introduce you to the reverend."

Reverend Saunders seemed surprised to see Aunt Sally and eagerly offered the ladies a seat. "Mrs. McFarlane! It's been quite a while since our last meeting. I do hope you're doing well. To what do I owe this unexpected visit? I've had the pleasure of meeting your great-niece, Katherine, and have been delighted to see her at worship services. Does this mean you're going to join her?"

"Well, Reverend, that depends on you."

The reverend raised an eyebrow. "And how is that?"

"You see, Reverend Saunders, we have a freed man in our employ who has recently begun attending your church. He would like to marry my Bessie but wants to have a real wedding, with a real preacher conducting the ceremony. Would you be willing to come out to my house next Saturday and perform the rite?"

The reverend stroked his well-groomed beard. "And how does this affect your attendance in church, Mrs. McFarlane?"

"I guess you can say I need to see how sincere you are to minister to all people, and that you're willing to do that outside the walls of the church, as well as inside. John is about as devout a believer as I've ever known. He loves the Lord and knows the Bible inside and out. His conduct is exemplary, and he has earned my respect. I would like to see him treated that way by others, especially by a man of God, such as yourself."

"I see. And if you are convinced that I am 'a doer of the Word, and not a hearer only,' you will return to worship with us at Trinity?"

"I see you're a man of great understanding, Reverend. Yes, I would come back to church again."

She would? Kate hadn't expected such a reply from her aunt. Even though Aunt Sally was uncomfortable being in church, she would make the effort for John and Bessie's sake. What an unselfish woman!

"Where is this man?" the reverend asked. "May I meet him?"

"He and his intended are right outside on the front porch, waiting for your answer."

"Well, then, let's not keep them waiting any longer. I'd like to meet this man who has made such an impression on you, dear lady. What time is the wedding?"

~

The rest of the week was a flurry of activity as they prepared the house and yard for the wedding ceremony.

Bushes were trimmed, weeds pulled, the porch rails washed, and the wicker furniture cleaned. John was exceptionally happy as he worked, singing aloud in his booming bass voice the spirituals so common to the Negroes.

Work stopped on Kate's ball gown while they created a dress for Bessie. Aunt Sally found some pink and white calico material in her trunk, which looked lovely against Bessie's caramel skin. They decided on a simple shirtwaist design, with a fitted bodice and full skirt, but with a collar trimmed in white eyelet lace at the neck. Aunt Sally recovered one of her old bonnets with the same fabric as the dress, trimming it with the eyelet lace as well. Kate added some white ribbon for ties on the bonnet and a bow at the neck of the dress.

When Bessie tried it on, she beamed with delight as tears welled in her eyes.

"Miz Sally, Miss Kate, dis da prettiest dress I ever did see! I thanks you so much fo' makin' it fo' me."

Kate and Aunt Sally brushed tears from their eyes as well, as they viewed the beautiful image in front of them.

"You look lovely!" Kate was thrilled with the result of their labor. The slender woman had been transformed. "I can't wait to see John's face when he sees you."

"Well, he'll have to wait a bit longer. He can't see her until she walks down the aisle. It'll be a sight to behold indeed!" Aunt Sally crossed her arms and nodded.

"And now that the roses are blooming, I can make you a beautiful bouquet to carry." Kate envisioned the bouquet with roses and pink ribbon to match Bessie's dress.

"Y'all done too much fo' me already. I know dis been takin' time away from makin' your own dress fo' de ball, Miss Kate."

"That's quite all right. This has been so much fun. Besides, my dress is coming along nicely. We'll have plenty of time to get it finished before the ball."

"I hopes John don' feel bad about his old clothes when he sees me in a purty new dress."

Aunt Sally looked startled then a big smile spread across her face. "Well, why didn't I think about that before? You go ahead and get out of that dress so we can finish it up. When you go outside, please ask John to come here."

Kate's heart warmed. What was her aunt up to now? Aunt Sally went upstairs to her bedroom and returned with an armload of clothes.

When John came into the house, Aunt Sally greeted him. "Here," she said, handing him the stack of garments. "Go try these on."

"What dese, Miz Sally?'

"Why, they're clothes, John. You need something better to wear to your own wedding than those work clothes you wear every day. We've got Bessie all fixed up with a new dress, and you need to be a fitting groom for her!"

"But, where . . . ?" John's voice trailed off as he searched the woman's eyes for answers.

"They belonged to Duncan. He was a heavier man than you, but you're about the same height. These clothes aren't doing him any good anymore, so they're just lying here useless. You go in there and try them on." She pointed to the dining room. "I'm sure we'll have to take them in for you, but that won't be a problem."

"Yes, ma'am. I better wash off some o' dis dirt befo' I put on dem nice clothes."

"Go ahead and clean up then so you can try them on, and we'll wait right here in the parlor. Time's awastin', though, so be quick about it."

When John returned wearing the new clothes, he looked like a different man. Tall and distinguished, hair graying at the temples, the freed slave had changed into a gentleman. The gray slacks were slightly baggy but long enough, and the coat was the same. The white shirt beneath stood out brightly against John's brown skin, and the black vest added to his refined appearance.

"Well, well, if you don't cut a fine figure in those clothes, John!" Aunt Sally walked around the man, grabbing a handful of material here and there. "Yes, indeed, we'll just take in these seams here and you'll look so debonair, you'll make Bessie swoon!"

"What about shoes, Aunt Sally? And a necktie?" Kate was anxious to complete the outfit.

"You're right. John will need those too. I believe you can wear Duncan's shoes too, John, with your big feet. And I still have his neckties, and can even add a handkerchief for your pocket."

"Ma'am, I don't knows what to say. You just too kine to me."

"Don't be silly, John. It's the right thing to do. Didn't we just read in the Bible, 'The man who has two tunics should share with him who has none, and the man with food should do the same?' Guess that goes for women too."

"Miz Sally, you is a fine Christian woman, and I thanks God fo' puttin' me here in dis place with you."

~

Saturday arrived with the promise of a beautiful spring day. Kate had cut bouquets of azaleas and placed them in vases around the porch and in the parlor. At two o'clock, Reverend Saunders arrived as promised. Soon the yard was filling up with Negroes from town. Household servants, maids, cooks, drivers, and dockworkers all gathered to chat excitedly about the wedding, enjoying some time away from their duties.

Promptly at 3:00, Reverend Saunders and John stepped forward to take their place in front of the guests. Whispers scurried through the crowd as they took in the fine-looking figure of John standing proudly in his suit, a rosebud pinned to his lapel.

Bessie walked out the front door to the gasps and

admiring eyes of her friends. Her gaze was fixed on John, though, as she floated toward him in her lovely new dress, carrying a bouquet of pink azaleas with a few white roses nestled inside.

John's face glowed as he watched his bride approach. The love emanating from his eyes was almost tangible, while his wide smile was dazzling. Kate observed the couple's adoration for each other as they joined hands in front of the minister. *So this is how true love looks.* She had been to many fancy weddings in Pensacola, but she didn't think any of them matched this one in its simple yet sincere celebration of two people joining together in a commitment of love. Would she ever experience that feeling? Could she feel the same way about Clay, and he for her?

Afterward everyone joined in congratulating the married couple, enjoying orange punch and cookies. When the festivities eventually died down and the guests left, Reverend Saunders faced Aunt Sally.

"Mrs. McFarlane, this is a fine thing you've done today and a brave thing too. You're a generous woman."

"Reverend, thank you for coming and marrying John and Bessie. That was a brave thing too."

"I believe God is pleased with us today. He told us to love each other, didn't He?"

"Aye, Reverend, He did. And I love these people here in my household."

"And it's obvious they love you too."

Turning to leave he looked back with a smile and said, "I look forward to seeing you tomorrow at the worship service."

"I'll be there, Reverend. I made you a promise. Your congregation will be so shocked to see me, they'll think there's been another resurrection!"

~

As time passed without another encounter with Eugene Blackmon, Aunt Sally's household resumed their activities without fear of intrusion. Nevertheless, the four tried to stay together as a precaution, making any necessary trips into town as a group.

On Palm Sunday Aunt Sally rode with Kate and Clay to church. Bessie and John walked by themselves, meeting friends along the way. Kate was still getting used to seeing her great-aunt in a dress ever since she kept her word to attend church after Bessie and John got married.

"This spring weather is delightful. We best enjoy it now before it gets too hot." Aunt Sally sat next to Kate, across from Clay and Cora. The older woman wore a simple brown dress with a lace collar. She refused to wear a hoop, though, no matter how stylish it was.

"I'm so happy to shed those drab winter clothes. I love seeing the springtime catalogs and new fabric in the store." Cora's hands fluttered about her like a butterfly while she spoke.

"And what do you like about springtime?" Clay asked, facing Kate. "Perhaps you're thinking about the upcoming ball?"

Kate's face warmed, and she smiled. "Actually, I was admiring all the lovely spring flowers."

Clay raised his eyebrows and pursed his lips while Aunt Sally's smug smile showed amusement.

They arrived at church, and while walking up the front steps, Kate overheard a conversation nearby.

"I heard they sent some soldiers over on the islands for border patrol. It's good to know we have men on guard here in town and over there too. Should keep us safe from enemy invasion."

Had Blackmon been sent to the islands? That would explain why they hadn't seen him.

Another man spoke. "Don't know how many we'll have left here after the big send-off in a couple of weeks."

What big send-off? Was Clay leaving? She couldn't wait to ask Clay about what she had heard. What if he left before the ball? Panic rattled her nerves as the possible cancellation of her plans loomed, dashing her dreams to bits.

On the way home she broached the subject.

"I heard that many of the soldiers will be leaving town soon."

Clay nodded. "That's correct. We're sending a hundred men to train at the Chattahoochee Arsenal before they get their final orders."

Aunt Sally joined the conversation. "Is that so? Where will they go next?"

"Probably Pensacola, to join forces over at Fort Barrancas." Clay glanced over at Kate, who tried to hide her anxiety as her hands grew moist inside her gloves.

"So will you be going too?" Aunt Sally asked the question Kate was thinking.

"No, I'm one of the few who will be staying here, at least for now. I'll probably get orders to move out later."

Cora chimed in. "You'll still be here for the ball, won't you, Clay? We can't let our Katherine go unescorted!"

Kate cringed, wishing she could hide under her hoop. The weather was getting warmer very quickly, and she fanned herself to curtail the beads of perspiration popping out on her face.

Clay smiled and leaned forward, fixing his eyes on Kate.

"Of course I'll be here. Miss McFarlane can rest assured I will not leave her unescorted."

The attempt to quiet her anxiety only partially worked. On the one hand, she hoped Eugene Blackmon would be sent far away and out of their lives for good. On the other hand, Clay might soon leave as well. And if he did, would that end any chance of a future with him?

Chapter Twelve

Perfect. Standing in front of the full-length mirror, Kate was thrilled with how beautifully her gown had turned out.

"Aunt Sally, it's lovely."

"It is a very pretty dress indeed. I don't think you could have done a better job of selecting a style and material that flatters you so well. With your slender form and tiny waist, the dress fits you just right."

The deep green satin evening dress came to a V in front, showing off Kate's ivory shoulders, without being too revealing. There were diagonal tucks running from the sleeves,   crossing in front on the bodice and creating another V at the waist. Trimming the edge of the short, puffed sleeves and the tucks were rows of wide lace, decorated with black velvet ribbon tied in bows. The skirt was actually two skirts, with a shorter one over the floor-length one. The shorter one was pulled up at intervals, creating the look of flounces, which were also accentuated by the bows.

"Thank you so much, Aunt Sally. You're a wonderful seamstress."

"Well, you're good with a needle and thread too. I've enjoyed working on a party dress; it's been so long since I made one, and I'm very pleased with the way it turned out, if I do say so myself. You'll turn a few heads, I dare say."

"I just hope Clay likes it."

"He'd be a blind fool if he doesn't."

The two women laughed aloud. Kate couldn't help admiring her reflection in the mirror. Surely Clay would be pleased as well. Kate paused, drawing closer to the mirror, her fingers touching her face.

"What's the matter, Kate?

"I'm afraid I've freckled, even with a bonnet on."

"Ah, you've the skin of a redhead, that's for certain. It's so hard to keep it from spotting. Don't worry, though. Those spots are light enough to cover up with some cornstarch so no one will see them. Now, what will we do with those glorious amber locks?"

Kate shook her head and sighed. "I know it might be impossible with my thick hair, but I did see an attractive style I particularly liked in the magazine. The hair is pulled up to the crown, then ringlets cascade down the back. Do you think we could do that with my hair?"

"Well, between the three of us – you, me, and Bessie -- I'm sure we can get the look you want. With your hair's natural curl, putting it in ringlets shouldn't be too difficult."

"Oh, I hope so. I also saw pictures where they wove ribbons through the hair, which was really pretty."

"Your hair is certainly thick enough to hold ribbons, and we have enough ribbon left over. I'm sure we can manage to make something you'll be pleased with."

Kate glanced down at her hands, red and rough despite the work gloves she wore in the garden. "I'm so glad you have nice gloves for me to wear, since I didn't bring mine with me."

"These have open fingertips, so they'll fit you just fine, even though you have longer hands." Aunt Sally handed her a pair of black lace gloves. "Now, you have your gloves, fan, nosegay, and chatelaine, but something's missing."

"Do you mean the shawl? I plan to wear your black one with the lace on it."

The older woman didn't respond as she walked over to an intricately carved wooden box on her dresser, opened it, took out a necklace, and returned to place the lovely piece of jewelry on Kate. Kate bent her knees so her aunt could reach her neck.

"Oh, it's exquisite, and so elegant! Do you really wish for me to wear it?" Kate's eyes widened as she caressed the large emerald brooch suspended from the gold and pearl necklace. She straightened and admired the reflection from the cheval mirror.

"This necklace belonged to my grandmother in Scotland. Her husband, who was also a sea captain, brought it to her from one of the islands he had visited on a long voyage. It was, in fact, accompanied by his proposal of marriage. He didn't think she would be able to refuse him after she saw that."

"But, Aunt Sally, it's too valuable for me to wear. Don't you want to wear it yourself?"

"No, dear. I want you to wear it proudly and be the envy of all the other girls. The color matches your gown perfectly. I thought of it as soon as I saw the fabric."

"It will be my honor to wear it." Kate gently touched the sapphire, admiring its reflection in the mirror, with tears stinging her eyes. Her aunt's thoughtfulness to share such a precious possession with her melted her heart.

Kate twirled around, her skirt rustling around her legs. "I'm so pleased you decided to accompany me as my chaperone! I'll feel much more comfortable to have you with me, since I still know very few people here."

"A few months ago I wouldn't have considered it, but now that I've returned to church, I suppose it's time to give society another try. Besides, I'm the only proper escort you have."

True enough, there was no one else suited to escort her, with her father and Aunt Elizabeth away, and it would not be acceptable for John to do so, even though he was capable.

"I know you'll enjoy getting out and visiting with the other people," Kate said. "It'll be such fun! After all I've heard about the Orman House, I'm eagerly looking forward to attending a party at so grand a home.

"Aye, it's the grandest house in town, no doubt. The Orman family knows how to impress all the investors that come here. But we better quit talking and get finished dressing before your gentleman friend comes to get us. And be sure to stand up straight. Tall women have a tendency to stoop, but it distracts from their appearance. And there's definitely no need to stoop next to Clay – he's plenty tall. Hold your head up high, and you'll look as graceful as a swan."

Your gentleman friend. Was he really hers? It seemed she seldom saw him, except on Sundays. Of course, he had an important job to do with his military duties, but she wished he would come visit more often. Even though they enjoyed each other's company, she didn't feel as if she knew him very well. Their conversations had been light and social, never about anything important. It irritated her how some men acted as though women were incapable of discussing matters of significance. Thankfully, her father had treated her as though she had equal intelligence with him.

There was no denying the physical attraction between her and Clay, but was it the beginning sparks of love? She wanted to feel what John and Bessie felt for each other, but would she know it when it was there? So many doubts assailed her, yet Clay had invited her to the ball, and no one else. Surely that showed his interest in her, so why was she worried? He was no doubt the most handsome bachelor in town, and she was still surprised he had asked her, with many other young ladies to choose from.

Just as the sun was setting, Clay arrived at Aunt Sally's. His face brightened when Kate appeared in her evening gown. A broad smile spread across his handsome face, revealing his dimples as his gray eyes radiated approval.

"Miss McFarlane, you are a vision of loveliness. How beautiful you look tonight!"

"Why, thank you, Lieutenant Harris. I'm pleased you like my gown."

"Not just the gown, my dear. The dress only accentuates your beauty." He took Kate's gloved hand and kissed the back of it, then turned and bowed to the older woman. "Mrs. McFarlane, you look very lovely tonight as well. I'm pleased that you're joining us tonight for the gala."

Kate's heart swelled as she smiled at her dashing escort - the perfectly groomed chestnut hair and mustache framing his finely chiseled face. Standing tall in his uniform, embellished with a gold sash and polished buttons, he exuded an air of nobility, reminding her of pictures she'd seen of England's Prince Albert.

A full moon was rising on the horizon with the promise of a wonderful evening. The late spring temperature allowed the air to be cool enough for comfort, but warm enough to be outdoors. As they neared the Orman House, the sounds of music and laughter could be heard before the house was visible. When it came into view, light poured from the floor-to-ceiling windows, onto the wide veranda, and into the gardens where gaslamps flickered.

A line of carriages formed behind the house as guests emptied out and onto the path leading to the imposing two-story Greek Revival-style mansion perched high atop the river bank. Clay led the women to the front door, where they were announced by one of the house slaves dressed in formal livery. Entering the parlor, they were greeted by Thomas and Sarah Orman, standing near a large round table, its magnificent floral arrangement commanding the center.

"Welcome to our home." Thomas Orman, the tallest man Kate had ever seen, towered over Clay. Mr. Orman bowed to Aunt Sally. "We're so glad you could come. Mrs. McFarlane, it is especially nice to see you this evening. It's been quite some time since we've had the pleasure."

Aunt Sally smiled and nodded. "I'm pleased to accompany my great-niece, Katherine."

"Katherine, you look stunning tonight. What a lovely gown!" Mrs. Orman grasped Kate's hands with both of hers in a warm welcome.

"Thank you." Kate curtsied.

Mr. Orman extended his right hand to Clay, while patting him on the shoulder with his other hand. "Clay, nice to see you. I appreciate your taking leave of your duties to attend our soiree. You know our son William shipped out with most of the other men last month." He swept his arm out toward the opposite side of the house. "Please get your guests some refreshments and make yourselves comfortable. There are chairs in the parlor and dining room, Mrs. McFarlane. But the air is quite nice outside this evening, so you may prefer the verandas or the gardens. We have some benches out there where you can sit down as well."

They excused themselves, and Clay led them back outside, where Aunt Sally seated herself on a wrought iron bench.

"May I get you ladies some punch?" The women nodded, and Clay disappeared among the other guests.

Kate sat next to Aunt Sally while they waited for Clay to return. The two women sat quietly as they took in the sights and sounds of the gathering. Women in elegant evening gowns on the arms of courtly gentlemen strolled throughout the gardens, greeting other couples with nods and curtsies.

Aunt Sally chuckled. "Looks like a bunch of peacocks strutting around, doesn't it?"

Kate hid her laugh behind her gloved hand. "Oh, it does, doesn't it?"

On one side of the house stood a large grove of orange trees, a crop Mr. Orman sold to ship captains, along with his cottom. The sweet scent of the blossoms wafted through the air. Kate tilted her head back and inhaled deeply. "What a delightful fragrance!"

"Those orange trees are Mr. Orman's pride and joy. If he could make more money selling oranges than cotton, he'd do it." Aunt Sally nodded at the orchard.

The front of the house faced the river, and a long boardwalk led down to it. From their perspective, the ladies could view the Orman dock, as well as others where ships were tied along the riverfront. Beyond them, the roofs of warehouses, hotels, and stores denoted the town.

Kate was the first to speak. "What a lovely view. I can almost see every building in town from here."

Aunt Sally nodded. "Yes, and Mr. Orman owns half of what you see."

"You mean, he owns half the town?"

"Practically. He owns half the cotton warehouses, two mercantiles, and at least five city blocks. Mr. Orman also owns other property outside of town, including the cotton plantation to the north."

Clay returned with china cups brimming with punch for the ladies. "Please forgive me for taking such a long time. I was detained by some of the men who were excited about our conquest of Fort Sumter. They're confident this war business will be over in a short time, with such easy victories."

Before Kate had a chance to ask him to explain about Fort Sumter, a servant arrived carrying a tray of smoked oysters and some small plates. "Would you ladies care for some oysters?"

The women declined the servant's offer, but Clay helped himself. "Delicious! I much prefer these smoked."

Kate had never developed a taste for oysters, smoked or not. Another servant appeared with a tray of barbecued pork. Kate shook her head. "No, thank you."

Hungry as she was, Kate was afraid she'd drop something on her gown or get food in her teeth and, truth be told, she didn't know how much food she could eat with her corset tied so tightly. Aunt Sally accepted the pork readily, though, as did Clay.

"Kate, aren't you going to eat some of this wonderful food?" Aunt Sally pointed to her plate as she nibbled some pork from her fork.

"Not yet. I'm really not that hungry now, but thank you, anyway. You go ahead and get what you want, though."

"Can I get you some more punch?" Clay lifted his cup. "I must be very thirsty, as I already need a refill."

"Yes, you may." Aunt Sally handed her cup to Clay. "This orange punch is delicious."

Before Clay could leave, Cora pranced up to their little group.

"There you are! I've been looking all over for you."

Cora glowed amid ruffles of her favorite color, pink. The dress had at least eight flounces, with rose-colored flowers adorning each one, as well as the bodice and the sleeves. In addition, her blonde ringlets were held in place by pink ribbons and more flowers, creating a look resembling sweet candy confection. Kate smiled and eyed the slender young man standing stiffly next to Cora.

The two men nodded to each other, and introductions were made. Clay did the honors. "Kate, this is Jacob Miller. Jacob, this is Katherine McFarlane, Mrs. Sally McFarlane's great-niece."

Cora beamed at Jacob. "She's the one I told you about."

Jacob Miller bowed. "It's a pleasure to meet you, Miss McFarlane. Mrs. McFarlane, nice to see you tonight as well."

"I was about to fetch refreshments for the ladies," Clay addressed Cora's escort. "Would you like to join me?"

A relieved look crossed Jacobs's face at the invitation. "Excuse us, please, ladies. We shall return shortly."

Cora's face sparkled as she beheld Jacob, impeccably dressed in his gray frock coat, striped vest, and starched white collar, the epitome of a banker. "Yes, Jacob, we girls can entertain each other. But just be back in time for the first dance. We'll meet you boys over near the dance pavilion."

The men left and Cora turned to Aunt Sally. "Mrs. McFarlane, would you like to accompany Kate and me to the dance pavilion?"

"You girls go on and socialize with some of the other guests. I'm fine right here, just watching everything."

As the two girls walked away, Cora turned to Kate.

"Isn't Jacob the most handsome man you've ever seen?"

"He's very nice-looking, and quite dignified." Kate spoke honestly, although she didn't think Jacob was nearly as handsome as Clay. In her opinion -- and apparently many other women, judging by their reaction to him -- Clay was clearly the best-looking man at the party.

Glancing in the direction of the carriages, Cora's attention was diverted to the arrival of more guests.

"Oh, there she is!"

"Who?" Kate turned to look as well, and her question was answered. Stepping down from a carriage was the woman she'd seen in the café, the Marquesa. Kate and Cora weren't the only ones with eyes focused on the woman. Every head was turned in her direction, which was not surprising, due to her dramatic appearance. The raven-haired woman wore a crimson silk gown with a black double-lace fall from the plunging low neckline. A single scarlet flower accentuated the décolletage, and a matching scarlet flower adorned her voluminous black curls cascading down the back of her neck. A black lace shawl was draped across her arms and she carried a matching black lace fan. Smiling at each gentleman in her path, she appeared to be pleased with the attention she garnered and enjoyed every minute of it.

"She's so brazen. Why, look at her low neckline! And the way she flirts with the men!"

Kate watched the Marquesa, who did indeed seem to be flirting with every man she saw, conveying numerous messages with her fan. Carrying it in her left hand, she opened the fan wide, extending an invitation to come talk with her. The men responded by following her like sheep led to slaughter, oblivious to the rest of their surroundings.

"Isn't a 'marquesa' the name of someone married to a marquis? I thought she was unmarried."

Cora tore her eyes away from the Marquesa to face Kate. "She's a widow. She was married to a marquis in Spain who was very old and very rich. When he died she inherited his fortune. Supposedly her father didn't want her to stay alone in their country, so he brought her here with him during the cotton season. I believe she's entertained herself by toying with our men."

"Why, whatever do you mean?"

"She's used her father to attain escorts while she's here." Cora's face reddened, and she turned away quickly to watch the Marquesa. "Isn't it deplorable the way those men are fawning over her?"

It was surprising, to say the least. Secretly Kate wished she could attract attention like the Marquesa. However she had never mastered the art of flirting. Looking down at her own plain palmetto fan, she sighed.

The music changed from quiet chamber music to a livelier dance tune, just as Jacob Miller appeared at Cora's side.

"Cora, dear, are you ready for our first dance?"

"Absolutely!" Putting down her shawl and fan along with their beverage glasses, Cora and Jacob strolled to the outside dance floor created on the grounds. Cora beamed over her shoulder at Kate. "Excuse us, please, Kate."

Kate scanned the area for Clay. Not finding him but hearing parts of a conversation nearby, she strolled over to listen. A small group of people had gathered around a distinguished-looking gentleman. Among them Kate found her aunt, absorbed in conversation with the man. Seeing Kate, her aunt reached out to summon her over.

"Katherine, I'd like you to meet one of my oldest friends in this city. This is Dr. Alvin Wentworth Chapman. Dr. Chapman has just published his book on flora of the Southern United States. Dr. Chapman, this is my great-niece, Katherine."

The kind gentleman smiled and bowed. "I'm very pleased to meet you, Katherine. Your aunt and I share an interest in plants. It's been some time since we've seen each other, as my field of study often carries me to other parts of the country. Of course, your aunt has been rather reclusive until recently, I understand. If you had anything to do with her reintroduction to society, I commend you."

Soon Kate was captivated as Dr. Chapman spoke about his many discoveries in the field of botany. She took the opportunity to query him about roses, and he respectfully answered, showing his appreciation for her interest. It felt good to be involved in a stimulating and enlightening discussion. She had almost forgotten about Clay until he arrived at her side.

In a voice a bit too loud, he said, "Katherine, I've been looking for you!" Clay's eyes sparkled in an unusual way, and she noted the smell of liquor and cigar on his breath. "Well, I'm glad to see you've been amusing yourself with plant talk. I'm afraid I got caught up in political discussions again." There was no mistaking the obvious tone of derision when he said "plant talk," as if the topic were foolish.

"Excuse us, Dr. Chapman. This young lady needs to dance."

Kate was embarrassed by Clay's rudeness, but she did want to dance. "I've enjoyed our conversation, Dr. Chapman.," she said.

"My dear, it has been most pleasant discussing our common interest. I hope we'll have another opportunity to talk. You young people run along now and enjoy the festivities."

Kate and Clay joined the other couples, and soon they were twirling amidst them. Clay's face glowed as he smiled at Kate in obvious enjoyment. "Kath . . . May I call you Katherine, as my sister does?"

"Yes, I believe we know each other well enough to use our given names."

"And you, charming Katherine, please call me Clay. Have I told you how radiant you look tonight?"

Kate's face warmed and she quickly turned away, sensing the heat of his hand on her waist while they danced. Her senses were flooded as she let herself be swept away with the music and magic of the evening. When she dared to look up at him, Clay gazed intently into her eyes, conveying a message too intimate for her comfort. She was certain she would melt; her senses were so overwhelmed.

Was this how love felt? She had yearned for his attention, yet this behavior was so completely different from his usual, reserved conduct. Was he beginning to display his true feelings to her, or was it the stimulation of the festivities? She was confused, unable to identify her own emotions.

Thankful for the gardenia nosegay she carried, she pressed it to her nose as the combined odors of liquor, cigar residue, and perspiring bodies threatened to overpower her. Their dancing was short-lived, however, as Clay soon became thirsty again, offering to get them more refreshments. Despite the servants carrying trays of punch among the guests outside, Clay once again retreated into the house. Apparently he preferred the stronger taste of brandy offered to the men inside over the orange punch.

After he left she accepted a glass from one of the trays, too thirsty to wait for Clay's return. She watched the dancing couples for a while and then decided to stroll around the grounds to cool off and breathe some fresh air. As she reached the opposite side of the house, she once again enjoyed the fresh aroma of the orange trees. How nice it would be to have one of those trees at Aunt Sally's house! She came back around to the front of the house then stood on the veranda facing the river.

Scanning the sights up and down the waterway, she noticed a couple standing down on the pier. Although it was some distance away and dimly lit, a note of familiarity struck her about the two people. A cloud covering the moon shifted, and Kate recognized the Marquesa's red gown, and standing extemely close to her was a man in a soldier's uniform.

With a gasp, she realized it was Clay.

Chapter Thirteen

Kate's heart stopped. What was Clay doing with the Marquesa? The way his arms encircled her waist as he lowered his head to hers, the way she held his face with her hands as she tilted her face up to his—there was no doubt the couple was very familiar with each other Perhaps too familiar. A rush of angry heat swept through her, and questions flooded Kate's mind as she tried to understand what she was seeing.

A bell sounded and someone called out, "Everyone gather 'round! It's time to present this year's Cotton Award!" Kate turned to see Mr. Orman standing at the front door, and before she knew it, she was swept along with the rest of the crowd toward the speaker. As she was pressed in, she tried to look back at the dock but found her view blocked by other guests.

Mr. Orman cleared his throat and scanned the crowd. "Ladies and gentlemen, as you know, it is our custom to award the planter with the best cotton crop for the year at the Cotton Ball. Mr. David Raney, president of the Apalachicola Chamber of Commerce, will present the award."

Mr. Raney stepped forward and lifted an elaborately

embossed silver pitcher for all to see.

"On behalf of the Apalachicola Chamber of Commerce, I'd like to present this year's award for best cotton crop to Mr. Howard Allen of Columbus, Georgia."

Cheers erupted as the guests applauded. A portly red-faced man stepped out of the crowd to accept the pitcher, which apparently was heavier than he expected as he almost dropped it in the exchange.

Mr. Allen withdrew a handkerchief from his pocket and wiped his sweating face. Spurred on by the onlookers and perhaps a bit too much brandy, he embarked on a long diatribe detailing the production of his prize crop.

Kate fanned herself to produce some relief from the oppressive heat of so many people in such close quarters. She wanted to leave, but her way was blocked by those behind her. As the man droned on, she couldn't get the scene by the waterfront out of her mind. What should she do? Leave? She desperately wanted to talk to someone about what she had witnessed, but whom? Oh, how she wished she could talk to John! He always had the best answers for any situation.

She couldn't think straight with so many emotions vying for her attention. Catching sight of Aunt Sally on the opposite side of the veranda, she worked her way through the throng to reach her aunt's side. With some difficulty, she finally managed to get close to the woman.

"Aunt Sally!" Kate whispered as loudly as she could to get her aunt's attention.

Unfortunately, several taller people stood between them, blocking her from the short woman.

"Aunt Sally!" Kate tried again, this time getting the attention of the gentleman standing behind her aunt. He tapped Aunt Sally on the shoulder then whispered in her ear. When she saw Kate, the curiosity on her face switched to concern. She forced her way through the crowd to reach Kate, who grabbed her arm and pulled her aside.

"Why, Kate, what on earth is the matter with you? Are you feeling well? You look rather flushed. Let's get away from all these people so you can get some fresh air."

The two women moved away from the crowd and found a place to sit in the garden.

"Oh, Aunt Sally, I don't know what to do! I've just seen the most alarming sight."

"Why, dear, what is it? What did you see?"

Kate, her eyes filling with tears, went on to explain the scene with Clay and the Marquesa down by the river.

"What does this mean? One minute Clay and I were dancing and having a wonderful time. He was telling me how beautiful I was. Then he went to get more refreshments, and the next time I saw him, he was with . . . that woman! How could he do this to me? I feel so humiliated."

"Dear, dear, calm down. Are you certain it was Clay you saw? There are other men here in uniform. Perhaps you mistook one of them for Clay."

"I'm almost positive it was he. If it wasn't, where is he then? It's been some time since I lsst saw him." Hope tried to take a small hold on her emotions as she considered the possibility that it might not have been Clay after all.

"I don't know, dear, but there are a lot of people here. Perhaps he's in the room where the men gathered - sipping brandy and smoking cigars or discussing politics. Of course, that doesn't excuse his absence so long from you, but men will be men."

Clay had previously told her that was exactly what he had been doing. Maybe she was mistaken. She really hoped so. She glanced up to see Clay approaching, his long strides moving swiftly across the lawn.

"Finally, I've found you! I've been searching all over for you, Katherine."

Kate stiffened. "You must have been searching in the wrong places. Surely I'm not that difficult to find. I'm not the shortest woman here."

Clay looked at her quizzically, his eyebrows raised.

"No, I'm afraid I have that distinction," Aunt Sally interjected.

Clay looked at Kate's aunt and smiled. Then turning to Kate, he reached for her hand. "Would you like to go for a little stroll?"

Kate's expression implored her aunt, who nodded in return. "That sounds like a good idea to me, Kate. Why don't you two take a walk?"

Kate reluctantly accepted Clay's hand as he led her away from her aunt. She was angry at him but wasn't certain she had cause to be. How could she know the truth?

"Did you see the presentation of the Cotton Award?" Clay turned to her as he asked the question.

"Yes, I did. Did you?" Kate raised an eyebrow as she studied his face.

"Why, yes, of course. I couldn't quite get out the door from the library where I'd been. Still, I heard the man drone on about his cotton. Where were you?"

"I was out on the veranda, wedged in between other guests. So you were in the library?" Kate stopped and faced him, trying to detect any hint of falsehood as he answered.

Clay met her gaze. "Yes, the men corralled me in there. They all wanted to discuss the possibility of war, and the likes of which I'm sure don't interest you."

"And why do you assume that, Clay? Shouldn't I be concerned about those things too? After all, they do affect me. Not to mention my father."

"Why, Kate, don't take offense. Most women don't typically enjoy those types of conversations."

"Well, maybe I'm not like most women." Kate's response was a bit sharper than she had intended.

Clay's eyes widened. "I can see you're not. But you needn't worry about such things. Those are problems for men to deal with. After all, it's the men who go to war to defend their country, as well as the women they care for."

Women they care for? There was that condescending tone again. But he'd said "care for." Was he telling her he cared for her? But what about what she had seen? She tried to brush the scene aside.

"But I am concerned about these things, Clay. I do want to know what's going on. I don't want to be kept in the dark. God gave women brains too, and I believe He expects us to use them." Kate tossed her escaping curls out of her way.

"Katherine, dear, must we argue about such things? I know you're a smart lady. I wouldn't be interested in you if you weren't. Why don't we just put this subject to rest?"

"I don't mean to argue with you either. I just want to know about the world I live in. If you remember, I've already suffered consequences from this impending war by being forced to leave my home. My father always tried to explain things to me, and I hoped you would do the same."

Clay placed his hands on her shoulders, peering into her eyes as if trying to understand her. "All right then. What do you want to know?"

With a sigh, she allowed herself to relax. Maybe Aunt Sally was right and it truly wasn't Clay she had seen.

"I want to know about Fort Sumter. Where is it? What happened there?"

"Fort Sumter is a fort at the entrance to Charleston's harbor in South Carolina. Last week Confederate forces demanded that Union troops holding the fort surrender. When they didn't, our forces fired on the fort, so they surrendered. It was such an easy victory for our side that we expect an early end to this war."

His confident tone was encouraging. "Truly? I certainly hope so. But were any lives lost?"

"Not that I've heard of. So you see, you have little to worry about. This business will come to resolution soon, now that President Lincoln sees we're a force to be reckoned with."

They walked on in silence as Kate considered Clay's remarks about Fort Sumter. If he was correct and there would be no long war, she'd soon be reunited with her father. Yet that thought posed another problem. Being with her father might mean leaving Clay.

Ahead of them a man dashed up the boardwalk into the house. Soon shouts sounded though the night air.

"What on earth is happening?" she cried as Clay's grip tightened on her arm and he steered her toward the house.

Inside excited voices rose from every direction. Clay grabbed the arm of the closest man. "Harold, what's this all about?"

"Didn't you hear, man?" He pointed across the room. "That fellow over there just arrived on a steamer with news that President Lincoln is retaliating to the Fort Sumter business by declaring a blockade of all Southern ports. He's planning to stop our commerce!"

"We'll see about that, won't we? He can't tell us what to do!" Clay crossed his arms in a defiant gesture.

Kate's heart pounded. What about Clay's assurances that the war would end quickly? Reaction to Lincoln's decision sounded like the war was heating up instead. She gazed around the room at the hardened faces of men ready to defend their land. The hope of being reunited with her father slipped from her grasp.

Other voices came from across the room. "I'm sure Europe will come to our aid. They need our cotton."

The foreign diplomats in the room appeared very uncomfortable as people questioned them about their countries' allegiances. Many gave vague responses, looking fearful and anxious to avoid answering questions.

One man shouted above the rest. "It's time all of us join the militia and fight this intrusion in our waters. I'm joining up right away, and I suggest the rest of you men stand up and fight for your rights as well!"

"Count me in!"

"Me too!"

"Every Florida county should have its own militia!"

"First thing in the morning, we'll meet at town hall and join up. We have to protect our property!"

Clay's commanding officer then took the floor. "I am encouraged by your support of our cause. I'll meet you in the morning and we'll sign you up for duty. Together we will defend our town and our state!"

The party no longer focused on cotton but on the impending blockade. Converesation turned to criticism of President Lincoln and his audacity to block their port.

Clay turned to Kate with a somber expression. "Katherine, I'm sorry, but I won't be able to accompany you to church in the morning. It looks like we'll be on duty tomorrow."

"It would appear to me that church is exactly where we all should be, to pray for this situation."

"Of course we need to pray about it. But you ladies will have to do that without us men."

And with that, Kate realized the party was over.

As Kate lay in bed later that night, thinking about the way the evening had turned out, her questions about Clay were replaced with concern for her father. How would the blockade affect him? Would he be able to return in September as he'd planned?

God help us, she prayed.

Chapter Fourteen

"I wonder if John and Bessie will enjoy going to a different church," Kate said as she and Aunt Sally walked to Sunday morning service.

"Oh, I'm sure they will." Aunt Sally nodded. "I hear the atmosphere in the Negro church is much different than at Trinity. A lot more lively, it seems."

Kate tried to fight the sense of loss threatening to overtake her. John and Bessie had decided to attend a church for Negroes instead of accompanying her and Aunt Sally to Trinity as usual. Of course, it was natural for John and Bessie to prefer attending a church with their own people. *Their own people.* Bessie and John felt like family to her, yet she understood their desire to be with other Negroes. No, it wasn't just that. She tried not to care, yet now that Clay wasn't with her either, she felt abandoned. She'd tried to put those nagging questions about what or whom she had seen on the dock out of her mind, but this sudden change in routine intensified her insecurity.

Seeming to read Kate's mind, the older lady took her hand and gave it a pat. "Our men have gotten all stirred up over President Lincoln's threat to block our river. They'll see to it that we're safe. They won't let anything happen to their livelihoods or their families."

"I'm certain you're right, Aunt Sally." Kate shoved her feelings aside to smile at her caring aunt. "It just seems so peculiar to be going to church without our usual escort."

The church was filled with mostly women. The few males present were either elderly or children. Every conversation Kate overheard was about the impending blockade.

"I heard those Yanks are planning to invade our city."

"Thank God our men will stand up for us and keep us safe from those marauders! There's no telling what they'd do to us poor women."

"Both my sons are joining up this morning. I hope they'll look out for each other."

Kate wanted to cover her ears, while at the same time she wanted to listen. She had heard this type of talk before, back in Pensacola when the state seceded. Everyone talked about the "enemy" as if it were a beast stalking their lives. However she knew some of the people who sided with the Union, and they were just normal people like everybody else. They were in the minority, though, at least among her neighbors, and were often ridiculed when they tried to defend their positions.

Kate and Aunt Sally sat with the Harris family, minus the men. The women nodded to each other as the organ began to play. Kate was surprised to see Cora's gloomy face. It was hard to believe that only last night she'd been surrounded by gaiety in a festive, carefree environment. Everyone had been happily celebrating a successful cotton harvest, with grand plans for the future. Now, in these somber surroundings, the memory was like a dream from a different era.

The reverend looked conspicuously alone as one of the few men in attendance. Even the music was different, without the normal balance of male voices joining in the singing. Some of the women wore anxious expressions, while others appeared lost. No one knew what to expect, but fear threatened to take hold, as minds tried to avoid the possibility of unfriendly forces overtaking their town or the danger to the men going off to fight a war.

After the service Cora reached out for Kate's hand. "Oh, Kate, I'm so sorry we didn't come get you today. With all the commotion going on, I just never thought about it until I saw you here. I hope the two of you weren't inconvenienced too much."

"You needn't apologize, Cora. When Clay told me last night he wouldn't be able to accompany me to church this morning, I didn't expect you to come. And when no one arrived at the usual time, we started walking."

"Aye, and it's a lovely spring day for a walk too," Aunt Sally added. "We might as well enjoy these days before it gets so hot."

"Cora, is anything else bothering you? You seem especially distraught." Kate studied the sullen face of her friend, unusual without its normal liveliness.

"Oh, Kate, Jacob is joining the militia. My Jacob! He's not a soldier; he's a banker. What will he do in the militia? How can he leave me like that? Why, who will be my escort?" The girl's eyes brimmed with tears as she blurted out her despair.

"He'll be fine, dear. He'll probably stay here, so you'll still be able to see him." Aunt Sally offered her sympathy.

"Do you really think so?"

"Of course, dear." Aunt Sally eyed Kate, nodding her into agreement.

"Yes, Cora. Aunt Sally's right. Clay's still here, isn't he? And with all this hubbub about a blockade, I'm sure Aunt Sally's right that Jacob will stay right here as well. Don't worry. He'll be fine. We women will just have to entertain ourselves while the men are busy protecting us."

Cora sniffed and wiped her eyes with her handkerchief. "I suppose you're right. I'm sorry to be such a ninny. I'll have to be strong for my soldier." And with that statement, she straightened up and stalked off.

"Well, I supposed that's settled, then," Aunt Sally said, as she and Kate watched the retreating girl. They covered their faces with their hands, attempting to stifle their laughter over Cora's sudden change of mood.

~

John and Bessie arrived home a bit later than Kate and Aunt Sally. John's deep baritone voice could be heard singing before they reached the house. "Sweet Jesus! Sweet Jesus! Lily of de valley. He's de bright and mornin' star!"

"Well, I take it you two enjoyed the service at your new church." Aunt Sally smiled as the couple strode up, arm-in-arm.

"Oh, yes, ma'am. We sho' did. We have us a real good time, singin' and praisin' de Lawd." John's wide smile was contagious.

"I hear the singing there is something to behold. Is it true that some of the visiting sea captains and their families go there while in town?"

"Dat's a fact. Dey was a family from one of de ships at de Negro church today, but dey said dey was leavin' port after de service. Dis blockade talk got 'em scared to stay here too long."

"So soon? Seems everybody is getting overwrought with anxiety," Aunt Sally said.

Bessie and John exchanged glances, and Aunt Sally's eyebrows lifted.

"Is there something else afoot?"

John's demeanor changed to a more somber one. He glanced at Bessie, who nodded, then he turned back to Aunt Sally.

"Well, some of de Negroes, dey thinks de blockade might be dere salvation."

Kate started at his comment. "Why, John, whatever do you mean?"

"Don't you go worryin' about nothin', Miss Kate. Me and Bessie, we not goin' nowhere. But some of de other folk think dose Union ships gonna come to set 'em free."

"You mean, they'll run away to the Union ships?" Kate's eyes widened as she visualized the exodus.

John nodded. "Dat's what some of 'em sayin' dey gonna do. Sounds plumb foolish to me. What dey think dose Union ship captains gonna do with 'em? Turn around and take 'em up north, like dey runnin' a ferry or somethin'?"

"You have a good point there, John. But I dare say some of the slave owners are concerned about the possibility as well," Aunt Sally said.

"Well, as far as I can tell, everybody's upset about something that hasn't happened yet. We haven't even seen any Union ships." Kate tried to sound convincing, despite her own doubts.

John shrugged and shook his head. "You'se right, Miss Kate. And I hopes to goodness we don't see none neither."

After lunch Aunt Sally said she was going upstairs for a nap. John and Bessie went back to their house, and Kate took her needlepoint out to the veranda. Her thoughts were consumed with what would happen to all the people in her life. Would she see Clay again anytime soon? What would happen to her father if he tried to pass the Union ships? Would John and Bessie stay with them or be persuaded to leave with their friends?

Restless, she had the urge to go back to the widow's walk where she could clear her head and perhaps see what was happening around them. She tiptoed up the stairs to the attic door then crept up the narrow stairs to the attic. Groping through the dim light, she climbed the ladder to the trap door and opened it. When she stepped out, her first sight was of the St. George Lighthouse, standing sentinel across the sound. Would its light mean safety or harm to her father if Union ships blockaded his path? Looking to the west of St. George Island, she saw tents pitched on St. Vincent's Island nearby. A shiver ran down her spine as she remembered that was where Eugene Blackmon had been sent. She hoped she'd never see him again.

When Kate walked around to the other side of the walk, the view jolted her. The army camp had doubled in size since she'd last been up on the walk. Rows of tents filled the cleared area, while throngs of men milled about. Surely the town would be safe with so many soldiers protecting it, both on the waterfront and on the land.

Suddenly Kate heard a sound coming from below. Hurrying back down to the door, she made out Aunt Sally's voice. "Who's up there? Kate, is that you?"

Kate had forgotten to pull the attic door closed behind her. It was time to confess to Aunt Sally that she'd been snooping around.

"Yes, Aunt Sally. I'm up here." Kate stood at the top of the narrow attic steps, looking down to the woman standing in the open door at the bottom. "I didn't mean to disturb you."

"I heard something moving on the roof and thought it might be a squirrel, but it sure sounded like a mighty big squirrel."

"I'm so sorry. I hope you don't mind that I came up here. I saw the widow's walk from outside and wanted to see what it would be like to go up there."

"It doesn't surprise me that you'd be curious about it at all. In fact, I would have told you how to get there had you asked, but I'd forgotten it even exists."

Kate came down the stairs toward her aunt. "Forgot it? How could you forget it? I find it intriguing. And the view is breathtaking! Do you never come up here anymore?"

"No, dear. After Duncan died, I lost interest in the walk. You see, he built it for me because I'd seen them on the houses in New England when we visited there early in our marriage, and I desired one on our new house. You know, they were built for wives of ship captains so the women could watch for their husband's return home. I'm afraid this one lived up to its name."

"Oh!" Kate's face warmed as she connected the widow's walk to her aunt's status. Trying to divert Aunt Sally from her bereavement, Kate recalled the items she'd seen in the attic. "I didn't touch anything in the attic, except to move them away from the door to the outside."

"The only thing up there is a box of old letters from Duncan, and his old sea chest. Oh, and there's a cradle and a box of baby things too. Duncan and our son Donovan built the cradle for our grandson, Bryce. Maybe someday you'll use it."

"Me?" Kate felt her face grow warm.

"Don't you be so surprised, girl. You'll be getting married before long. Perhaps Lieutenant Harris will be asking for your hand."

"Oh, Aunt Sally, you do go on! I doubt Clay has given marrying me a second thought. Even if he wasn't consumed by this war, I'm not sure he's the man for me anyway." An image of the two people down by the river invaded her mind.

"Is that a fact? Do you still doubt his integrity? I thought you'd decided you saw someone else on the dock last night."

"I'm not sure why I have this doubt. I do have feelings for him, but I don't know what they are. He's certainly attractive and can be quite charming, yet something appears to be missing. Even though we've spent a good amount of time together, I don't feel as if I really know him, and I wonder if he truly cares for me."

"Time will tell, dear. Time will tell. Come on now and let's get some supper." Aunt Sally hesitated, looking over her shoulder at Kate. "Would you do me a favor before you close the door?"

"Of course. What is it??"

"Get that box of letters and bring them down. I haven't looked at them in years, and I feel like spending some time with Duncan again."

Kate returned to the attic to find the box. If Clay were sent away, would she feel the same as Aunt Sally did when Uncle Duncan sailed away? Would Clay send her letters too?

Chapter Fifteen

Kate wasn't prepared for the changes she saw in town. As she and Aunt Sally stepped onto Main Street, she immediately noticed the absence of cotton bales that had previously filled the streets. No ship whistles or shouting came from the docks. Gone too were the draymen and dockworkers.

Instead the town was filled with soldiers. Troops walked down the street in both directions, as they went from their encampment to the waterfront. Along the edge of the water where the river ran into the bay, officers shouted orders.

As they made their way to the mercantile, several offices in town appeared closed, dark, and empty. Entering the Harris mercantile, the women saw Cora and her father, who were inundated with uniformed men buying merchandise.

"Give me some of that gun powder too." One of the men pointed over the counter.

"Yes, sir, I'll do that. Would you men like anything else?" Mr. Harris reached behind him for the merchandise.

"Do you have any knives?" another man asked.

"In this case right over here."

Cora looked up from her tallying and greeted them with a somber smile. When she finished adding up the soldiers' receipts, she edged her way around the men to Kate and Aunt Sally.

"It's been like this all week. Men coming in, constantly looking for provisions." Cora glanced over her shoulder.

"I must say, I was surprised to see so many soldiers." Aunt Sally nodded. "I haven't seen this many since March, when we watched the departure of the Franklin Rifles."

"Yes, I know. Ever since the announcement of the blockade, our town has been filled with men coming to join the militia."

"What are they doing down at the waterfront?" Aunt Sally asked. "There's a lot of commotion over there."

"They're building up the battery where I hear they're going to place cannons. Cannons in town!"

"Have you seen Jacob?" Kate peered down at her distressed friend.

"Occasionally I see him march by with other men, but he can't take time to be social. He's too preoccupied with his duty." Cora's eyes stared off into space. Then, as if remembering the ladies, she brightened as she smiled. "But he looks so fine in his uniform! It was made by the best seamstress in town." Cora's blonde ringlets nodded in agreement.

"At least he's still in town and hasn't been ordered elsewhere," Aunt Sally said.

"Yes, he is, for now. He and Clay are needed to help build up our town's defenses."

So Clay was still in town. Kate hadn't seen him since the ball and wondered if he had been required to go to another assignment. Was that relief she felt or disappointment? Even though he was here, he hadn't come by to visit her. Perhaps his duties didn't permit such things anymore.

"But where's all the cotton?" Kate asked. "And where

did all the businessmen go? It appears some of the offices are closed."

"Oh, that's just typical of this time of year. The cotton is usually all shipped out by now, and the merchants who have come here for the cotton shipping business have left as well. This year, however I believe our foreign consulates closed earlier than normal. I heard they were in a hurry to get away before the blockade began and interfered with their plans to go home. At least you don't have to worry about the Marquesa bothering Clay anymore. She and her father left town right after the ball."

Kate tilted her head, brows furrowing. "I don't understand, Cora. How did the Marquesa 'bother' Clay?"

As her face turned beet-red, Cora suddenly appeared to remember some unfinished business she had to attend to as she scanned the room for an escape. "I, uh, I'm sorry, but you must excuse me, ladies. I'm afraid my father needs my help with the books." She spun around and scurried away through the door in the rear leading to the office.

Kate watched Cora depart with realization dropping like a weight in her stomach. The scene of the couple on the dock replayed in her mind, but this time she saw the man's face more clearly, and she was certain that face belonged to Clay. "Aunt Sally, there's more to this story than I've been led to believe. I knew something wasn't quite right."

"She certainly acted like she'd let the cat out of the bag. I must admit, her remarks raise questions. The truth will come out, though. It always does."

The ladies finished their business with Mr. Harris, whose brow was speckled with perspiration as he moved sacks of goods. "Thank God, I still have what you need. Those men have certainly diminished my inventory. In fact, I'm almost out of gunpowder. I hope my next delivery comes soon, or I'll be out of everything."

As the women exited the mercantile, Aunt Sally fanned

herself against the warm humid air of the early May day. "Let's get some lemonade while we're in town," she said, nearly gasping for breath.

Walking down the boardwalk to the café, Kate was intrigued by the assortment of "uniforms" worn by the passing soldiers. Some of the men sported sashes of different colors, while others had coats and caps of various designs and fabrics. Still others had no uniform of any sort.

"Aunt Sally, why are these uniforms all so different? In Pensacola, men from the Naval yard and those who manned the forts wore similar uniforms."

"More than likely the uniforms you saw there came from factories up North. These were made by mothers or wives back home, with whatever fabric they had to use. Like so many things, the men from the wealthiest families have the best uniforms. Nevertheless, they still have unity of spirit, even if they don't have unity in their clothing."

"I suppose you're right." Kate couldn't help thinking of Clay in his splendid-looking uniform, showing he was from the more privileged families. Her stomach tightened, as another surge of anguish gripped her.

Kate and Aunt Sally entered the café, which overflowed with soldiers. Mary was running between the tables, waiting on the many men who had stopped in for some refreshment. Several of them flirted with her as she passed by. "Where's your man? Is he off to war yet? He better be careful about leaving you alone."

"My husband is right behind those doors back there in the kitchen," she answered firmly, "and you better watch your tongue if you want to keep it. He's got a way with scoundrels like you."

"I didn't mean no harm, ma'am. Just teasing. Tell that husband of yours we're just here to protect him and his family."

"Well, I'm sure all of us here in town appreciate your selfless duty." Mary refilled a cup of coffee for a soldier.

Wiping her brow with her apron, the plump woman spied Kate and Aunt Sally waiting to be seated.

"I'm sorry you ladies have to wait on me. These men are running me ragged. I sure hope they don't behave like this when they're at their mama's house!" She chuckled under her breath. "Some of them aren't half bad-looking, but others are young enough to turn over my knee!"

A couple of men at a nearby table stood. "Ladies, you may have our seats."

"Thank you, gentlemen, but I need to sit near the window." Aunt Sally motioned with her head. Turning to Mary, she said, "Can you get us a seat somewhere away from the more boisterous ones? I need to rest a little while before we head home."

Kate frowned. Aunt Sally seemed more tired than usual.

"Of course. It's getting hot already, isn't it? I'll put you two right over there at that empty table. Maybe you'll catch a breeze through the window. I believe this is the hottest day we've had so far this year. We can expect it to get even hotter before long."

As she walked them to the small table, Mary continued her banter. "Quite a different scene these days than before, isn't it? None of our refined foreign guests are in town anymore. Just all these men. But I bet you're glad those foreigners are gone, aren't you? Especially that Marquesa." Mary stretched out the last word derisively, looking straight at Kate.

Kate didn't reply but instead waited for the woman to continue. Aunt Sally prodded the woman as she fanned herself with the menu. "Yes, we were wondering when all the consulates would close and their representatives would leave."

"They ran like scared cats when they heard about the blockade coming. Sure was glad to see the Marquesa leave. The way she hung onto Clay, sashaying down the boardwalk in her fancy clothes, like she owned him or something." Mary shook her head. "It was a sight to see, and I was tired of seeing it. Of course, Clay didn't seem to mind having her on his arm either. I heard he'd been quite the ladies' man back in Boston when he was going to school up there. I bet she was mighty upset about him taking your niece to the ball instead of her. Oh, but what I would've given for the look on her face when she found out." She chuckled. "Guess her daddy couldn't help her with that."

Kate exchanged glances with her aunt.

"What would her father have to do with Clay taking her to the ball?" Kate had to ask.

"Oh, she made him use his influence to get whatever she wanted. Seems like she had asked him to request Clay to be her escort around town. In fact, I heard the reason Clay stayed here instead of shipping out with the rest of his company in March was because her father used his influence to keep him here."

"Is that so? I didn't realize the man had so much power." Aunt Sally untied her bonnet and removed it from her head, fanning herself with it in the process. "My, but it's warm today. Mary, could you please get us a couple of glasses of lemonade? I need to cool off before I faint."

"Oh, yes, of course, dear. I'm sorry to make you wait. I'll be right back with it." The woman hurried off.

Kate felt her own temperature rising, but it wasn't from the weather. "Aunt Sally, I just don't know what to think about Clay. If he was escorting the Marquesa around town, that would explain why he didn't come visit me more often. However if he had no choice, should I be upset with him?"

"Choice or not, he could have been more forthright with you. Even more so if he cared about you. Seems like Lieutenant Clay Harris wanted to have his cake and eat it too."

"I agree. Why wouldn't he have told me if he truly didn't want to be the Marquesa's escort and was forced into it? I never saw them together in town, but now I'm certain it was the two of them down on the dock. That would also explain his absence during most of the evening."

"I'm afraid you're right. The man has been deceitful."

Anger replaced her former hurt and disappointment. Just thinking of Clay strolling down the street with the Marquesa on his arm turned her stomach. And to think the whole town knew about it! Everyone except her, and she felt like he'd made her look like a fool by pretending to be interested in her. All this time she assumed it was his military duty keeping him away. No wonder she questioned his feelings about her. He was an impostor, a charlatan! She hoped she never had to lay eyes on him again, lest she say something she might regret.

When they finished their lemonade, Kate was eager to go. "Aunt Sally, do you feel like walking home now? I believe I've had all I can take of this town today."

"Yes, I believe I've rested enough. Let's pay our bill and start back."

As they took their leave, the café door opened and Clay stepped inside.

Chapter Sixteen

"Katherine! How are . . ."

Kate brushed past Clay and out the door. He followed her outside, catching her by the arm. "Wait! I need to speak with you."

Shaking off his hold, she tried to maintain her composure. "I'm afraid we're in a hurry, Clay. Aunt Sally needs to get home and rest." She twisted her face away, refusing to look at him as she turned to go.

"Katherine, I've been meaning to come see you, but with the blockade upon us, I've been forced into duty preparing for it."

By then Aunt Sally had joined them on the boardwalk. "Been preoccupied, Clay?" The irony of her statement wasn't lost on Kate.

"Please, Katherine, wait a moment. Why won't you look at me?"

Raising her head to look at his face, she scorched him with her eyes. He flinched then frowned.

"Katherine, whatever is the matter? Are you upset about something? Has someone done anything to offend you? Have I?"

As calmly as she could manage, she responded. "Clay, I

do not have time to discuss anything with you. Please allow us to get on our way."

He stepped back and, with a sweep of his arm, complied with her wish. "Yes, of course. Please excuse me for interfering with your business." And then in a soft, imploring voice he added, "I miss seeing you, Katherine. I hope we can have some time together soon."

Kate didn't reply but strode briskly away as Aunt Sally hurried to catch up with her. After they had put some distance between themselves and Clay, Aunt Sally gasped, "Kate, please slow down. I can't keep up with you."

Kate halted and waited for her aunt as the older woman struggled to catch up. "I'm so sorry. I wasn't thinking. I just couldn't get away from that scoundrel fast enough. I never wanted to see him again, and he surprised me by his arrival at the café."

"It's all right. I can imagine your discomfort around that young man. I'm very disappointed with Clay Harris myself. I thought he was a more respectable Christian than his behavior has shown. But could we continue walking home at a slower pace now?"

"Of course, Aunt Sally. I'm sorry. I apologize for being inconsiderate."

"I understand, my dear. You just put him out of your mind, Kate. He certainly isn't worth your time. Someday you'll meet the right man for you, an honorable man who will respect you and want to be with you and only you – someone who will truly love you."

"I'm not sure I believe that anymore. Clay is the first man I was ever truly interested in, and now I discover he wasn't really the man I thought he was. How can I ever trust a man again? How does one really know when the right man comes along?"

"You mustn't let Clay's character color your impression of all men. There are many honorable men like my Duncan was. Don't give up hope, dear. You're still young." Beads of perspiration peppered Aunt Sally's face as they continued down the sandy road.

"But, Aunt Sally, I believed that if Clay was a Christian, he would've been honest. Even when I doubted his feelings or suspected his activities, I clung to the hope that his beliefs would verify his character. Obviously I was wrong. His behavior has shown no moral character."

The thought of her recent deception with Aunt Sally when she held back the truth about Gene Blackmon flitted through her mind, but she brushed it away. It wasn't the same at all. She'd only been trying to protect her aunt.

"Aye, that's true. But you don't know if he's truly a Christian or not. Only God knows that. And just because the man attends church, it doesn't mean he's a Christian, any more than going into a henhouse makes one a chicken."

Aunt Sally's remark caught Kate off-guard and before she could help herself, she burst out laughing.

"You have such a way of bringing things into perspective. I can see your point. However I don't believe I'll ever trust Clay Harris again."

"Perhaps not. Sometimes when things don't work out the way we expected, we have to understand there must be a reason. We must look for God's plan in the matter. What lessons can we learn? Is there anything He wants to teach us?"

"Not to trust men?"

"Now, Kate, that can't be true. Think of a man you can trust."

"My father. He's the only man I could ever trust."

"And what about John? Don't you trust John?"

"Of course. John would never betray me."

"Well, then, that's two men you can trust. And I'm sure if you think about it awhile, you'll remember others as well."

"I'll try, Aunt Sally." Kate let her arms drop to her side.

"I'll try."

Reaching the house, they stepped up to the veranda. The oppressive heat and humidity of the day had fatigued the older woman, and she retired to her room for a nap.

Kate needed to cool off as well, both from the temperature and her anger. She picked up the heavy Bible from the parlor and took it outside to the veranda, where she collapsed in a wicker chair.

Once more, she ran her fingers over the leather-embossed cover, tracing the outlines of the design with her fingers. She felt the letters "HOLY BIBLE" and continued along the edges of the floral motif, coming to a stop where she felt an unusual lump. A flaw in the workmanship was not obvious to the naked eye, hidden among the petals and leaves.

"Lord, please help me find the answer in Your Word. I'm so confused and disturbed. How will I ever know whom to trust again? That evil Eugene Blackmon was obviously wicked, yet I thought Clay was a decent person. But I was so wrong about him. I need You to speak to me and help me to understand, to give me wisdom and ease the pain I feel of being betrayed."

When the book fell open to the center, Kate started reading the Psalms, which she had always enjoyed. Today, however, she found herself identifying with the travails of David.

"LORD, how are they increased that trouble me! Many are they that rise up against me." The first line of Psalm 3 spoke to her heart. *Oh, it does seem that way, Lord.* She read on to Psalm 6. "Let all mine enemies be ashamed and sore vexed; let them return and be ashamed suddenly." *My enemies! I didn't realize I had enemies. But now, I can count three: Eugene Blackmon, Clay, and the Marquesa. Yes, Lord, let them be ashamed.*

"Help LORD: for the godly man ceaseth; for the faithful fail from among the children of men. They speak vanity everyone with his neighbour; with flattering lips and with a double heart do they speak," Psalm 12 warned.

Flattering lips. That was Clay, all right. Why hadn't someone told her about Clay's infidelities? Not even Cora, whom Kate considered a friend. No one. Instead the whole town allowed her to believe she was the only woman Clay was interested in. The more she thought about it, the more upset she became. How long had he been seeing the Marquesa? Kate had arrived in February, but the Marquesa had been in town since the cotton season began in October. Had he been seeing her all this time?

And there had been nothing she could do about it. Oh, for relief from this weight of despair! Her roses. Leaving the rocker, she put the Bible back inside, then went around the house to the rose bushes. A deep crimson rose blossom hailed her, beckoning with its beauty. Instinctively she grabbed the stem to inhale its aroma and savor its loveliness.

"Ow!" She jumped back when a thorn pierced her thumb and put the wounded finger into her mouth.

Tears spilled out and raced down her face. She turned and ran to look for John.

John and Bessie sat outside the open door of their little house, shaded by the huge oak tree stretching over the building. The couple was laughing as usual, until they noticed her approaching them.

John's brow furrowed. "What de matter, Miss Kate?"

"Everything." Kate sank down on an old stump nearby and began to pour out her heart and her frustrations. "I feel like I've been made such a fool. I'm angry with the whole town. Everyone knew what was going on except me. I just hate them. I hate them all!"

Bessie came over and put her arms around Kate as she sobbed.

"Now, now, Miss Kate. You don't mean dat."

"But I do. I really do! Just like David's enemies in the

Bible, everybody is against me."

Bessie patted her on the back. "Miss Kate, everybody not yo' enemy. Just 'cause folks see somethin' goin' on dat don't seem right, it don't mean dey go tell ev'rybody else. Dat's gossip, and smart folks stay out of it. It just nobody's business what other people does."

"But what about Cora? I thought she was my friend. She didn't tell me the truth either."

John rubbed his chin. "Well, now, you knows Miss Cora's his sister. She prob'ly scared he be mad at her if she done tole you about dat other woman."

Kate recalled the comment Cora had made in the carriage ride coming back from church one day. What had she said? Something about another woman being unhappy to see Kate with Clay. She remembered Clay's silent rebuke to his sister. Now it made sense. Cora must have been referring to the Marquesa, and Clay probably swore her to secrecy. Apparently her brother's reproach was more important than her friendship with Kate.

Kate stood up, placed her hands on her hips, and stomped her foot. "I will never forgive him, and I hope God punishes him for being so deceitful!"

"God gonna do dat, sho' nuff," John said. "You just gotta leave dat in God's hands. But you gots to fo'give him."

"Why? He doesn't deserve forgiveness."

"Maybe he don't, but God says we has to fo'give each other anyways."

"Well, I can't do that. And I'm sure God will understand why. Clay hurt me, humiliated me, and deceived me. I can't forgive him for that. No one could."

John and Bessie exchanged glances, and John said, "You just pray about it, Miss Kate. Sometime it don't seem pos'ble fo' us to fo'give somethin' or somebody, but you gotta ask God to he'p you."

"I'll pray, but I don't think I can ever forgive him. One

thing I know for certain -- I'll never trust another man. I guess I'll just end up a spinster like Aunt Elizabeth."

~

Kate wiped sweat off her brow with the edge of her apron. The taste of sweet corn would be worth this heat. That reminder and John's singing made working in the garden bearable.

Aunt Sally sat on the veranda, escaping the scorching sun. Kate wove her way through the corn stalks and joined her. The box containing Uncle Duncan's letters lay in her aunt's lap, while she dabbed her eyes with a handkerchief.

"I'm sorry, Aunt Sally. I didn't mean to intrude on your privacy."

"Oh, that's quite all right, dear. I do miss my Duncan. These letters just remind me of the love we shared."

"How wonderful it must be to find your true love. I don't think I ever will."

"Of course you will. You're still young, dear."

"But I'm almost twenty years old!"

Aunt Sally chuckled. "You still have plenty of time to find your true love. God has someone for you. You just have to be patient and wait for him."

"I hoped Clay might be that person. But I was sadly mistaken."

"Didn't you tell me you had doubts about him?"

"It's true. I did. Now I understand why."

"When the right man comes along, you'll know, Kate. You'll just know."

The women quit talking and watched John and Bessie tease each other.

"They found it, didn't they? They truly love each other; it's so evident. And to think how they came together! It's amazing, isn't it?"

"Only God could have done that. He surprises us sometimes with the way He does things. Often it's not at all how or what we expect."

Kate lowered her voice. "I hope Bessie's all right. She hasn't felt well the past few mornings. She appears to be all right now, though."

Aunt Sally glanced at Kate, then back at Bessie and smiled. "Bessie, you and John come on out of the sun and rest now. Get you some of that lemonade and sit a spell."

The couple obediently left the garden and joined them on the veranda. Bessie plopped down on the settee, while John went inside and got the lemonade.

"You look pretty tired, Bessie. Are you feeling puny?"

"I'se just tired. Feels like I could curl up like dat old cat over dere and take a nap."

"So you've been sick in the mornings lately?" Aunt Sally arched her eyebrow.

"Yes, ma'am. Cain't keep nothin' down. Guess I better quit drinkin' coffee. It's too hot, and I don't like de way it smells no mo'."

Aunt Sally laughed out loud. "Looks like we need to get that old cradle ready!"

Chapter Seventeen

They all stared at Aunt Sally. John's mouth dropped open, and Bessie gasped.

Kate covered her mouth with her hand then exclaimed, "Bessie's with child? Oh my, John. You're going to be a father!"

John had been leaning against the porch column, but his legs gave way and he sank down on the settee beside Bessie. Taking her hand, he looked at her with eyes misting over.

"Me? Ol' man like me gonna be a papa? Lawd, who woulda thought? I feels likes Abraham in de Bible!"

Aunt Sally guffawed. "John, you're fifty, not a hundred like Abraham was. But I must say, I don't know too many men your age having their firstborn. See, Kate, God still has surprises for us."

John shook his head in disbelief, while happy tears streaked Bessie's face. Kate's heart swelled with joy for John and Bessie. What a surprise indeed.

"Bessie, you don't need to spend so much time out in that hot garden now. You need your rest. Oh, I'm so thrilled to know there'll be a baby in this old house again!" Aunt Sally slapped her knee.

John gazed at Bessie with awe. "Praise de Lawd! Thank you, Jesus! I never thought I'd see de day I'd have my own chile'. I'm gonna take real good care o' you, Bessie."

Bessie smiled lovingly at John. "I didn't think I'd have a chile' either, John. Didn't even think I'd be getting married befo' you come here."

Aunt Sally rose from her chair. "Come on, Kate. Let's go through that trunk in the nursery and see what we can find. I better get my knitting needles out too. If my calculating's right, this baby'll be born in the winter and will need some warm clothes."

The small room adjacent to Kate's bedroom had once served as a nursery for Aunt Sally's grandchild. The older woman went over to the trunk in the corner and opened it. She reached inside and carefully lifted out a christening gown and cap.

Kate gasped. "How exquisite! Did you make it?" She reached out and gently touched the delicate clothing.

"Sure did. I made it for my son, Donovan, who was christened in it twenty years before his son was."

Kate admired the small white linen gown with its tiny tucks across the bodice, accentuated by delicate Ayrshire embroidery. The little cap with satin ribbons was embroidered to match. Kneeling down beside Aunt Sally, Kate peered into the open trunk, eager to see what else lay within. There were a few baby blankets and a small pictureframe that held a lock of fine blond hair.

"Was this the baby's hair?"

"Aye, that's Bryce's hair, from his first haircut. We had a time trying to get him to sit still." Aunt Sally took the picture frame as her eyes gazed at a memory.

"How old was he when he and his mother moved away?"

"He had just turned two, right after Donovan died. Cristina was afraid to stay here much longer and risk the two of them catching the fever too. Of course, after the mayor ordered the ship quarantine, no one else got sick. Christina was finished with this country, though, and wanted to go back home to her mother and father in Cuba, where she felt safer. I suppose I don't blame her for that."

"And you've never seen or heard from them since?"

"For a few years she'd send an occasional letter. But in the last one, she said she was getting married again, and that was the last I heard."

"And your grandson? You have no idea of his whereabouts?"

"No, and I'm sure he doesn't remember me either. He would be about twelve now. He was the spitting image of his father when he left. I've often wondered what he looks like now."

Kate's heart ached for the old woman. How unfair that all her family was gone! No wonder she had worn black for so many years.

"But now we have a new wee one to look forward to." A smile crept across Aunt Sally's face as her spirits brightened. "I'm ready to start knitting again. I need to go to town and see what yarn the mercantile has. I may need to order some. Do you knit, dear?"

"I'm afraid I've never learned. I tried, but I kept dropping stitches until Aunt Elizabeth got frustrated and quit trying to teach me. But I can crochet – and embroider and needlepoint. I can crochet a blanket for the baby."

"Wonderful! We'll have plenty to keep our hands busy and give us something to do in the shade during these long, hot days."

"Aunt Sally, are you a bit concerned about Bessie having a child?"

"Because of her age? Some people think babies born after a woman is thirty won't be healthy. But Bessie's strong, and we'll pray the good Lord will protect her and her baby. And we'll make sure Bessie is taken care of."

"But she's so thin." A chill ran down Kate's back. Aunt

Elizabeth had told her the reason Kate's mother died in childbirth was because she was too thin.

Aunt Sally glanced at Kate. "Aye, so we'll just have to see to it that she eats. Usually the sickness goes away in a couple of months. Then a woman eats as usual. And some of us eat too much." Aunt Sally laughed. "Duncan said I looked as though I'd swallowed a horse when I was carrying my babe. I ate like one too!" Aunt Sally stretched her arms out over her stomach to demonstrate.

Kate smiled, imagining what Aunt Sally must have looked like. They closed the trunk, then she helped the older woman to her feet. "Is that all you want from this room?"

"Yes, for now. John will have to get that cradle out of the attic and clean it up before the baby comes, but there's plenty of time for that."

As they rounded the stairwell to go back down, Aunt Sally eyed the attic door. "You know, Kate, I believe there's another trunk in the attic that has baby things. We'll have to get it down too."

Kate remembered a small trunk in the attic, as well as another chest. "Shall I get it now?"

"No, it can wait. Let's see what we can get Bessie to eat now."

~

It turned out there were a few things Bessie could eat without getting sick. She loved cornbread, for one, and wanted to eat it hot or cold.

"We better buy another sack of cornmeal next time we go to town," Aunt Sally told Kate as they sat husking corn on the back porch.

John came up to the house just in time to hear her. "Miz Sally, can we gets some buttermilk too? Bessie gots buttermilk on her mind and keeps sayin' how she'd love some with her cornbread."

"Of course. Next time you get milk at the Richardsons',

152

ask them if they have any."

Bessie soon kept John busy going to the Richardson house for buttermilk on a regular basis. Aunt Sally often sent some of her canned food in exchange. One day while she searched the pantry for another item to send with John, Bessie eyed the canned pickles on the shelf. "Dose pickles sho do look good, Miz Sally. Do you mind if we has some fo' dinner?"

Aunt Sally smiled as she grabbed the jar of pickles. "Well, of course not, Bessie. Remember when we put these up last year? I thought we had so many cucumbers we'd buy the mercantile out of Mason jars. We have plenty of pickles now, so we might as well eat them before the next crop comes in."

"Um, mm! Cornbread, buttermilk, and pickles! Dat sho do sounds good!"

Kate raised an eyebrow, questioning Bessie's taste, and sent Aunt Sally a glance.

Chuckling, the older woman winked back at her. "Sometimes women get peculiar tastes when they're carrying a child. I can remember I enjoyed some strange food combinations myself."

Kate grinned. "You did? What kind of strange things did you eat?"

"Figs. I wanted canned figs on everything – biscuits or cornbread. I could eat them all day long. I liked salt pork too, fried crispy. Yes, figs and salt pork. But I got so tired of eating them that I've never liked either of them much ever since."

Kate's attention turned to the younger woman. "Bessie, do you want a boy or a girl?"

"John and me, we just wants a well baby. We don't care what de good Lawd wants to give us. We just be thankful if it turns out to be a fine baby, girl or boy."

"Have you thought of any names yet?"

"We's talked some about dat. But we ain't made up our

minds."

"Nor should you. You have plenty of time for that. Now you go get some rest, and I believe I'll do the same." Aunt Sally pointed to the pregnant woman, emphasizing her words.

When Bessie and Aunt Sally departed, Kate fetched the embroidery piece she'd been working on. A sampler, it had letters, numbers, and flowers cross-stitched around the edges. She hadn't planned to do anything particular with it when she'd started. She had just enjoyed busying her hands while she sat and let her mind wander. As she studied the piece, an idea came to her to turn it into a gift for the baby. She would leave spaces for the date and name and then stitch those in place when the details were known. Kate grew more excited as she thought of ways to arrange the piece. She couldn't wait to see John and Bessie's reaction when she gave them the finished, framed memento. Did Aunt Sally have any more colors of thread she could use? Perhaps she had some in the extra trunk in the attic.

Aunt Sally wanted to bring it down anyway, so she knew the woman wouldn't mind. Kate tiptoed up the stairs so they wouldn't creak and wake the older lady while she napped. When she opened the attic door, a blast of warm air hit her, reminding her summer was in full swing. She left the door open, hoping for some light and air as she mounted the narrow attic steps.

When her eyes grew accustomed to the dimness, she found the trunk. She moved toward it, brushing cobwebs aside, and shivered as she caught a glimpse of a spider scurrying up the wall. Curiosity got the better of her, and she wanted to investigate the contents before carrying the trunk downstairs, but the stale, hot air, combined with the musty smell of things long forgotten, was suffocating. She opened the hatch to the widow's walk for some ventilation, then fanned herself with her hand and wiped perspiration from her face. When she had cooled off a bit, she returned to the trunk and gingerly lifted the lid.

Inside she found wooden toys some loving hand had made for a child. She reached in and touched a little pony with a cornhusk tail. A bundle wrapped in cloth and tied with ribbon caught her attention. Opening it, she found a silver cup and spoon. Her eyes misted as she considered the child, now gone, and the memories gone with him. Why had Donovan's wife not taken these items too? Perhaps Aunt Sally had asked her not to. Kate studied the small serving pieces, wondering if Aunt Sally would want John and Bessie's baby to have these items. She sighed. Would she ever have a baby of her own? With no husband in sight and no man she could trust, the prospect seemed doubtful. Besides, she too was thin – like her mother had been.

Kate closed the trunk lid, glancing across the attic at her great uncle Duncan's sea chest. A sea captain like her father, he likely kept similar items there. The heavy lock on the outside looked as though it hadn't been touched for years. Did Aunt Sally have the key? She'd left it there, unopened. After all, why would she need those items anyway? But if there was a telescope inside, it would be nice to use on the widow's walk.

A gust of welcome breeze blew in through the open hatch, inviting her outside. She accepted the invitation and stepped out to bright sunshine reflecting off the nearby water. She never tired of the view of turquoise water and white sand. A flock of pelicans dipped and dived in the water, apparently following a school of fish. She watched a large heron move stealthily along the shore. The tall, long-legged bird had an awkward gait. Did she look that way when she walked? Aunt Elizabeth had often criticized her for not walking like a lady. Her heart twisted. Who would be attracted to someone who walked like a giant bird?

The white tower of the lighthouse on St. George Island rose across the channel from the militia tents on St. Vincent's Island. The world was so peaceful from her perch above it all. What an odd juxtaposition of serenity and wartime. Who would believe there was a hint of war in this quiet place?

She scanned the water beyond the islands toward the entrance to the bay. Gone were the merchant vessels that had once dotted the scene awaiting their cotton cargo. Where was her father now? How she missed him! Would she be able to spot him when he arrived? The thought shook her as she realized he would be in danger if these waters were indeed blockaded.

As if in response to her question, she caught sight of a ship out at sea, drawing closer to the entrance of the bay. The ship stopped, and she could tell this was no ordinary merchant ship. This ship flew the Union flag, and cannons could be seen jutting from the sides.

The blockade had begun.

Chapter Eighteen

A heavy weight sank in Kate's chest at the unwelcome sight. No longer was there a question about whether the blockade would reach them; it had arrived. What would happen to the town, to its inhabitants? Would the ship fire its cannons at them?

Kate had to tell the rest of the household, but should she wake Aunt Sally and alarm her? The old woman seemed to be getting frailer each day. And what about Bessie? She didn't want to upset her and harm the baby she was carrying. John. She'd talk to John first. She hurried downstairs and ran outside.

He was leaning on a hoe and standing in the shade when she found him. His eyebrows knit together at her breathless arrival. "Miss Kate, what's de matter? Is Miz Sally all right?"

"John, they're here! I saw them with my own eyes!"

"Hold on, now, Missy. Who's here?"

"The blockade! There's a Union ship out in the water, just beyond the opening of the bay. What will we do?" Kate gestured to the water with waving hands.

"Calm down now, Miss Kate. Dere's nothin' fo' us to do right now. Nobody gonna harm us. We got soldiers ready to shoot at any ship dat come to town. Dey been waitin' and watchin', workin' on dat batt'ry so dey be ready, ever since dey hear about dat blockade. And any o' dem Union fellas gonna have to come around de island by our soldiers at St. Vincent's to get to us. We gots to trust dem and trust de Lawd to protect us."

"Oh, John, do you really think they can keep the Union ship away? And what about Bessie? Aren't you worried about her?"

"No, Miss Kate. I trusts God to take care o' her. I learned a long time ago dere's lots o' things I cain't fix, and dis be one o' them."

Kate's lips quivered. "John, what about Father? What will happen to him when he comes for my birthday? Will they shoot at him?"

"Yo' papa's a smart man and he know how to stay out of dang'rous places. It's not time fo' your birthday yet, and lots o' things can happen befo' he come back. Don't be borrowin' trouble, like my maman used to say. Dat's in de Bible too, you know. It say don't worry about tomorrow 'cause today has 'nuff to worry about."

Calming down a bit, Kate took a deep breath. "Well, I have to tell Aunt Sally. I'm concerned about her lately and hate to upset her too much. She seems to tire so easily these days."

"It's dis heat, mo' than likely. It tires anybody out, 'specially an old lady like Miz Sally."

At that moment Aunt Sally walked outside and called to them from the porch. "What's all the fuss about? Where's Bessie?"

"Bessie all right, Miz Sally. Just takin' a little nap, dat's all," John called back.

They walked over to where the old woman stood on the back porch. Searching the expressions on their faces, she crossed her arms and frowned. "All right, you two. Out with it. What's got you so excited?"

Kate remembered the last time she'd kept a secret from Aunt Sally – the business about Eugene Blackmon, a mistake she'd regretted.

Casting a sideways glance at John, she said, "Aunt Sally, I went up to the attic to fetch the box of baby things you told me about. While I was up there, I got hot and went out on the widow's walk to cool off."

"What happened up there?"

"Well, when I was out there, I watched a Union ship arrive and anchor just beyond St. George Island. Oh, Aunt Sally, they're here! The enemy is here. What should we do?"

Aunt Sally gazed out at the water, its blue hue just visible through the trees along the bank. She heaved an audible sigh. "You don't say."

John cleared his throat and spoke up. "Miz Sally, dere anythin' you wants me to do?"

"I need to think about this. Think and pray and see what God tells me. Meanwhile, we go on about our business as usual."

Later in the day some local soldiers arrived, approaching from the shore. As they walked up to the house, a familiar voice was heard through the open windows. "Company halt!"

With a sinking sensation in the pit of her stomach, Kate knew it was Clay before he came to the door. Although he was one of the last people she wanted to see, she went to open it and spare Aunt Sally the effort of getting up.

Standing at attention on the front porch, Lieutenant Clay Harris greeted her in an official tone. "Good afternoon. I'm here to let you know that an enemy ship has positioned itself at the entrance to the bay in an effort to block our harbor. We've had no contact with them yet, but we'll be patrolling the shoreline on a regular basis to make sure they don't sneak ashore during the night. Let us know if you see anything unusual or any strangers around here."

Aunt Sally had made her way over to the door before Kate could respond. "Clay, do you really think we're in any danger here? Why, they'd have to get through the pass by the lighthouse and St. Vincent's before they'd get to this place."

"We mustn't discount that possibility. We do have troops on St. Vincent's, and the lighthouse keeper is watching for enemy movement, but there's a chance they could elude us."

"Well then, we'll keep an eye out. Thank you for warning us."

Clay tipped his hat then let his eyes rest momentarily on Kate as if he had something else to say. But he turned on his heel and called to his soldiers, "Attention! March!"

Kate watched the soldiers march away, feeling as though she'd just seen a total stranger. There was no hint of a former relationship between her and Clay, just a cold space separating their past from the present. Could this possibly be the same man in whose arms she had danced just two months before? He'd made no attempt to contact her since they'd run into each other in town, the day she found out about his liaison with the Marquesa, the day she found out who he really was.

Apparently, he'd comprehended the reason for her actions, knowing he was guilty of wrongdoing. Or he'd decided she wasn't worth the effort of explanation or apology. Whichever it was, she realized her anger toward him had subsided, yet evolved into something worse. Was it hatred? No, that involved too much emotion. It was bitterness, and with a coldness that chilled her to the bone even in the summer heat, she disliked him intensely. She didn't like the way she felt about him either, but it couldn't be helped.

~

Aunt Sally started the next morning with renewed determination. "We need to stock up on supplies. Let's all go to town today and see what we can fetch home. We'll need more canning jars, salt, sugar, and paraffin, to name a few. We've got to get busy and put up all that's coming in the garden this month. The tomato plants are full, and those blackberries and figs need to be picked before the birds get to them. Be sure and remind me if there's anything else I'm forgetting."

When the group arrived at the mercantile, Mr. Harris was already running low on goods. "Don't know when the next steamer will be down. Guess you know about the Union ship. Folks are getting skittish about the blockade, plus a lot of our suppliers are selling their goods to the military. This is my last sack of salt."

Kate scanned the store, noting the empty shelves as well as Cora's absence. Where was she? Had she hidden when she saw them coming? Was she trying to avoid a conversation with Kate?

"Well, salt's one thing we can make ourselves if we have to," Aunt Sally said. "We've got plenty of saltwater we can boil. I'll take some more of that cornmeal though. Thank the Lord, we've got our garden coming in now."

"Yes, ma'am, that's for certain, Mrs. McFarlane. Aren't you worried about being so close to the water, so far away from town?"

"No, sir, your fine son has assured us his men will be looking out for our safety."

Kate's face warmed. *Fine son*? Indeed!

Aunt Sally continued. "And with the swamp on the other side of us, I don't expect anyone to come from that direction. I think the gators would take care of them before they got very far."

Mr. Harris guffawed. "Ma'am, you've never been one to be afraid of anything. Don't know where you get all your courage."

"Mr. Harris, the good Lord's taken care of me this long; I don't expect He'll stop now. I just trust Him to do it,

MARILYN TURK

that's all. Didn't He say in the Good Book, 'Fear not, for the Lord is with thee'?" Aunt Sally handed one of the parcels to Kate.

"Yes, you're right," Mr. Harris agreed. "I just hope those Union soldiers read the same Book."

"We're all God's children, aren't we? Whether we're from Florida or Scotland or Boston."

Mr. Harris shook his head. "You take care now, Mrs. McFarlane." He turned his eyes toward Kate. "Young lady, you look after your great-aunt and make sure she doesn't do anything foolish."

On the way back home, Kate struggled with what Aunt Sally had said. "Do you really believe we're all God's children? Even the Union soldiers?"

"Well, of course I do. I don't see anything in the Bible about any of us being any better than people from the North."

"But they're our enemy. How can God be on both sides?"

"Now that I can't explain. I just know He loves them as much as He loves us. We can't blame Him for people arguing and fighting. People have been doing that since Cain and Abel."

John and Bessie walked behind them, John pulling a small cart loaded with supplies as he joined in the conversation. "Sometime yo' enemy can be right here under yo' nose. Dey don't has to come from some place else."

"Like that dreadful Eugene Blackmon. And to think he's supposed to be one of the soldiers protecting us!" Kate tossed her head in disgust. "I hope he's still over on St. Vincent's after Aunt Sally reported him to his superiors."

"That's one man who seems to be everyone's enemy – yours, John's, and probably more people in town. But at least he's on our side against the Union," Aunt Sally said.

"So now we gots one enemy protectin' us from another

162

one." John gave a low whistle, shaking his head.

"Well, let's just pray they both stay away from us!" Kate added.

She remembered her latest interaction with Clay, whose name was right after Eugene's on her list of adversaries. Knowing he was in charge of her protection gave little comfort. What did she ever do to acquire all these enemies?

As if sensing their fears, Aunt Sally refocused their attention. "We've got plenty to keep us busy besides worrying about what's going to happen next. We've got blackberry jam to make, tomatoes to pick and can, plus I noticed the cucumbers are almost ready to pick too."

John began singing. "Ride on, King Jesus! No man can a'hinder me!"

Just hearing his triumphant voice lightened the mood. How Kate loved to hear him sing. It never ceased to lift her spirits. No matter how bad things were, John managed to be cheerful. Bessie joined in with her high voice, while Kate and Aunt Sally hummed along.

~

The long, hot days of summer were filled with activity as the garden produced on a continual basis. Kate worked harder than she ever had in her life, especially since Aunt Sally and Bessie had to rest more often. Bessie, whose thin body was blossoming into the form of a woman with child, helped Aunt Sally with the canning, while Kate worked outside with John.

Although she pinned up her thick amber curls under her sunbonnet as best she could, she considered cutting them all off if would make her any cooler. Her clothes were wet with perspiration, whether inside the house or out, but at least outside, there was a chance to get a breeze off the water.

John's singing through the chores helped to keep their minds off any threat of danger, if only temporarily. When he wasn't singing, he'd take out his harmonica as he rested in the shade, and play a tune that provided soothing comfort to their weary souls.

Tending the roses in Aunt Sally's yard was Kate's favorite pastime, as she lovingly trimmed and watered each plant accordingly. Sometimes she splashed them with soapy water to keep insects from damaging the tender flower buds. The rich colors of the flowers, some deep crimson and others various hues of the sunset, were a pleasant contrast to the dry summer grass. Each day she inspected every plant, inhaling their wondrous scent as she checked to see how many flowers had opened.

"You treat dem roses like dey you chillen," Bessie teased.

"Like you treat your chickens," Kate said.

Their Bible reading was now taking place in the late afternoon shade of the porch, where they fanned themselves with palmetto fans, trying to cool off before the mosquitoes began to attack. The group clung to words of comfort they found in the Scriptures. Kate read from Psalm 27 verses that evoked safety. "'The LORD is my light and my salvation; whom shall I fear? the LORD is the strength of my life; of whom shall I be afraid?'"

"Whom indeed?" Aunt Sally said. "Why, the Union soldiers aren't stronger than our Lord!"

"Praise be to God!" John said.

"Amen! Thank You, Jesus," Bessie added.

"I wonder what it means by 'the Lord is my light'?" Kate looked at Aunt Sally for an answer.

"I suppose it means He guides us, like a light does in the dark."

John nodded in agreement. "Dat's what I thinks too."

"Like the lighthouse guides ships to shore, don't you agree?" Kate pictured the St. George Light guiding her father to her.

"Aye, that's right. It guides us to safety and keeps us

out of danger." Aunt Sally's head bobbed up and down as she spoke. "What a comfort that is."

~

The next day, while they were in the garden, John broke into song with "This little light o' mine, I'm gonna let it shine."

Kate smiled and joined in the singing, as did Bessie and Aunt Sally. They were enjoying themselves so much they didn't hear soldiers arrive from the beach. Startled, they turned around and Aunt Sally addressed the man in charge, which wasn't Clay but a young man who looked as if he were wearing his older brother's clothes, gathered at the waist with a belt.

"Young man, you shouldn't steal up on us that way. You could scare an old woman to death, coming up behind us like that!"

"I'm sorry, ma'am. I believe the singing prevented your hearing us."

"Perhaps. So tell me, son, is there some news? Or are you just roaming up and down the beach, looking for enemies?"

The young soldier winced at Aunt Sally's words but managed to keep his demeanor polite. "We're here to make you folks who live by the water aware of recent events which may affect you. Three of our city officials visited the Union ship under a flag of truce. When they boarded the ship, they were issued a warning that no vessels can enter or depart our port; therefore, any ship attempting to do so will be fired upon.

"In retaliation, we have removed all buoys and channel markers, and extinguished the light in the lighthouse. We'll not help the Yanks navigate our waters, but we'll hope they run aground trying. Colonel Hopkins has ordered a battery erected on St. Vincent's so we'll be ready for them." His official tone and military stance, with shoulders back and chest out, exuded pride.

Kate barely noticed them leave, her mind reeling from the words she had heard. No light in the lighthouse? How would her father be able to find her? Even more frightening, what if he was fired upon while trying? She had to find a way to warn him.

Chapter Nineteen

"In dat great gittin'up mornin', fare you well, fare you well . . . ."

Kate smiled at John's cheerful voice. The way he started each day in such good spirits was a blessing to everyone else.

"Good mornin', Miss Kate!" John greeted her with his big grin and warm eyes as she stepped outside, tying on her bonnet in the early morning sunlight. "Looks likes we can start pickin' de beans today. Um-um. I can taste 'em already. We gots us a good garden, yes suh, thank the Lawd."

Picking beans wasn't her favorite thing to do, especially in the summer heat, but she did enjoy the reward of good food afterwards. Kate looked around for Bessie.

"How's Bessie today? Is she up yet?"

"She feelin' just fine. Says dat baby o' ours is dancin' in her belly." John's laughter rang with pride. "Bessie's makin' biscuits right now. She hungry all de time and cain't wait to eat!"

Aunt Sally stepped outside next to Kate but fixed her gaze on John. "With all your singing, I'm not surprised that child is dancing."

Kate smiled and nodded. "I certainly agree with that notion."

Bessie came out of the cabin, stretching and rubbing her stomach. "Did I hear y'all talkin' about my baby dancin'? He sho is, I do believe. Kickin' me all over my insides."

"Well, tell John to sing something less lively, and maybe the babe will settle down."

While they laughed at her remark, Aunt Sally studied the sky out over the water. Darkness loomed on the horizon.

"I believe we're going to have some rain today. We certainly could use it, but we better hurry and get these things picked before it starts," she noted.

Kate grabbed baskets for each of them, and they set to work going down each row, picking beans, tomatoes, squash, and cucumbers as fast as they could while approaching thunder boomed a warning. Giant raindrops started to fall as they were finishing up. A blinding rip in the clouds, followed by a loud crack, exploded a pine tree at the edge of the property. Bessie screamed and Kate jumped. They each grabbed their baskets and ran into the house before the deluge began.

"Lawd, dat scared me half to death!" Bessie shivered.

John put his big arm around her. "We be okay in here now. Miz Sally, do you mind if we sits de storm out in here?"

"Well, of course I don't mind. I wouldn't have you going back out in that torrent. Let's sit in the parlor and snap beans until it lets up."

The thunderstorm lasted the rest of the day, giving them a much-appreciated rest. Bessie jumped at each loud thunderclap, but John tried to soothe her and drown out the sound with his singing. The weather cooled the temperature to a more pleasant one, and when the storm passed, a breeze blew off the water and through the house. A cacophony of frogs croaking and crickets chirping serenaded the group as dusk approached, keeping rhythm with the grandfather's clock inside.

Kate jolted awake in her chair. She glanced at the others and discovered they too had dozed off. John slumped in his chair, while Bessie's head drooped over the pan in her lap. Aunt Sally's head hung backwards, a slight snore emitting from her open mouth. Kate smiled at the scene, then quietly as she could, stood and stretched, gently placing her pan of beans on the table. Through the window she glimpsed a hint of orange as the sun dropped over the horizon. She suddenly wished to get a better view of the colorful sunset without the obstruction of trees.

Grabbing her skirt she raced up the stairs on tiptoe, trying not to wake anyone. When she stepped out onto the walk, her breath caught. The sun's scarlet sphere melted into the waters, coloring the waves crimson gilded with gold, as bands of purple streaked the sky amidst splashes of orange, pink, and yellow like brushstrokes painted by a heavenly artist. *Lord, what a glorious sight. Thank you for this wonderful display of your creation.*

As she watched the grand finale of the sunset, her eyes swept the water's horizon, stopping on the dark outline of the lighthouse over on the island. She still couldn't believe soldiers from her own side had put out the light. What a foolish thing to do! Foolish, sad, and frightening. A beacon that provided safety was not allowed to function or protect either side. She shook her head as she tried to make sense of the situation. War didn't make sense. How neighbors could choose sides and become enemies was beyond reason.

No sooner had the sun disappeared than the sky became dark, and Kate had to carefully find her way back inside the attic. As she stepped off the ladder, she groped the sides of the wall with her hands, feeling her way around. She bumped her leg against a sharp edge, hurting her shin. "Ouch!"

Gasping from the pain in her leg, Kate reached down and rubbed the injured spot. She felt the edge of the object she'd hit. The sea chest. She'd forgotten about it. Now more than ever, she wanted to open it and examine its contents. If it held a telescope, she could keep an eye on the Union ship and the islands. But the key was missing, and Aunt Sally didn't know where it was. Was there any other way to open it? If they tried to pry it open or hit it with an ax, the contents might get damaged in the process. She'd ask Aunt Sally if it could be brought downstairs. Maybe they could figure out how to get it open out in the light.

She lit the kerosene lamp in the upstairs hallway then went downstairs to the parlor, where the others were beginning to awaken.

"My goodness, it's already dark! I must have fallen asleep in my chair." Aunt Sally straightened her spine and adjusted her position.

Bessie and John both woke with a start. "Looks likes me and Bessie tooks us a little nap too. Sorry, Miz Sally."

"Sorry? For what? We must have needed the rest, and the good Lord sent the rain and gave us a chance to get it. Kate, dear, what did you do while the rest of us catnapped?"

"I took a little nap too, but I woke up when the sun was setting and went up to the widow's walk to get a good look. It was glorious!"

"Sometimes it seems the sunsets are more beautiful after the worst storms. When I see them, I think the good Lord is smiling." Aunt Sally smiled as she spoke, emphasizing her words.

"He must be. It looked like an artist creating a masterpiece."

Aunt Sally nodded. "'The heavens declare the glory of God,' Psalm nineteen-one. I don't think God stopped creating after six days. True, he rested on the seventh day, but I think He's still creating."

Kate had never considered that idea. But then every time she saw a new bud blossom on the rose bushes, she marveled at its uniqueness. No two were ever alike -- just as two people were never alike, even if they were twins.

John stood and stretched his arms out to the sides, then pulled Bessie up out of her chair. "We needs to get busy and get some supper ready. Bessie'll be feelin' puny if she don't eat somethin' soon. I gots to go check on things and see what dat storm did to de garden."

"We have biscuits left over, and some cucumbers and tomatoes, so we can eat pretty soon." Aunt Sally pushed herself up from the arm of the chair.

"I sho was lookin' fo'ward to a mess of fresh green beans." John rubbed his stomach in anticipation.

"It's too late to cook them today. We'll just have to have them tomorrow instead." Aunt Sally picked up a pan of the snapped beans.

"Hungry as I is right now, I couldn't wait fo' dose beans to cook no way," Bessie said as she went out the back door with John.

"The rain cooled things off a bit." Aunt Sally rubbed her shoulders.

"Are you too cool? I can get your shawl, if you'd like," Kate offered.

"Not right now. I think I just need to move around some."

Kate bent over and gingerly touched her aching shin.

Aunt Sally raised an eyebrow. "What's wrong with your leg?"

"Oh, that. I'm afraid I bumped it on the old sea chest in the attic when it got dark and I couldn't see my way around."

"Let me look at it."

Kate lifted her skirt high enough to reveal a red and blue lump on the front of her leg. "I must have hit it right on the corner of the chest."

"You've got quite a bump there. Get a rag and dip it in the cool water out of the bucket outside. Wring it out and hold it on your leg. I don't see a scratch, so I don't think you need a poultice. If you keep a cool rag on it, the swelling should go down."

Kate did as Aunt Sally directed and sat down on the porch to prop her leg up while she held the rag to it, glad no one else was around to see her exposed leg. As much as possible, she covered the rest of her leg with her skirt.

"I should be helping with dinner," Kate lamented.

"There's not that much to do. Bessie and I can handle supper. We need to move that chest out of the way, though, so you won't hit it again."

"I've tried, but it's pretty heavy. Do you mind if John brings it downstairs?"

"I don't mind, but why?"

"I'd really like to see what's inside. The men in our family have always been mariners. I'd like to find out what kind of things Uncle Duncan kept in it. There might be a telescope I could use on the widow's walk. Would it be all right with you if we opened it?"

"Of course. I don't mind a bit. I suppose there could be some interesting things in it, or maybe just some personal mementoes. But I don't know how we'll get it open. I have no idea where the key is now. Maybe John could pry it open, but I'd rather not break it and destroy anything inside."

"I've thought about that too. I wouldn't want to damage anything either."

"Remind me tomorrow to ask John to go up and get it when it's daylight. Maybe if we all put our heads together, we can figure out how to get it open."

Chapter Twenty

The sea chest hit the floor with a solid thud.

"Whew! Dat a heavy trunk." John wiped the sweat from his brow.

"It hasn't been moved since Donovan and one of his crew put it up there after Duncan died. I told Donovan I didn't want to see it then." Aunt Sally stood by the chest, hands on her hips.

Kate nodded, staring down at the object. "I can see why. Nobody could've moved it except a man as strong as John. I know none of us women would have been able to."

"There's been no reason to move it anyway. It's been years since I went up to the attic, and I frankly forgot all about it."

John knelt down by the object, feeling along the edges. "It shut tight, dat fo' sho. I thinks it be rusted shut."

Kate knelt alongside him. For the first time, she was able to get a good look at the object that had resided in the dark attic for the past ten years. The heavy old chest was made of large oak boards, dovetailed together at the edges. Two sturdy iron hinges joined the top to the back, with two thick metal carrying handles on either side. An iron lock on the front securely kept the contents hidden with its vacant keyhole.

"That old chest was built to last. Duncan's father had two of them built in Scotland, one for each son." Aunt Sally leaned over and rubbed her hand across the smooth boards.

"What's this?" Kate pointed to a brass plate, dulled by dust and years of neglect.

Aunt Sally removed her kerchief from her pocket and rubbed it on the plate. Gradually some letters appeared on the metal.

"Captain Duncan McFarlane," Kate read.

Her eyes misting over, Aunt Sally continued to rub until the brass regained some of its sheen. "Aye, my dear Duncan's nameplate."

Kate put her arm around the older woman. Maybe she shouldn't have asked to bring the chest down and arouse painful memories for her aunt. "I'm sorry, Aunt Sally. I didn't mean to upset you. We can put it back in the attic."

Aunt Sally patted Kate's hand on her shoulder. "No, keep it here. I'm all right. But I still miss him and always will."

John continued examining the box. "Don't knows how we gonna get it open 'cept fo' bustin' it wid de axe."

"No, let's not do that just yet. Maybe I'll remember where the key was. Now that Kate's got me curious about the contents, I don't want to break them. After all, a sea chest was a sailor's most private possession. He only kept his most important things in it, and he carried it with him everywhere he went. I wonder what Duncan kept in there. Let's leave it here for now and go have our scripture reading for the day."

Kate carried the heavy Bible from the parlor to the veranda, where the others waited. She settled into one of the large rockers and opened the book to the ribbon-marked place. "We left off in Psalm 119, the longest chapter in the Bible."

"Dat a long one, all right." John nodded. "Too much fo' dis head to take in all at once."

Bessie nodded. "I know dat's right."

"That's why I'm only reading five verses each day," Kate said. "It gives us more time to think about the meaning. I'll begin with verse 103.

"'How sweet are thy words unto my taste! yea, sweeter than honey to my mouth!

Through thy precepts I get understanding: therefore I hate every false way.

Thy word is a lamp unto my feet, and a light unto my path.'"

Kate quit reading and looked up. "What do you think these verses are talking about?"

"Sounds like it's talking about obeying God's laws," Aunt Sally suggested.

"Um hum. I thinks so too. Doin' de right thing and stayin' out o' trouble," John said.

"I likes de part 'bout de honey, 'sweeter than honey to my mouth,'" Bessie declared. "God's word bein' sweet like honey, dat's a nice thing. Ummhmm. Make me want honey too."

Kate smiled at Bessie, who seemed hungry all the time these days.

"Well, let's get you some honey fo' dat baby den." John reached over and patted her growing stomach.

Kate suddenly stood upright, the Bible sliding off her lap to the floor. "I've got it! I think I know where the key is."

"What on earth?" Aunt Sally's eyes widened.

John leaned over and picked up the fallen Bible. Kate sat back down and ran her hand over the cover. "John, can you get me a small knife?"

"What are you planning to do with a knife, Kate? Cut the Bible?" Aunt Sally reached for Kate as if to stop her.

"Please trust me, Aunt Sally. I think I know where the

key to the chest is hidden."

John returned quickly with a knife and handed it to Kate. Feeling along the edge of the cover, her hand stopped when she came to the unusual lump she had noticed before. Taking the knife, she carefully slid the point along the edge of the inside cover underneath the lump. After cutting a slit large enough to put two fingers into, she reached inside and pulled out a key.

Kate held it up, smiling at her discovery.

"Well, I be," John said, shaking his head.

"Let me see that." Aunt Sally stretched out her hand to Kate, who placed the key in it. As she turned it over in her hand, she smiled and nodded. "That Donovan. He was always hiding things from me. Now I remember that when he asked me where to put the key to the chest, I told him, 'Somewhere safe.' Of course he would hide it in the Bible! Duncan always said, 'The key to life is in God's Word.'"

"Can we try the key now to see if it fits?" Kate placed the Bible on the nearby table.

"We certainly can."

They returned to the parlor where they had left the chest. Aunt Sally handed the key back to Kate. "Here, you try. I believe I'm shaking too much."

Kate took the key and put it into the lock. It was a perfect fit. With both hands and some effort, she turned it until there was a "click." She glanced up at Aunt Sally, who nodded.

"Go ahead. Open it."

Kate motioned to John. "John, will you help me lift the lid?"

The two pushed, and with a loud groan, the lid opened. Aunt Sally leaned over to take a look inside. A captain's hat lay on top. Reaching down, she grasped the hat with both hands and clutched it over her heart. "Duncan's hat. I remember how dashing he looked in it."

"This looks like eating utensils." Kate unfastened a

small leather pouch, which revealed a silver spoon, fork, and knife.

"I sees some books in dere." John stood over the chest, watching as Kate lifted out each object.

"Captain's logs." Kate opened each book, mentioning the dates and notes within. "These are like the ones Father keeps."

Kate continued to remove things from the chest, placing them on the floor. A sewing kit with pins, needle, and thread was wrapped in some scraps of clothing. A metal tin contained a shaving brush, knife, shaving soap, and mirror. She also found a hairbrush-and-comb set.

"Duncan took great care in his appearance. His hair and beard were always meticulously groomed." Aunt Sally beamed with pride.

A beautiful dark walnut box turned out to be a humidor containing two hand-carved meerschaum pipes with a silk tobacco pouch. Another box contained an inkwell, pens, writing papers, plus a packet of letters wrapped with a ribbon.

"Let me see those." Aunt Sally took the letters and gasped. "Why, these are letters I wrote to Duncan! He saved them all."

"Look, a Bible. And a hymnal." Kate removed the two books, holding them up for the others to see.

"That was Duncan – such a devout man. He conducted church services onboard the ship, leading most of his men to their Savior. Many ships had trouble with sailors being wild and rowdy, especially when they were on shore. But Duncan's men had a reputation for being well-behaved, honest, and decent. They may not have been that way when they joined his crew, but when they met the Lord, their lives changed. Duncan used to write me stories about the different men whose backgrounds were full of all kinds of trouble. He believed God led them to him so they could find the Lord."

"What a special man he must have been." Kate smiled. "And did he sing these hymns?"

"Oh, yes, he did. Why, his booming voice would have rivaled John's."

John beamed. "Someday we be singin' together, Miz Sally. We all will, yes, ma'am."

Kate's attention returned to the sea chest where she was finding her way to the bottom. She removed an old blanket that hid another box, this one mahogany with a brass anchor inlay in its top. Opening it carefully, she found a mariner's brass spyglass lying inside on a black velvet lining.

"Oh! This is wonderful!" Kate exclaimed as she removed the instrument. "Look. It opens out to double its length." She held the telescoping spyglass by its brown leather grip and stretched it out, looking through the end. "I wonder how far one can see with it?"

"You try it and find out," Aunt Sally suggested. "I imagine you can see clear out to the island with it from the walk."

"I can't wait to use it. Let's see what other surprises we have in here."

Another small leather pouch revealed a brass pocket compass, with its blue sundial hands still in working condition. "I gave that to Duncan for a wedding present." Aunt Sally took the piece and sighed.

"What dat?" John pointed to an item in the bottom corner that had been covered by the other objects.

Kate reached inside and brought out a brass lantern. "Why, Father has one of these! I saw it in his cabin. He told me it was a signal lantern he inherited from his father."

"Oh, yes, I remember that lantern. Duncan and Donald each had one. They used to send messages to one another when they were on their ships. Sort of played a game with them. No other ships had them at the time because they were a new invention. I believe they used Morse code with lights."

"That's what Father said too. I wish I knew how to work it."

Aunt Sally frowned. "Do you want to send a signal to someone? Who would you send a message to – the Union ship?"

"Why, Father, of course!"

Chapter Twenty-One

"This heat will be the death of me!" Kate wiped her brow with the back of her sleeve. "What happened to the breezes off the water?"

Aunt Sally replied from the veranda. "We don't get any in August. Come on out of the sun and try to cool off. John can finish up."

Kate joined Aunt Sally and Bessie, who had been having backaches lately. Aunt Sally made her rest as much as possible, despite her complaints. Bessie was helping them make a quilt for the baby, so she was busy sewing some pieces of fabric together. Kate untied her bonnet, fanning herself with it. "Aunt Sally, I am so tired of all this hair! I am quite tempted to cut it off."

"I understand the way you feel, but you would regret that decision if you did, and then it would take years to grow it back. Let me see if I can tie it up tighter."

Kate sighed and reluctantly went over to the older woman, kneeling in front of her while her hair was attended to. "Why don't men have to worry about their hair? It's not fair!"

"The Bible says if a woman has long hair, it is her glory."

"I know, but it doesn't feel very glorious right now." Kate leaned back into Aunt Sally. "And mine is so thick and curly! Why can't it be straight like yours?"

"We always want what we don't have and what someone else has. Women with thin, straight hair would love to have yours."

"I wish I could give them some."

"Hold still now."

"How 'bout some nice juicy watermelon?" John walked up from the garden carrying a large green-striped one.

"That sounds heavenly. I didn't realize we had anymore. Bring it over here and we'll cut it." Aunt Sally patted Kate's secured curls. "There you are, Kate. That should hold awhile. Would you go get us a knife, please?"

John washed off the melon in the dry sink on the porch.

When Kate returned with the knife, John cut the watermelon into wedges and handed each one a piece. Sweet juice ran down their hands, arms, and chins as they devoured the moist fruit.

"This is delicious!" Kate managed to speak in between bites.

"Might be's de last one, too. I think dose vines 'bout played-out," John replied, holding his piece in one hand and pointing to the remaining melon with his other hand.

When they were finished they went to the well and took turns pumping out water so the others could rinse off.

Kate paused and looked around. "Something's strange. I don't hear any birds."

They all stood still, listening and scanning the trees surrounding the house. "You're right. It's quiet as a church mouse," Aunt Sally said.

"Dey gone." John walked out into the yard, searching the sky.

It was too still. No breeze. No birds. Nothing. The overcast sky appeared to be hiding a secret.

Kate was perplexed. "Gone? Where? Why?"

John and Aunt Sally exchanged concerned looks. "Let's go look at the water," the woman said.

When they reached the water's edge, the tide was out. Way out. The shallow water extended much farther than usual.

Kate pointed. "It must be low tide."

"This isn't a normal tide. John, are you thinking what I am – that there's a storm brewing?"

John looked out to the Gulf. "Yes, ma'am. I thinks so. A big one too. We best get ready. Don't know how long befo' de storm gonna hit us."

"Do you think it's a hurricane?" Kate remembered tropical storms that had struck Pensacola, flooding many of the downtown streets.

"Could be. Dis be de time o' year fo' them, and de way dat water's been sucked out, it sho nuff might be." John started heading to the house, helping each woman up the steep bank.

"John, get some nails and start securing the shutters. Tie down anything you can't nail down or bring in. Let's pick up everything that might blow away and put it inside. And Kate, you get a basket and go pick anything that's almost ripe. A bad storm will destroy the garden. Bessie, get the eggs before John nails the henhouse shut. Fill up every pail and pitcher we have with water from the pump in case salt water gets in the well. John, get your cabin door nailed up too. You and Bessie will have to stay in the main house until the storm has passed."

They all hurried to do their assigned tasks, following Aunt Sally's instructions. Every match was located and all the lamps filled with oil. Even the furniture from the veranda was brought inside to keep it from blowing away. Kate ran to her roses, cutting the stems that held promising buds and blossoms, returning to put them in a large vase filled with water. A lump formed in her throat at the prospect of her precious flowers being destroyed.

The wind picked up in the afternoon, and whitecaps appeared on the water. Angry dark clouds covered the southern horizon over the Gulf as if a giant beast were creeping toward them. Strong wind gusts blew intermittently, making the trees bow down to them.

Just as it was getting dark, the rain began. "Time to get inside," Aunt Sally commanded. "We'll have to ride this out."

With the shutters nailed against the windows, the house was uncommonly dark. The wind blew stronger and stronger, whistling and roaring around the house. Blowing rain pelted the sides so hard it sounded like nails were being driven in.

"Is that hail?" Kate asked.

"No, just driving rain. But it's still hard enough to ruin the garden. Good thing we got the last of the tomatoes and beans before it started."

Kate peeked through the slats of the shutters and saw the trees bending low to the ground. The din of the storm was so loud they could barely hear each other speak without raising their voices.

"Let's pray for the Lord's protection." Aunt Sally bowed her head and the others repeated the posture. "Dear God, please keep us safe during this storm. Look over us and protect our home from damage. And dear Lord, we pray for our neighbors who are in the same situation. Amen."

"Amen," they all repeated.

Bessie spoke up. "Does you thinks dem soldiers is out dere in dis storm with jus' dey tents? Dat won't be no protection in dis storm."

"I'm sure they have enough sense to seek shelter somewhere safe," Aunt Sally said.

"What about the ones on St. Vincent's Island? Do you think they had to stay there during the storm?" Kate couldn't help but pity anyone, even Eugene Blackmon, riding out the storm on one of the islands.

"I hope their leaders realized soon enough they needed to get off the island. I've seen storms like this when the whole island was covered with water."

"Lawd, I'd hate to be on one o' dem boats out dere. I gets sick just thinkin' 'bout it." Bessie held her stomach.

"Sometime it be better on a boat 'cause it can ride out de storm, so longs it don't wash up on sho' or hit somethin'." John nodded, asserting his opinion. "I's heard stories 'bout people ridin' out big storms on dey boats."

"Duncan had to ride out a few, but I'd rather be on land than sea myself."

Bessie looked fearful and turned to Aunt Sally. "Does you thinks de chickens be all right? I's so worried 'bout my poor babies."

"We'll pray for the chickens too Bessie." Lifting her eyes heavenward, Aunt Sally spoke. "Lord, please watch out for our chickens. They're your creatures too, and we hope you will take care of them for us." She patted Bessie on the arm.

Kate kept moving from window to window, trying to peer out.

"Let's get in the parlor. We can work on our sewing in there," Aunt Sally said as she walked down the hallway.

"John, you stays right here by me." Bessie grabbed John's arm and pulled him along with her.

"Yes, ma'am, Bessie. I won't be goin' nowhere fo' a while." He smiled down at his nervous, bulging wife.

John removed his harmonica from his pocket and tried to play over the noise of the fierce storm outside. The wind roared and thrashed like a wild beast trying to break into the house. Sounds of cracking limbs were heard as trees gave in to the force of the gale. A deafening crash reverberated through the house, followed by a loud thud. Kate and Bessie both screamed.

"What was that?" Kate asked.

"Sounds like a tree hit the house," Aunt Sally said calmly.

"I'se gonna give it a look-see." John stood.

"You not goin' out in dis!" Bessie wailed.

"No, Bessie. I'm gonna looks 'round inside and sees if a branch done broke through an' is lettin' water come in de house."

"Take that lantern over there with you." Aunt Sally pointed to the kerosene lamp sitting on the hall sideboard.

John took the lamp and moved from room to room, checking for damage. The women listened to his steps as he went upstairs, exchanging worried glances when the noise stopped.

"He must've gone to the attic," Aunt Sally ventured. "I sure hope this old roof holds out."

John's welcome footsteps were soon heard coming back down. Anxious faces greeted him when he returned to the parlor.

"Well? Do we have a leak?" Aunt Sally's forehead puckered.

"No, ma'am, not dat I could find, no way. Up in de attic, I hears somethin' beatin' 'gainst de roof, but I didn't see no water comin' in or no holes. Must be a branch done fall on de roof."

"Thank you for making sure everything is all right. I'd hate to have water coming inside."

"Yes, ma'am, Mis Sally. We jus' has to get dat branch off when de storm passes. If dat's de most damage we has, we can thanks de good Lawd."

The storm continued to pummel the house for several more hours, while the house creaked and groaned in self-defense.

"It sounds like the house is going to blow apart." Kate continued to hope and pray the old structure could stand against the force of the storm.

"This house was built with sturdy heart pine, perhaps

the best built house in town," Sally announced. "Duncan knew the hazards of living near the water, so he built it to withstand storms like this. It's been through storms before and survived just fine."

"I pray you're right. I remember some houses in Pensacola blew apart or washed away in a hurricane. I wonder how high the water is here now."

"We can't see out to tell. But we do have the advantage of being on a bluff above the water. Those people on low ground are the ones in danger of flooding."

Kate nodded. "As I recall, those homes in Pensacola that were destroyed were in the part of town where the land was flat. Our home was on higher ground and fared much better. We had wind damage but no flooding."

"Likes in de Bible. Dat man dat done build his house on a rock," John said.

"Aye, John. Duncan thought about that verse when he chose this high property. Even though we were farther away from town, he decided this site was better for a home. And I believe he was right. Some of the townspeople suggested, and still do, I might add, that we're too far away. But I like it just fine where it is. Close enough to town to get what I need, and far enough to stay away from nosy neighbors."

While they were laughing at Aunt Sally's remark, the noise of the storm abated, becoming suspiciously quiet. Kate noticed first, turning to listen.

"The storm seems to be letting up. Do you think it's over?"

John shook his head. "Not just yet. Dis here's de middle o' it. I seen dis befo'. It blows and blows and rains buckets, den stops fo' a little while. Next thing you know, it start up all over again, but de wind, it blows de other way."

"John's right. I've seen it that way too. The wind changes direction," Aunt Sally said. "Just when you think everything's going to settle down, it all get stirred up again."

"I wish we could see outside," Kate said, "but it's too dark."

"And too dangerous to venture out yet. You never know what the storm has blown over that you might run into."

"We needs to watch out fo' snakes too. I remembers even back when I's a boy in Louisiana, dem snakes come up to higher groun'. Water moccasins and all kines o' snakes be tryin' to get in de house."

"Lawd, he'p us!" Bessie shrieked. "I cain't stan' snakes!"

"We better put some rags and old blankets at the bottom of the doors then," Aunt Sally suggested. "That'll keep the water out, as well as any snakes that try to come in. And we better check the windows, too, to see if any water came in around them."

After they checked all the doors and windows for leaks and plugged the gaps with rags, Aunt Sally covered her mouth to hide a yawn.

"Bessie, you and John can sleep on cots here in the hallway. I'll get you some blankets. Kate, let's you and I head to bed."

Just as they were going up the stairs to their bedrooms, the rain began again. Soon the wind was howling and swirling around the house as before, shaking the windows like an intruder trying to force its way inside. Kate reached out for Aunt Sally's hand, helping her up the stairs. "Aunt Sally, do you mind if I sleep in your room tonight?"

"I was going to suggest that myself. I would feel a lot better knowing you were all right. Not to mention I would appreciate the company on a night like this."

As they settled into Aunt Sally's big bed, Kate turned to Aunt Sally. "Do you think Father is all right? I do hope he's not out there in this storm."

"Your father has been sailing the seas for many years and knows how to ride out a storm—and even better, how to avoid sailing into one. He'll be fine, I'm sure. He's more than likely somewhere far away from here and not close to the storm. Pray for him, dear. We can trust God to take care of him."

As Kate lay there, listening to the sound of the gale raging beyond the walls, she worried about her father's safety. *Dear Lord, please keep him safe in this storm, wherever he is.*

It was August 16, just over a month until her birthday when he had promised to come see her. She had to warn him not to come, though. Perhaps she could learn how to use the signal lantern and send a message to keep him away from danger.

Chapter Twenty-Two

Kate woke to a quiet morning. The storm had passed through during the night, and based on the light trying to get into the room through the closed shutters, the sun was shining.

She sat up and discovered Aunt Sally already getting dressed.

"Sleep well?" the older woman asked her.

"I must have. I listened to the storm for a long time before I fell asleep though."

"Yes, it was a noisy one. But it's gone now. Time to see what it left in its wake."

Kate threw on her clothes and helped Aunt Sally make the bed. When they got downstairs, Bessie was putting the kerchief on her head, about to go out the door. Outside John was removing nails from the shutters. As Aunt Sally and Kate stepped out onto the veranda, Kate gasped. "Oh my! What a mess!"

"Sho is. Soons I gets done with dese here shutters, we can let some air get in de house. Den I'se gonna start cleanin' up de rest of de mess."

Kate's mouth dropped open as she surveyed the foreign landscape bearing little resemblance to its former appearance. The yard was covered by leaves and pine needles, the trees stripped bare by the fierce wind. Tree limbs were strewn around the yard, having been ripped from their trunks. In the adjacent swamp, gray denuded trees stood like skeletons. In one area the trees appeared shorn off at the same height. She pointed. "What happened there?"

John glanced over. "Must've been a little twister. Sometimes you gets 'em when de 'cane comes. Good thing it stayed over dere and didn't hit de house."

"Well, we certainly have a better view of the water now." Aunt Sally gazed out at St. George Sound, where trees that had formerly provided a barrier between the house and the water were now either gone or naked. All turned to look at the receding waves, still choppy and dark, unlike the normally peaceful blue surf they were familiar with. The lighthouse stood out across the way, even lonelier than before without any foliage around it.

"Do you think Keeper Williams and his family stayed on the island during the storm? That would be terrifying." Kate envisioned the tempest assaulting the keeper's home and lighthouse.

"I heard they left the island when the Guard took the light out. After all, they have no reason for being there now," Aunt Sally said.

"Oh, my Lawd, he'p me!" Bessie exclaimed as she ran over to where the henhouse was supposed to be. It was gone. Boards and parts of the house were scattered far and wide. "Where my chickens? Prissy! Pecky! Pokey! May! Red!"

Kate and the others ran over to Bessie to try to calm her, as well as to help find her chickens. John put his arm around the sobbing woman, trying to console her. "We'se gonna fine yo' chickens, honey. I'se sho' they be safe." Peering over her head at Aunt Sally and Kate, he shrugged as if he couldn't think of anything else to say to the distraught woman.

Kate hoped his words would prove to be true.

"But dey house is gone. Gone! Chickens don't fly! What happened to 'em? De wind done blowed dem away! Dear Lawd, dem po' things!"

John held Bessie close and patted her on the back. "Lets just keep prayin' and trust de Lawd we fine 'em all right." Raising his eyes toward heaven, he said, "Lawd, please he'p us fine Bessie's chickens. We done asked You to protect dem in de storm, and we knows You did."

He then pushed her gently away and took her hand as he started walking to the big house. "I needs to get to work gettin' dat limb off de house first. Might needs to patch the roof too. Come on with me. We can looks fo' de chickens soon's I finish."

They all walked around to the front corner of the house where a large limb from the oak tree leaned against the house. John took the axe and went to work chopping it into pieces. The women gathered branches, picking up anything they could lift and carry away. Kate tried to carry more than the other two women, concerned for Bessie's condition and Aunt Sally's age.

Aunt Sally pointed to the pile of limbs. "Some of this will be good firewood. Let's stack some of the shorter pieces over there."

Kate and Bessie did as Aunt Sally directed. Hot, humid air pressed down on them as they worked, with occasional relief when a gust of wind, the last vestiges of the storm, blew through. Everything was soaked from the deluge the night before, the ground making squishing noises as they walked.

Kate checked on her rose bushes, which didn't seem the worse for wear, having been protected from the wind's fury by the house. No buds were evident, yet the bushes were still alive. Kate wished she could say the same for Bessie's chickens. Much as she wanted to trust God, she wasn't sure

He truly cared about the chickens. Yet she kept her misgivings to herself lest she upset Bessie any more than she already was.

They stopped their labor for a simple lunch of sliced tomatoes and cold biscuits left over from the day before. The porch furniture was returned to the veranda, where they sat quietly in the shade, resting up before they went back to work.

Wanting to break the silence, Kate was about to ask John to sing when Bessie sat upright and said, "What dat?"

Each of them turned to listen. Was that a rooster crowing somewhere? "I hear it too!" Kate got up from her chair and walked around the house in the direction of the sound. Bessie quickly joined her, followed by John and Aunt Sally. "There!" Kate exclaimed. "I heard it again."

"Me too! Oh, dear Lawd, could dat be Red?"

They continued toward the noise, heading away from the house and the water. At the far edge of Aunt Sally's property, where the yard ended and the woods began, something in one of the trees caught their eyes. Bessie started running, yelling as she ran.

"It's Red! It's Red clear up dere in dat tree! He alive!"

Sure enough, the rooster was in the tree, about twenty feet above the ground. He looked a little disoriented, but alive nonetheless. "I'll get de ladder and fetch him down," John said.

When he returned and propped the ladder against the tree, Bessie held the ladder steady and shouted instructions.

Kate and Aunt Sally plopped down on a nearby fallen tree to watch the rescue and to rest. Soon Kate's eyes began to water . . . and then she started sneezing.

"Must be something in the air setting you off," Aunt Sally remarked.

Kate sneezed again. She wiped her nose with the kerchief she had tied around her neck then jerked her head, listening.

"I hear a noise coming from under this tree."

Kate leaned over to see below. Soft clucking sounds replied.

"Bessie, I think we've found the rest of them!"

Bessie ran over and knelt down where Kate pointed.

"Dey here! De girls is all here! Praise de Lawd!"

John chuckled as he stepped down from the ladder with the rooster under his arm. "How 'bout dat? See, Bessie, de Lawd, He done watch over yo' chickens."

Bessie smiled through moist eyes. "He sho did, and I'se so thankful!"

"I'll have to make a box to put 'em in 'til I builds a new henhouse so dey don't wander off or somethin' else gets 'em," John announced.

He immediately set to work and made two crates with loose boards found in the yard, one for the hens and one for Red, and soon all the chickens were safe and secure. Bessie beamed with happiness. "We's gonna keep 'em in our cabin 'til we can put 'em back in dey own house."

As it turned out there wasn't much damage to the roof of the main house, so John was able to patch the corner. When Kate gazed up at the widow's walk, though, she saw a disturbing sight. One of the railings had broken and lay against the side of the attic.

Aunt Sally also spotted the damage. "That must've been the noise we heard hitting against the house last night."

"Yes, ma'am. Dat railin' done been hangin' loose and bangin' up against de house. I'll have to fix it befo' you goes out dere again, Miss Kate."

"I can help you, John. I'm not afraid of heights."

"You don't need to go out there until the railing is fixed, Kate," Aunt Sally asserted, hands on her hips. "We don't want you falling off the rooftop."

"But Aunt Sally, somebody has to help John. He can't do it by himself, and I don't think you or Bessie can help him."

Bessie's eyes grew wide and she stepped back, shaking her head and pushing away with her hands. "No, ma'am. I cain't go up dere on dat roof. It so high I gets dizzy just thinkin' of it. John, you be real careful. I don't want you goin' down off dat roof either."

"All right," Aunt Sally conceded. "I don't think I can climb those steep stairs to the attic anymore, so Kate, I suppose you're the only other person who can assist John. You just stay close to the door and don't lean out too far."

"Trust me, Aunt Sally. I'll be careful, and John will, too." She glanced at Bessie.

Kate grabbed a small bucket of nails, and John took a couple of boards and stuck a hammer in his pocket. They went up through the attic outside to the widow's walk, where the broken railing dangled over the side.

"Dis won't be too pretty 'cause dese boards ain't painted like de other part, but it'll keep de railin' from hangin' loose and maybe fallin' all de way off. I'll squat down out dere and reach it, and you hands me a nail when I asks fo' it."

As she passed John the nails, she surveyed the surrounding area. The scenery looked scrambled, with treetops twisted and broken in every direction. She could see farther downtown, now that much of the foliage had been removed by the wind. Trinity's steeple still stood, a welcome sight to the otherwise strange landscape.

She gazed out at the lighthouse standing sentinel on the island. There appeared to be fewer outbuildings near it than before. No tents were visible over on St. Vincent's Island either. The soldiers had abandoned camp for the storm, or the tents had blown away. Hopefully, the former was true.

Out beyond the entrance to the bay she could still see the Union ship, though it appeared to be farther away. Scanning the water closer to shore, she saw debris floating in the water, possibly the remnants of someone's property.

Her eyes caught sight of an unusual piece of drifting rubble. What was it? And what was lying on it? She squinted against the reflection of the sun on the water.

"John, do you see something out there in the water?"

John chuckled. "Yes'm, Miss Kate. Dey's lots of things floatin' in de water right now. Lots of things dat used to be somewhere else, maybe even somebody's henhouse."

"No, John. This is different. I think there might be a person out there. When you're finished, I'll run get the spyglass we found in the trunk and come back to get a better look."

John brushed off his hands. "It's done. Dat'll hold it 'til I can get back and make it right." He turned to look in the direction Kate was pointing, then shielded his eyes with his hands. "Don't know fo' sho' what dat is."

Kate ran downstairs to get the spyglass then returned to the walk. As she extended the instrument, she focused on the piece of debris. "John, it's a body! See for yourself!"

John peered through the instrument as well. "Sho' do looks like some po' soul. Cain't tell if he's dead or alive."

"We have to go find out. Whoever it is might need our help. Did our boat stay tied?"

"Yes'm. I checked on it, and it held fast 'tween those two trees where I tied it upside down."

"Hurry! I'll tell Aunt Sally and get a blanket."

The two rushed outside, where Kate found Aunt Sally. "Aunt Sally, we saw a person floating on a piece of wood out in the water. John and I are going out to see if we can help them."

Kate grabbed her skirts as she and John scrambled down the bank. John untied the boat from the trees, turned it upright, and pushed it into the water, helping Kate to climb aboard. As he rowed Kate kept the floating object in sight. When they pulled alongside, they saw a man barely atop what appeared to be part of a ship. John touched the form with one of the oars, and they heard a moan.

Kate felt her eyes go wide. "He's alive. Quick! Get him in."

John reached over the edge, as Kate leaned the opposite way for balance. Lifting the man with both of his strong arms, John hauled him into the boat, where Kate promptly wrapped him in a blanket. The fellow was alive but badly bruised and unconscious, his clothes in rags and soaking wet. A large lump protruded from his forehead.

"Don't looks too good. He real pale, and we don't know how hurt he be. Dat's a big ole bump on his head. Somethin' hit him real hard." John pointed to the man's head.

"His skin is very cold. I hope this blanket helps warm him up. Maybe we can get some hot tea down him when we get him back." Kate held the man's head up in her lap while the rest of his body lay in the bottom of the boat.

"Don't knows how you can make him drink when he out like dat."

"We have to try."

When they got back to shore, John hopped out, pulled the boat back on the sand and tied it up. Then he lifted the man out and carried him up the bank to the house. Kate ran ahead to tell the others what they had found.

Aunt Sally took over. "Let's lay him down on the porch in the settee for now. Get him comfortable and make some tea. I'll go upstairs and get the little bedroom ready, and then we can move him up there."

"Good thing he not too heavy, or we couldn't get him upstairs." John eyed the frail figure on the cot. "Looks pretty skinny. Wonder how long he been out dere?"

"Since the hurricane, I'm certain. Not long enough to lose a lot of weight. I don't think he weighed much before the storm either." Aunt Sally stared down at the man. "He's pretty young. About your age I'd say, Kate."

An involuntary shudder shook Kate as she leaned over the still figure, biting her lip while studying the sandy brown hair curling over his ears, the chiseled contours of the face. "Wonder where he came from? Do you think he was one of the soldiers over on the island?"

"We can't tell by looking at him. Maybe he'll come to and tell us who he is. We'll have to get those wet clothes off him. I'll go see what else I can find to put on him. From the looks of these things, his will need mending before he can wear them again."

Kate went upstairs to help Aunt Sally get the nursery ready for the injured man. The two of them agreed to take turns checking on him. She'd seen many soldiers, but never one in such a weakened condition. Who was he, and what had happened to him? Her heart went out to the young man, creating a desire to comfort him and nurse him back to health.

When the room was ready, John carried him upstairs to the single bed they had prepared. The young man was tall, and his feet hung over the end. Aunt Sally retrieved some of Duncan's clothes from her armoire and handed them to John. "Here, put these on him. And try to cover his feet up with the quilt. Got to try to keep him warm. He's shivering."

Kate waited outside the bedroom while John and Aunt Sally got the man changed into warm clothes. Then she and her aunt went downstairs and out back, handing the wet clothes to Bessie who was standing by the washtub. Bessie held up the clothes, examining them.

"Dese clothes be pretty tore up. Don't knows if we can mend 'em or not. Lawd, what dat poor man musta been through out dere in dat water all night!" Bessie shook her head as she rinsed the clothes.

Aunt Sally stood by watching. Reaching out for what appeared to be a jacket, she said, "Let me see that." As she examined the garment, she looked closely at the remaining buttons. "My, my, what have we here?"

"What, Aunt Sally? What is it?" Kate leaned close for a

look.

"That young man is apparently a sailor from a Union ship."

Chapter Twenty-Three

"A Union soldier?" Kate's eyes widened, as a weight lodged in her stomach. "How do you know?"

"These buttons here. See the eagle on that anchor? That's the US Navy insignia. He must have been on one of the Union ships out in the Gulf."

"But the blockade ship is still out there. Do you think he washed overboard in the storm?"

"It's possible, I suppose."

John joined them downstairs and overheard the conversation. "He be hangin' onto a piece of somethin', like a ship dat broke up. Must be mo' pieces if a ship wrecked."

"So what are we supposed to do with him? Do we turn him in to the Guard?" Fear threatened Kate's senses.

"We're not turning him in to anybody right now. He's hurt and needs looking after," Aunt Sally declared.

"But he's the enemy," Kate argued. Wasn't he?

"He's our fellowman, one of God's children, just like we are. If you remember, God told us to love our enemy, feed him, and give him something to drink if he's thirsty."

Kate vaguely remembered reading those words in the Bible but didn't think it applied to Yankees.

"But these are the same people who would shoot at us, at our ships, at my father's ship! And we're supposed to be nice to them?"

"Yes, we are. I hope you can put aside your anger and fear and show some compassion to the young man. Wouldn't you want someone to do the same for one of your loved ones?"

Kate nodded reluctantly. It didn't seem fair, but she knew Aunt Sally expected her compliance. "Yes, ma'am."

"I think he got fever. He still shakin', and dem cuts and scratches needs cleanin'. Does you wants me to do dat?" John asked as he joined them outside.

"I can clean him up, but I'll need you to help me move him," Aunt Sally said. "Kate, get some clean rags, rinse them in cool water from the pump, and bring them upstairs to me. We need to put one on that big knot on his head. I'll go get the bottle of liniment to put on his cuts."

~

In the dim light of the lantern, the pale man looked like a corpse lying on the bed. Kate wrung out the rag in the basin of water then applied it to his head. The light stubble on his face indicated he was usually clean-shaven. His cheekbones were high and prominent, squaring his face with a strong chin. The man was thin, though muscular, and Kate tried to avert her eyes from the sight of his bare, bandaged chest. Although it was improper for a young single woman to look on a man so exposed, she had little choice as his nursemaid. She pulled the thin cotton sheet up over his body in case he was too cool.

So this is what the enemy looks like. She had not expected him to appear so normal, yet she didn't know how she expected an enemy to look. He wasn't the menacing, fearsome being she had imagined. This man seemed so harmless. At least for now.

Aunt Sally stepped into the room and motioned to the man. "How's our patient?"

Kate faced her aunt with a curious gaze. "He's still out. Whatever caused that bump on his head knocked him out cold. Do you think he'll recover?"

"Time will tell. We don't know how badly he's been hurt. You go on to bed, and I'll take over from here."

Kate started out of the room then turned back. "Should we go get a doctor?"

"No. We won't tell anyone about him. Not yet. They'll want to drag him off to some prison before he can recover properly."

Kate nodded and retired to her bedroom, where she poured some fresh water into the basin and washed herself. She was bone-tired after such a harrowing night and exciting day. She put on her nightgown and collapsed onto the bed. As she drifted off to sleep, she couldn't get the man lying in the bed in the next room out of her head. Where did he come from? Who was he? How had he ended up drifting on a piece of wreckage so close to them?

During the night an unusual noise awakened her. She sat up quickly, listening. From the next room came the sound of moaning. Kate hurried to the room, not bothering to light a lantern. Moonlight came through the open window, illuminating the figure moving restlessly on the bed. Each movement produced a groan from the man's mouth. Apparently Aunt Sally had gone to bed, and Kate was afraid she'd awaken from the noise. Kate crept over to the restless man, picked up the cloth that had been on his head, and reapplied it.

"Shhh!" She patted his arm while whispering. "Be still. You're hurt."

The man stilled. She sat on a chair by the bed and rubbed his arms gently until she heard steady breathing as he went back to sleep. When his body relaxed, so did hers. She felt his head and noticed his fever had abated. She sighed with relief, surprising herself. Did she really care about this man's health? A thump in her heart assured her that she did.

~

The next few days the women treated the injured man, taking turns trying to make him comfortable. While Kate sat with him, she worked on the piece of embroidery she was making for John and Bessie's baby. She had just started making a row of baby chicks walking along the bottom of the piece, a special tribute to Bessie's chickens. An occasional glance at the man allowed her to assess his condition. The bump on his head had begun to go down, and his skin color was regaining some normalcy. Good thing they had been the ones to find him and not someone else. She shuddered to think what might have happened to him otherwise.

When Kate went downstairs to get fresh water for the pitcher, Aunt Sally asked about him, expressing concern that he had been unconscious so long. "He needs to eat. It's been a long time since he's had anything in his stomach. Let's try to get some soup down him again."

They had tried several times before, but the patient had been unreceptive, coughing each time they put the soup in his mouth. "All right. I'll take some up to him." Kate put a bowl on a tray to carry upstairs. As she passed the parlor with it, she heard voices outside the house. One of them was familiar.

Clay Harris had arrived with a few of his men. Aunt Sally went out to greet them, while Kate stayed inside, listening to the conversation through the open window.

"Good morning, ma'am. We've come to see how you people fared in the storm."

"Aye, we did just fine. The Lord looked after us, and we're getting things back to order slowly. How's everyone else in town?"

"Some of the warehouses down by the river were flooded, but the cotton's all gone, so there was no great loss besides water damage. Although the ice in the ice house

202

might not taste so good anymore. And several houses lost parts of their roofs when trees fell on them. One man was hurt lying in his bed when a tree fell on his roof and crashed through the ceiling."

"My word! How terrible. Will he be all right?"

"Yes, ma'am. He has a broken arm, but he was pretty lucky he wasn't killed. Is there anything we can do to help you?"

"No, but thank you for asking, Clay. We're finished with most of the cleanup. How about your soldiers? How did they fare?"

"The ones that stayed did fine, but the battery downtown was flooded during the storm. We'll be rebuilding it as soon as the men come back. Many of them went to their homes to check on their families and livestock. Any man who wanted to take a leave was allowed to do so."

"That's good to know. Some things are surely more important than the blockade."

Kate peeked through the window to get a look. Clay was still handsome, but he no longer held any attraction for her. She felt like she could see right through him now and knew exactly what kind of character he was, the kind she did not want to associate with ever again. She saw him raise an eyebrow at Aunt Sally's remark.

"I can assure you the blockade remains our biggest concern. The Union ship is still out there, despite the storm; however we have reports that another vessel shipwrecked over near the island. We haven't found any bodies or survivors yet, but some wreckage washed up on the shore, and we suspect it was from another Union ship."

"Oh, my. I do hope it wasn't one of ours."

"We'll find out. We're in the process of rebuilding the camp over on St. Vincent's, and we're patrolling the islands again." Clay paused, looking out at the water toward the islands. Then, apparently remembering his mission, he turned back to Aunt Sally. "Well, if you don't need any assistance, we'll be on our way. Yours is the last house we've checked on."

"Because we're at the end of the road. Glad we didn't need any help." Aunt Sally smiled as she adjusted her hat. "You men take care."

The men turned and marched off, leaving Kate full of questions. What would they do if they found out about the Union sailor in their home? Would that be considered treason? He must have been on the boat that shipwrecked. But was it another blockade boat? And where were his shipmates? As she carried the soup up the steps toward his room, she wondered if she'd ever have a chance to find out.

~

That night Kate was again awakened by the man's moans. Once more she scrambled out of bed and went to his room. This time she found him thrashing around and speaking incoherently, apparently having a nightmare. Kate quickly sat down by the man and spoke in low, soothing tones, stroking his hair, rubbing his lean muscular arms, and patting his hand. He calmed, and Kate hoped he would rest the remainder of the night.

As she stood to move away, he suddenly grabbed her hand. Kate gasped.

"Stop," the man said in a soft, hoarse voice. "Who are you? Where am I?"

Kate's heart caught in her throat as she glanced at his face and saw his eyes trying to focus on her. Thankful the darkness hid her in her nightgown, she didn't know what to say. Her free hand flew up to her hair, as if she could hide the mass of unbound tresses flowing down her back.

"Please. Are you an angel?"

"No. I'm someone who's taking care of you." Kate spoke softly. "You were in a storm, and we found you. You're in our house now."

The man started to cough. "Can I please have some

water?"

Kate rushed to fill a cup from the pitcher then returned to the bed with it. She leaned over and lifted the man's head so he could drink.

"Thank you." This time his eyes looked straight into hers, as if trying to see her more clearly in the moonlit room. "You're beautiful."

The words startled Kate and left her speechless. The man must be delirious, or the bump on his head had affected his vision. She offered him more water then stood to leave again.

"Please stay," the man whispered.

His plea touched her in such a way she couldn't refuse him. "I'll stay until you fall asleep, but then I must go do the same."

"God bless you."

She sat back down and put her hand over his. His fingers hooked over hers as if to keep her there. The innocent gesture flooded her senses with its warmth and sense of intimacy. Although she wanted to move her hand, she sensed his need for the security, and allowed his grasp. She hated to admit she enjoyed the feeling of closeness it conveyed.

"Thank you," he whispered again with his eyes closed. Soon he was sleeping peacefully.

Kate slipped her hand away from his and quietly stood. Something touched her inside as she gazed down at the sleeping man. Was it pity? No, the tenderness in his voice, the touch of his hand, the genuine appreciation he had shown had stirred her emotions, had created a connection to him she didn't understand and hadn't desired.

An instinct surfaced within her, and she knew she must protect him, whatever the cost.

Chapter Twenty-Four

When Kate entered the man's room the next morning, she was surprised to find him wide awake. His gaze followed her as she walked. "I know I'm not dreaming now. You must be my angel."

Kate looked into his warm hazel eyes and saw a hint of a smile on his lips. Her face warmed with his gaze.

"Glad to see you're awake. How are you feeling?"

"Alive, but with quite a headache. So you're the one who's been nursing me? I want to thank you for your kindness."

"It hasn't been just me. My aunt Sally and I have both been looking in on you."

"My gratitude to you both then. And do you mind telling me where I am?"

"You're in Apalachicola, Florida. We found you hanging onto a piece of wreckage out in the sound."

"And you and your aunt brought me back here by yourselves?"

"No, John carried you."

He raised his eyebrows. "Oh, is that the Negro man I've seen? Is he your slave?"

"No!" Kate's emphatic answer made the man flinch.

"John is a freed man who works for us. He and his wife, Bessie, are both free."

"I didn't mean to offend you, but I thought everyone in the South had slaves."

"Everyone doesn't, but some do. We don't own anyone."

Abruptly changing the subject, it was Kate's turn to ask questions. "Where are you from? Do you remember what happened to you?"

"My home is in Ohio, but last I remember I was on a supply ship bringing provisions to the USS Montgomery. The weather got bad and the seas became very rough. We lost sight of the Montgomery and were pushed aground by huge waves. We sent out a distress signal, and the Montgomery tried to help us, but we started breaking apart. That's all I remember. Did you find anyone else?"

She shook her head. "No, no one else. Maybe the rest of the men stayed on the other side of the island, the Gulf side. Somehow you got pushed through the pass and ended up in the Sound. You were alone out there on a piece of the ship."

The young man closed his eyes while his lips moved silently. When he looked up, his eyes were moist. "I pray my shipmates were rescued. Only God knows why I ended up here."

They paused in their conversation as Aunt Sally walked in. Studying the situation, she smiled at the man and set her hands on her hips. "Good morning! I see you're feeling better. We weren't certain you'd still be with us. What's your name, son?"

Kate was embarrassed she hadn't attempted any introductions yet.

"My name is Joshua Jones. And who are you, dear lady -- my rescuer?"

"Sally McFarlane. I see you've met my great-niece, Katherine."

Joshua turned his head to look at Kate. "Not officially. Pleased to make your acquaintances, ladies. Thank you very much for your kindness."

"Joshua. That's a good Bible name, and you're quite welcome." Aunt Sally smiled. "Are you about ready to eat? You must be starving, since you haven't eaten for at least three days."

"I am indeed very hungry. If you can help me up, I'll dress and join you at your table." Joshua tried to sit up, then groaned and fell backwards.

"I don't believe you're ready to get up yet. We'll bring you some food. Maybe you can sit, though. Kate, help me lift him and put a pillow behind his back."

The women lifted him to a sitting position. "Can you tell me where your pain is?"

"My head and my sides. I think I may have a cracked rib."

"I thought as much. That's why we wrapped your chest. You had a nasty bump on your head, but it's about gone now. Just a purple knot today. We've been putting cool rags on it to bring it down. Would you like a fresh cloth on your head?"

"Not right now, please, but maybe after I eat." Joshua's gaze moved to the window. "Am I on the second floor? I can see sky."

"Aye, you're upstairs at my house."

"It's very warm here."

"No, Joshua, it's downright hot. Sometimes we get breezes off the water, but in August they don't come often. We've tried to keep you cool by keeping some water in the basin there and rinsing your head and arms off with wet rags."

"Thank you, Mrs. McFarlane. God bless you for your kindness to me."

"Thank God, we found you."

The women left, and when Kate returned carrying a tray

with a bowl of soup and cornbread, Joshua gave her a big smile.

"My angel returns!" His eyes twinkled.

She felt her cheeks flush. "This should make you feel better."

Joshua bowed his head over the tray and said, "Lord, thank You for this good food. Please bless it to my nourishment and bless the hands that have taken care of me and prepared it. Amen." Lifting his eyes, he turned to Kate. "Would you please sit with me while I eat? I would enjoy the company."

"I really need to go help the others." Why couldn't she just leave? Her mind told her to, but her feet remained planted on the floor.

"I wish I could help too, and I will, as soon as I can get up and about."

"That might not be such a good idea."

He raised his eyebrow. "Because I've been injured? I should be good as new in no time, especially with all the good care I've received."

Kate searched for an answer. "If you're discovered here, you'll be taken prisoner."

Understanding flashed in his eyes. "Of course. I forgot I'm the enemy. Are you planning to turn me in?"

"No. We wouldn't do that." The reality was that Kate didn't know what they would do. They couldn't hide him forever. "You have our protection as long as you need it."

Kate stood rigidly while Joshua slurped. "This soup is delicious, maybe the best vegetable soup I've ever had." Looking up from his poised spoon, he said, "Have you always lived with your aunt?"

"No, only since February." Kate wasn't certain she was ready to divulge any personal information to this man who was still a stranger, albeit a friendly one. "I'm from Pensacola. My father is a sea merchant. Did you say you're from Ohio?"

Without further encouragement, he began talking about himself. "Yes, I am. I suppose you wonder how I ended up on a ship in the Gulf of Mexico."

Kate nodded, and he continued. "I grew up on a farm where I lived with my parents, grandparents, four sisters, and three brothers. We're a big family, and we have a grand time together. But one time my father took me to Cleveland to pick up a new wagon, and I saw the lake. Lake Erie. It's so big, it looks like the ocean. I saw the ships out there and decided that's where I wanted to be – on a ship." He took a sip from the spoon. "When the war broke out, my brothers joined the Army, but I joined the Navy. It took some getting used to, but I love it. I love being out on the open water. Did you say your father is a sea merchant?"

Kate had to get away from this man before she disclosed too much about her father. After all, Joshua was still the enemy, and her father's safety was at risk. How did she know she could trust this Yankee? Taking the tray with the empty bowl on it, she said, "I really need to go now. Can I get you anything else before I leave?"

"Do you have a Bible I can read?"

The large Bible they usually read from was too heavy for the man to handle in his present condition, much less carry upstairs, but then Kate remembered the smaller one in Great Uncle Duncan's sea chest. "Yes, we do. I'll get it for you."

She went downstairs to the chest and retrieved the Bible, glancing at the other objects in the process. Returning upstairs, she handed the book to Joshua.

He took it from her as if it were fragile and smiled at her. "Thank you. Perhaps when you have time we can read it together."

"Perhaps."

Kate hurried back downstairs, trying to erase Joshua's pleasant smile from her mind as she returned to the sea chest. She had noticed the signal lantern again when she retrieved the Bible and impressed with a sense of urgency, wanted to examine the device.

Removing the lantern from the chest, she studied it, trying to remember how Father had explained its operation. He'd said the signals were adapted from the Morse code to a series of light flashes. Did Uncle Duncan have a book of instructions?

Digging down further in the trunk, she discovered a small leather book. Inside were handwritten notes detailing how to create the lantern's code. What would she say in her message, and where would she send it from? Maybe John had used one of the lanterns before, or at least knew how to use it. Grabbing the book and the lantern, she raced outside.

"John! John!" She found him putting the finishing touches on the new chicken house.

The big man wiped his hands on his pants; taking a kerchief from his back pocket, he wiped his brow. "Dere. It be finished. Bessie's chickens gots a new home. Dey should be happy now."

Kate smiled. "Bessie or the chickens?"

John laughed. "All of 'em." Then his gaze fell on what was in her hands. "What you got dere? Ain't dat de lantern from Mr. Duncan's old sea chest? What you gonna do with it?"

"John, I have an idea, but I'll need your help."

John raised his eyebrows, drawing back his head to look down on Kate. "Dat right? Let me wash up and come up to de house so's you can tell me all 'bout it."

"Listen, John. For now this needs to be kept private, between you and me."

The big man frowned. "I sees trouble comin' when you wants me to keep yo' secrets."

"Please, John. Just listen to me. Is there any harm in that?"

"No, ma'am. Meet you up on de porch."

When John came up to the house, Kate glanced each

way then motioned him around to the side, just in case Aunt Sally or Bessie was in earshot.

"So what be dis idea of yo's, Miss Kate? What you needs my he'p fo'?"

"John, you know Father is coming here for my birthday. He promised he would, and he has never missed one of my birthdays."

"I knows you's right 'bout dat."

"But, John, I don't want him to risk coming here now. He'll either be fired on by the blockade ships or maybe by our own soldiers. It's not safe, and we need to warn him."

"You plans to warn him wid dat lantern? Hows you gonna do dat?"

"Did you ever see Father operate the one he had?"

"I did. He pulled dat knob dere and made dat piece slide back and fo'th over de fire so's de light flashed."

"That's correct. But did you know any of the signals?"

"No, but he had a book dat 'splained it."

"I found this book in the trunk too. It explains the Morse code, and Uncle Duncan made notes about using the lantern to send it."

"Miss Kate, I don' thinks I can 'cipher dat."

"You don't need to. I believe I can do it. I just have to decide what message to send to him so he'll understand and know I'm the one sending it."

"Whats you needs my he'p fo'?"

"I need you to row me over to the island so I can get into the lighthouse. I think it's the best place to send the signal from. Father will be looking for the lighthouse, expecting to see its light."

John stepped back, covering his mouth with his hand and shaking his head. "Miss Kate, dat's a dangerous thing to do dese days, what wit' dem soldiers patrollin' de island."

"I know, John, so we need to choose our timing perfectly. Before we actually send the signal, we need to discover how long it would take to get to the island, get in the lighthouse, and when to send the signal. Since Father will be here in four weeks, we should go soon. Will you help me?"

"I needs to thinks 'bout dis, and pray 'bout it too. I sees why you don't want your Aunt Sally to know. She wouldn't let you do it, no suh."

"But do you think it's possible?" Kate implored.

"All things be possible with God, but I's not sure He 'grees with dis idea of yo's."

"Please think about it."

"I said I will, and I will. But hows you plannin' to get in dat lighthouse if de do' be locked?"

"I don't know yet. Perhaps you can help me figure that out also." Kate tipped her head sideways and smiled her sweetest smile at John.

"Don't you go givin' me dat little girl look o' yo's. I's gonna think on it."

"Do you promise you won't mention it to anyone?"

"I don't like keepin' things from Bessie, an' if I tell her, she won't tell Aunt Sally if'n I tells her not to."

"But she probably won't want you to do it."

John nodded then turned and started singing as he walked away. "I want Jesus to walk with me."

As Kate watched him, she heard a sneeze coming from above. She glanced up, and her breath caught when she realized they'd been standing below the open window of the room where Joshua Jones was. Had he heard anything?

Chapter Twenty-Five

"Good morning, Miss McFarlane. You look radiant this morning."

Kate raised an eyebrow, and Joshua chuckled then coughed as he held his side. Sitting on the edge of the bed, he looked much healthier with the bruises gone and scratches healed. However, Uncle Duncan's shirt and trousers – held up by suspenders – hung on his lean frame.

"Here's some fresh water for you." As Kate replaced the water pitcher on the washstand, she mulled over his compliment as heat rushed to her face. Radiant? Wearing her everyday gingham dress and apron, with her hair pulled back into a braid, hardly qualified as radiant. But it didn't matter. She had no intention of being on friendly terms with this Union stranger.

"I apologize if I make you feel uncomfortable. May I ask you a favor, please?"

She faced him, holding the pitcher in one hand, with her other set on her hip. "What do you need?"

"I'd like to stand up, and I need someone to lean on. I'm quite tired of sitting and lying all day and night. It's time I begin to tend to myself and relieve you kind people of that burden."

"I'll go get John. He can help you when he's finished with his chores." Kate headed out the door.

"Miss, I would really like to stand now. I was hoping you'd let me lean on you. You're a tall woman and look strong enough to support me."

Kate bristled at the familiar reference to being tall, but Joshua's pleading expression forced her to give in to his wishes, and she put down the pitcher and returned to the bedside.

He pushed off from the bed, placing his left hand on top of the bedrail for support, then reached for her and let his right arm drape over her shoulder. With a grunt and a grimace, he stretched himself as tall as he could comfortably do. She put her arm around his waist to help steady him.

As she looked up at him, Kate was astonished to realize how much taller he was than she. He was even taller than Clay. Carefully they took a few steps, with Joshua leaning on her.

"Where would you like to go?"

"I'd like to look out the window right now and get a better view of my surroundings."

When they reached the window, he rested his hands on the sill and peered out. The room was on the side of the house facing the marsh, now gray and brown, having lost its greenery in the storm.

"If it weren't so hot, I'd say it looks like winter, with everything being so barren."

"That's a result of the hurricane. Salt water blew in from the storm and burned the leaves or blew them off. Even the pine tree needles are brown."

"I see." He directed his gaze to the south. "So there's the water. I wondered how close the house was to it. And that's where you found me?"

Kate nodded. "Yes, in the sound."

"The water's beautiful here, so peaceful and unlike the

way I remembered it."

"It usually is calmer on this side of the island."

"Do you ever go boating?"

"Not lately. The others like to fish, but I haven't developed an interest in it."

"You're not afraid of the water, are you?"

"Certainly not." Kate scowled at him. "My father's been taking me sailing since I was a small child."

Her anger only seemed to amuse him. With a boyish grin, he replied, "You are most fortunate. When I was a boy I dreamed of being on the water, but working on the farm was my future. Until I signed up for the Navy."

Her mood calmed as she reflected on what he said. "I've lived near the water my whole life and have always enjoyed sailing with my father."

"So your father joined the Confederate Navy?"

Kate bristled at his reference to her father. Why was he so interested in Father's activities? "No. My father doesn't approve of the war and has removed himself from it."

Joshua raised his eyebrows. "Is that so? I thought one had to choose which side he would fight on."

"My father has no interest in fighting. He traded with the North, but we live in the South, so he has sympathies for both."

Joshua stared out at the water, seeming to mull over her remarks. "I pray to God the fighting will be minimal and short-lived. Heaven forbid there is any more loss of life."

"Then tell your President Lincoln to remove the blockade. Why should innocent people have to suffer?"

"I can't answer that question, nor do I have the authority to tell the president what to do. I just follow orders from my superiors."

He was beginning to slump, so Kate reached out her arm and put it around his waist again. "I think you need to rest now. Perhaps you can walk some more tomorrow."

Joshua nodded and allowed Kate to help him back into

the bed. "Thank you." He lay back down then gazed intently at her. "You have the most beautiful green eyes."

Her face warmed, but before she could respond, he closed his own eyes and emitted a tired sigh. As she hurried to the door, he spoke once more. "When will you see your father again?"

"I have no idea." And she marched out.

Kate stomped out the back door onto the porch, slamming down the metal bucket she had used to refill Joshua's pitcher. Aunt Sally stood at the washstand, rinsing off some just-picked squash. Jumping at the loud intrusion, the older woman wiped her hands on her apron then placed them on her hips, eyeing Kate quizzically. "What's got you all fired up this morning?"

Kate shot an angry glance toward her aunt and pointed upstairs. "That man!"

"Well, what on earth did he do, Kate? Was he rude or ungentlemanly?"

Kate blew out a disgusted breath. "No. He just...just...he's too nice!"

Aunt Sally threw back her head and laughed. "That's a problem?" The woman tried to cover her smile with her hand as she spoke. "And since when does being a nice person make you angry?"

"Oh, I don't know. I just don't trust him."

"Because he's on the other side, or has he done something else?"

"He asks me questions about Father." Kate related the conversation she'd had with Joshua. "I don't care to discuss my personal life and my family with a stranger, nor do I want to put Father in danger. And I won't give him any information that could possibly cause Father harm."

"What can he do from here to hurt your father? Perhaps he's just trying to make conversation with you. After all, you've not been very friendly."

"I do not care to be friends with the enemy!" Kate

strode away to find John.

He was working on the fence around the new henhouse. He straightened to remove his handkerchief from his trouser pocket and wipe his brow then nodded to Kate as she approached.

"All right, Miss Kate. I's gonna he'p you. Has you figured out how to work dat lantern yet?" The big man folded his arms across his chest.

"Oh, John, thank you so much. Won't you feel better knowing Father won't be captured trying to come here?"

"I feels better when dis plan o' yo's is done. And . . . de lantern?"

"Almost. I just need to practice a little more."

"So what's you gonna tell him?"

"God go with ye."

John tilted his head and rubbed his chin with one hand as he considered the phrase. "I thinks dat's good. Um hm, I thinks so. He'll get de meanin' to go and know nobody but family be sendin' him dat message."

"I think so too. But first we have to go to the island to time everything. How soon do you think we can do that?"

"We needs to go when de tide's goin' out so we can go fast, and we needs to go when it's still dark. Dat way we has less chance o' bein' seen by dem soldiers guardin' de island. Let me watch it fo' a couple mo' days, so's I can tell when dat is."

"Of course, we're not enemies, so our soldiers shouldn't suspect us, but I'd hate to have to explain why we're there."

"Dat fo' sho.' And dey could thinks we's workin' fo' de other side too."

"I didn't think of that. Perhaps we should have a reason for being there that they'd accept. Can you think of one?"

"Well, you wouldn't be visitin' de lightkeeper's family, since dey done moved off de island now. Hmmm . . ."

"Could we go fishing or oystering or something like

that?"

"Could be. Could be. O' huntin' fo' wild boar."

"I don't think I'd go with you to hunt for boar."

"No, you pro'bly wouldn't. So we bes' bring our fishin' poles and nets and be ready to do some fishin' so we won't be lyin'. Is you bringin' de lantern?"

"Not this time. I can't risk losing it."

"Good thinkin'. I be lettin' you know 'bout de tides."

As she had for the past few nights, Kate went back up into the attic to practice the code with the lantern. A series of short and long flashes would convey the message, she hoped, to her father. She also hoped the Union ship wouldn't pick up the signal, but if it did, that it would not react. Stepping out onto the widow's walk at night was an eerie feeling. The summer air was still, except for an occasional breeze off the water. The night sounds of the animals were loud – sounds of frogs, crickets, owls, and God knows what else roamed at night. The moonlight streaked across the water toward the house, the only light she could see besides a few campfires over on St. Vincent's Island where the soldiers had re-established their lookout since the hurricane. St. George Island was dark, with no light from the lighthouse or the keeper's house.

Kate shook her head, dumbfounded that the Confederates dismantled the light. What a senseless thing to do, when it could jeopardize the lives of many besides those on Union ships. Mosquitoes droning around her face brought her attention back home, and she quickly went inside before the pests feasted on her.

She tiptoed through the house, trying not to call attention to herself. Just as she entered her room, she heard Joshua's voice calling quietly to her. Had he heard her upstairs? "Miss McFarlane, is that you?"

To keep him from waking Aunt Sally, Kate went to his room with her finger to her lips. She whispered as she entered. "What do you need?"

Sitting up with his back against the headboard, Joshua smiled when he saw her. "I've been doing a lot of thinking since I've been here and have come to a new understanding about this war and those affected. I want you to know I'm not your enemy. I would never harm you or your family. I hope you can believe me. I'm an honest man."

Though the light from the window was dim, she could still see his warm hazel eyes looking at her, studying her. Had he heard her conversation with Aunt Sally or read her mind? Which was worse, she didn't know, but a pang of guilt attacked her.

"Will you trust me?" Joshua implored.

Sighing, she relented. "I'd like to believe you, but I just don't know if that's a prudent thing to do. There are very few men I trust." She slapped her hand over her mouth, regretful that she'd revealed any personal information. But she couldn't take back the remark, and Joshua didn't miss it.

"I don't know who's caused you to mistrust men, but you mustn't judge every man by the scoundrels that exist. We're not all evil."

Joshua appeared to be sincere, but did she dare trust him? If she did, would that make him her friend? That could not happen.

"Very well then. I'll try to trust you. Now I need to retire, and so do you."

Joshua was still staring at her, studying her face. "I wish I could see you better in this light, but at least I can still remember the lovely green of your eyes."

Kate spun to leave the room, but Joshua continued speaking softly. "I'm telling you the truth. You do have beautiful eyes. Please accept my compliment."

"Thank you." Then she hurried to her room, anxious to get away from this man who made her so ill at ease. She had more important things to think about. If only she could forget the gentle sound of Joshua's voice when he spoke to her.

Chapter Twenty-Six

"We has to leave 'bout three in de mornin' wid de high tide. I thinks it gonna take 'bout a hour to get over, but it mights be mo'. We just has to fine out." John spoke in low tones, his eyebrows knit together. "You sho you wanna do dis, Miss Kate?"

Kate glanced around to make sure Aunt Sally and Bessie were still on the opposite side of the house.

"Yes, John, I'm certain. It's only a few weeks before Father comes, and we must be ready."

"If you says so. I figures we gots to have time to get over to de island, looks aroun', and see hows we gonna get in dat lighthouse, so's next time we knows what to bring wid us. I spec we be back home befo' de rooster crow. Dat way, Miz Sally won't know we been over dere. I be thinkin' we should tell her, though."

"Why? She'll just be worried about us, and it won't be good for her heart."

"Maybe so, but befo' we goes back to send dat message to de cap'n, we has to tell her and let her knows we gots everythin' figured out so she won't worry so much."

Kate mulled it over. "I'll agree to that. When are we going?"

"Tonight. I's gonna throw a pine cone at yo' window to makes sho you wakes up. Den you meets me down by de boat."

Tonight? Kate's heart raced with nervous anticipation. How was she going to keep Aunt Sally from sensing something afoot? Kate knew she would have to act normal so her aunt wouldn't get suspicious.

She left John and went to check on her roses. Finding a budding flower on the bushes, she couldn't wait to show it to the others. She broke off the stem then hurried around the house with it.

"Aunt Sally, look! The first blossom since the hurricane."

She froze, dropping the rose when she saw Joshua standing on the back porch. "Oh!"

"Good morning to you, Miss McFarlane. What a pretty rose." He eyed the scarlet flower lying on the porch.

Kate reached down and snatched up the blossom then narrowed her eyes at him. "How did you get out here?"

"Very slowly, I'm afraid." His eyes twinkled at her reaction.

"B-but . . ." Kate stammered, trying to avoid his gaze.

"I thought I'd try to move around a bit, get some fresh air. I hope you don't mind. I'll try not to get in your way."

Aunt Sally walked up from the garden then, holding a basket of yams. "Well, look who's up and about! You must be feeling better, Joshua."

"Yes, ma'am, I am, and getting mighty tired of lying around all day."

Despite his confident words, his stance began to sag, and Aunt Sally motioned to the rocking chair nearby. "Your mind may be ready to get up, but I can see your body isn't quite ready yet. Sit down in that rocker and rest a spell. You don't want to do too much too soon."

Joshua obeyed her command, heaving a great sigh as he plopped down.

Aunt Sally seemed relieved that he had settled into the rocking chair. "Can we get you anything? Coffee? Tea? Lemonade? Or are you hungry?"

"Coffee would be nice, if it's not too much trouble. Have you all eaten your breakfast?"

"We have, but we have some biscuits left and we can cook you some eggs."

"That sounds grand, but I don't want to be a bother."

"Nonsense. Not a bother at all. Kate, please go ask Bessie to cook Joshua a couple of eggs and get him a biscuit too."

Kate glared at Joshua, then spun and tramped out to the kitchen. Why, he acted like a guest!

"I'm afraid your niece doesn't care for me." The sound of Joshua's voice behind her reached her ears.

"Care for him? Why should I?" Kate muttered under her breath.

When she returned with his food, he and Aunt Sally were deep in conversation. Joshua stroked his patchy chin whiskers while he talked.

Aunt Sally noted his action. "Would you like to shave? I can get you some soap, a razor, and a mirror, if you'd like."

His gaze, intent on Kate's arrival, diverted to the older woman, and a big smile spread across his face. "Now that would be wonderful! I've never been able to grow a nice beard, and these whiskers are beginning to itch."

"I'll get you the shaving necessaries. Now go ahead and eat before it gets cold. You can shave when you're finished."

Kate set down the plate of food on the small table in front of him, handing him the tin coffee cup as Aunt Sally went inside.

"Thank you. This looks delicious. Won't you please sit with me while I eat?"

"I really need to help the others." Kate's glance shifted

to the garden, where Bessie and John were working. But for some reason she couldn't understand, she didn't leave. Instead she sat on a nearby cane chair while he ate.

Aunt Sally came back out on the porch, carrying a shaving brush, soap, razor, and a small mirror. Noticing how quickly Joshua's food disappeared, she said, "Looks like your appetite has returned. That's a good sign."

"Yes, ma'am. I'm feeling much better today."

Kate jumped up to carry his empty dishes over to the dry sink to rinse them, while Aunt Sally took him the shaving articles.

"You can sit over there on that stool where there's better light." Aunt Sally nodded in the direction of the opposite side of the porch.

He rose slowly and moved to the stool, and Aunt Sally brought him a pan of water. After making a good lather with the soap, he brushed it on his face and began to strip off the unwanted facial hair. "Here's a towel." Aunt Sally handed him a fresh cloth to dry his face. "Why, Joshua, you look quite handsome!" She stepped back to admire him.

"Thank you, ma'am. I do prefer being clean-shaven."

As Kate looked over her shoulder to catch a glimpse, her eyes widened at the change in his appearance. Her heart raced and her skin tingled as she stared at the handsome face.

Aunt Sally glanced from Kate to Joshua with a bemused smile. "Doesn't Joshua look nice now that he's had a shave?'

Realizing she was staring, Kate didn't answer, but instead returned her attention to the dishes, averting her gaze as heat crept up her neck. After wiping her nervous hands on the edge of her apron, she reached up and struggled to tuck her hair back under the sunbonnet.

"You shouldn't hide such lovely hair. It's the most glorious color I've ever seen," Joshua said, his voice hinting amusement.

Ignoring the compliment, Kate turned and shot him a glare. "It's too hot. I've a mind to cut it all off."

Joshua leaned back with a look of shock. "No. You wouldn't consider such a thing, would you? It would be a real shame. I remember how pretty it was when you came into my room at night, that long red braid hanging down your back."

Kate struggled to hide her unease. Why did he have this effect on her?

"If you'll excuse me, please, I must go help the others." She turned toward the garden.

"Of course. Say, may I ask you a question before you go?"

"Yes?"

"The old Bible in your parlor. Do any of you ever read it?"

So he snooped around the house when he came downstairs. What else would you expect from an enemy? "As a matter of fact, yes. We all get together right after breakfast and read it; that is, I read, the others listen, and then we talk about it."

"That a fact? I would very much like to join you tomorrow morning, with your permission."

Tomorrow morning? Hopefully she and John would be back in time for the Bible reading.

Aunt Sally nodded and clapped her hands together. "Why, that's a grand idea, Joshua. We would indeed like for you to join us. Don't you agree, Katherine?"

Kate gave Aunt Sally a hasty glance. "Yes, of course." She hurried away to join John in the garden.

For the rest of the day, Kate pushed thoughts about Joshua aside as she anticipated the trip to the island. After she went to bed, she tossed and turned, unable to sleep as she waited for John's signal, counting every chime of the grandfather's clock. It didn't seem she had been in bed very long when she heard something hit the window. She bolted out of bed and ran to look. Outside, John's form was barely visible as he walked to the water. With shaking hands, she dressed then grabbed her shoes. On silent, stocking-clad feet, she tiptoed across the floor, slowly opened her bedroom door, then rushed down the stairs and out the back door.

Even in the summer the humid night air felt cool, and she was glad she had grabbed her shawl. The deafening sound of frogs and cicadas followed her as she ran across the yard and scampered down the bank. John was getting the boat ready to put into the water. He motioned to it and whispered, "Climb on in. I'm gonna push us out."

She did his bidding, and once he shoved the boat off, he hopped over the side to join her. John grabbed the oars and started rowing to the island. Going out with the tide made the boat move quickly across the water. Unfortunately it was also moving eastward toward St. Vincent's Island and the army camp instead of St. George Island, so John had to continuously row to keep the boat on course.

Once away from shore, all was quiet. The only sound came from the oars splashing into the water. The clear night sky was lit by a brilliant half-moon, whose reflection streamed across the waves as the stars winked a knowing salutation. On any other night Kate would admire these sights and praise God for them, but tonight her prayers focused for Him to still her trembling limbs and racing heart. She pulled her shawl tighter. John always knew how to calm her spirit, but they couldn't risk speaking on the open sea and being heard by the soldiers on St. Vincent's. The eerie silence served to intensify Kate's fears.

Kate whispered, "I wish you could sing right now," longing for the soothing effect of his melodic voice.

John motioned with one finger over his mouth to be quiet. Then he whispered back. "I does too."

Finally, they made landing on the sandy beach. John dragged the boat out of the water and tied its rope to a spindly tree near the shore. The deserted beach revealed damage from the hurricane's assault on the few buildings near the lighthouse. Shingles were missing off the keeper's house, shutters hung loose, and two of the three outbuildings were leaning, with boards missing.

Waves crashing on the Gulf side of the island grew louder as the stealthy pair made their way across the deep white sand to the lighthouse. A wooden bar crossed over the sturdy door, held by a chain and padlock on the other end. John studied the mechanism.

"Do you think you can break it?" Kate asked, looking from the lock to John.

"I thinks so. I needs to bring de heavy mallet, and I thinks if I hits it hard nuff, I can bust it."

Kate gazed up at the towering building. It was half as tall as the Pensacola lighthouse she had climbed before. Judging by the height, it should take her less than ten minutes to scale the staircase once they got in. The climb, plus getting the door open, and the trip across had taken longer than she expected. She didn't know how long it would take to send the message. On the next trip, they would have to leave the house much earlier.

After surveying the area they started back to the boat as the lighter sky gave hints of approaching morning. They had gone only a few steps when they heard voices coming from the other side of the lighthouse.

"Hurry! Someone's coming!" Kate picked up her skirt and ran with John close behind.

"Hide in dis building here. We cain't make it to de boat." John pulled her into one of the dilapidated small outbuildings. The two of them peered through cracks between the boards. Soon a detachment of soldiers appeared.

"Dey must be de soldiers from St. Vincent's, patrollin' de shore," John whispered.

As the dawn revealed the area, the soldiers stepped into

sight. John and Kate recognized the leader at the same time.

"Eugene Blackmon." Kate muttered under her breath. One of the boards she leaned against made a cracking sound.

"Who goes there?" Blackmon called out. "Come out and show yourself!" Peering between the cracks, Kate saw the scowl on his face and the gun he pointed at the building.

"You stay put, Miss Kate. I'se gonna go out." John pushed her gently back.

Kate held her breath as John moved over to the open doorway. When she glanced around for a way to escape, she saw hay on the ground and on shelves, along with a few feathers. Oh no! Their hiding place was an abandoned chicken coop. Kate's heart raced and she pinched her nose to avoid breathing the hostile air.

As John stepped out with hands outstretched, Blackmon's face contorted into a crooked grin. "Well, look who's here. If it ain't Miz Sally's nigger! Now what on earth would you be doin' way over here? Plannin' to catch a ride on that Union boat over there?" Blackmon motioned to the water with his gun.

"No suh. No suh. I was just out fishin' and ended up over here. Thought I'd do some crabbin' on de island, but I needed to relieve myse'f so I slipped in dat ole shed."

"That right, huh?"

Kate's eyes itched and her nose started running. Her throat tickled, and she held her breath, straining to listen to the conversation. Blackmon didn't sound convinced by John's explanation. She moved toward the doorway. Perhaps she could help by confirming John's story. Unfortunately her sensitivity to chickens prevailed.

"Aa choo!"

Instantly Blackmon reacted by pointing in the direction of the sound. John jumped between him and the henhouse as Blackmon fired a shot. John crumpled to the ground as the bullet entered his body.

"No!" Kate screamed. She ran out to the man lying on the sand, a trickle of red running from his body into the gritty sand beneath him. "John!" Kneeling beside him, she touched his face. "John!"

John moaned and looked up at her. "I'se sorry, Miss Kate." Then he closed his eyes, wincing in pain.

Kate turned to Blackmon. "How could you! He wasn't armed. You shot an innocent man!"

Blackmon stared at her, his mouth hanging open. Just then another man ran up, alerted by the sound of gunshot. Blackmon's superior officer saw the gun dangling from Blackmon's hand and the bleeding, injured man lying on the ground.

"Blackmon! What's going on here?" he demanded.

"Captain, sir, I thought they were the enemy," Blackmon began to explain.

"Would somebody please help us?" Kate's wail diverted their attention.

John looked up at her pleadingly and murmured, "I wants to see Bessie."

"Can you help me take him home where we can take care of his wound?" Kate entreated the captain while tears ran down her face.

"Yes, ma'am. Men, go get our boat and let's lift him into it. Where's your home, ma'am?"

Kate motioned across the sound to Aunt Sally's house. "Over there. Sally McFarlane's house."

The man raised an eyebrow. "How'd you get here?"

She pointed to their boat tied farther up the other side of the beach. He nodded then singled out one of the men. "Private Warner! Untie that boat over there and take it back to the McFarlane house. We'll follow in our boat."

The men sprang into action. All but one. Blackmon still stood staring at Kate and John. His captain turned to him and ordered, "Blackmon, I will deal with you later. Right now we need to help get this man home."

Chapter Twenty-Seven

Kate leaped out of the boat and ran up the bank to get Bessie and Aunt Sally. They jumped from their chairs on the porch as Kate rushed toward them.

"Aunt Sally! Bessie! John's been shot!"

Bessie screamed and raced to the water as Kate and Aunt Sally followed. Soldiers were carrying John up the bank when Bessie saw her husband, a deep crimson stain spreading across his chest. "Oh, my Lawd Jesus!" She scowled at the soldiers. "What you done to my man?"

"Take him in there to the dining room and put him on the table," Aunt Sally ordered, pointing to the house. "Kate, run get some blankets, a pillow, and some rags. Quickly!"

Kate rushed to the house, grabbed the items and met the men as they entered the back door carrying John. Bessie tottered on unsteady legs, wailing and crying behind them. Aunt Sally put her arm around Bessie's shoulders, helping to steady her.

"Shh, Bessie. Let's not upset John anymore. Think of the babe you're carrying and calm down. John needs us to take care of him." She continued speaking in a low, soothing voice until Bessie settled down. Kate moved ahead to lay the blankets and pillow out on the table. "Kate, go fetch a bucket of water," Aunt Sally ordered.

When Kate returned, the soldiers were leaving, and Aunt Sally was removing John's shirt to look at the injury. She wet a cloth to clean the wound, as Kate and Bessie stood helplessly alongside, watching. Bessie's lips moved in silent prayer as tears made trails down her face.

"Looks like the bullet went clean through his shoulder," Aunt Sally said.

John moaned and moved on the table. Aunt Sally placed her hand against his forehead. "John, you be still now. We need to stop this bleeding."

Kate searched Aunt Sally's face for answers. "Will he . . . ? Is he . . . ?"

"He'll live if he hasn't lost too much blood, good Lord willing. Looks like the bullet missed his heart. His shoulder will hurt for a while, though." As Aunt Sally padded the wound with more cloths, John flinched from the pain.

Bessie glanced heavenward and said, "Thank You, Jesus." Then she laid her head on her husband's chest and sobbed.

John reached up with his good arm and patted her head, muttering softly. "Now, now, Bessie. I cain't leave you and our baby. Everythin's gonna be fine."

"Kate, I need your help. You lift him up while I pass that strip of cloth under him."

Kate moved to Aunt Sally's side and they wrapped John's shoulder, binding his upper arm to his chest.

John opened his eyes and peered up at Kate. "Miss Kate, you all right?"

She nodded, unable to find the right words. He had done nothing wrong. He'd only protected her as always, and yet he was shot for it. Her guilty conscience battled with anger at Blackmon. He had shot an unarmed man. How she wanted him to pay for his misdeed!

"Let's let him rest now. Kate, can you go to the Richardsons' and ask them to send for the doctor? I've done the best I can, but the doctor might have some medicine to give him."

Kate grabbed her shawl and rushed out of the dining room. Passing the stairs she halted when she noticed Joshua on the landing. Their glances met as his tender eyes conveyed sympathy. In a gentle voice he said, "Is there anything I can do to help?"

She could only shake her head as she turned and hurried out the door.

~   ·

"Would you like to tell me what you and John were doing over on the island?" Aunt Sally's rocking chair kept a steady rhythm as she and Kate sat on the veranda, waiting for the doctor to come out.

Should she tell Aunt Sally the truth or retell John's explanation? Kate's fan fluttered as she considered how to answer. Didn't the Bible say God hates a "lying tongue," and hadn't she felt guilty when she lied to her aunt before?

Aunt Sally's eyebrows lifted. "Well?"

Kate sighed. She couldn't dodge the truth anymore. Lying to Aunt Sally now would only increase her transgression. "Do you remember what Father said about coming back to see me on my birthday?"

"Yes, I recall him saying that."

"My birthday is next month, but now that the blockade ship is out there, I'm afraid he'll be in danger when he comes."

"Could be. But what could you do about it?"

Kate told her aunt about the signal lantern and her plans to warn her father.

"So we needed to go over to the island to time everything first."

"That was a very dangerous undertaking. Why didn't you tell me before you left, or ask permission, for that matter?"

Kate bowed her head, afraid to look her aunt in the

eyes. "I don't know. I'm sorry, though. So sorry about John. It's all my fault he got shot."

"Not all your fault. He's a grown man and a free man and can make his own decisions. I'm sure he just wanted to protect you."

Tears welled up in Kate's eyes. "I know. And that's why it's my fault." The tears trickled down as she sniffed and retrieved her handkerchief. "And now Father could be harmed, and I won't be able to warn him either. So it'll be my fault if he gets hurt or captured too. Oh, Aunt Sally, why is it that even when I try to do something good, something bad happens?"

Aunt Sally reached over and patted Kate on her leg. "Sometimes life does seem that way, I know."

"What can I do? I feel so helpless. I can't row the boat and get into the lighthouse by myself."

"Pray about it. Let God provide the answer. And I'll pray about it too."

Bessie appeared at the door holding John's blood-stained shirt. Kate and Aunt Sally exchanged anxious glances. Bessie sighed, looking as though she would collapse. "He be sleepin'. Doc Walker says I can leave him awhile. I wants to stay with him, but I needs to wash his shirt and sew up dis hole." An anguished sigh escaped her.

Kate stood and took the shirt from her. "Bessie, you sit here and rest. I'll take care of the shirt."

Bessie nodded and slumped into the chair.

"I'll get you some lemonade." Aunt Sally pushed out of the rocker. "You need to take care of yourself. Why don't you go take a nap?"

"Thank you, ma'am, but I wants to stay close by. I'se just gonna rest out here a spell, den go back in and see 'bout John."

The doctor appeared at the open door, a slight smile showing on his face. "He had a close call. In fact, it's a miracle he didn't get shot through the heart, but it looks like the bullet glanced off something and went through his shoulder instead. You ladies did a good job cleaning up the wound. I've given him a little laudanum to help ease the pain. It'll hurt for a few weeks, but I think it'll heal if you keep it clean."

Aunt Sally smiled. "Thank you, Dr. Walker. I appreciate you coming out to see about John."

"He's a good man, and I don't mind treating good men. The scoundrel that shot him, though, that's another story. I wouldn't have felt as obliged to treat him, had it been the other way around. Still odd how John ended up all the way over there on the island." The afternoon sun glistened off the white beard dominating the doctor's face and matching his snowy hair.

"Yes, the current is mighty strong sometimes." Aunt Sally nodded, rocking on her heels with hands on her hips.

"Hmm. Yes, I suppose you're right. Well, I'll be off. You send for me if there's any change, but I think he'll mend well."

As the doctor's buggy pulled away, Kate felt something heavy in the pocket of John's shirt. Pulling out the object, she gasped. "Oh, my!"

"What is it, Kate?" Aunt Sally asked.

"It's the miracle." Kate held up John's harmonica, which displayed a heavy dent in the metal.

A rustling sound came from inside the house. All heads turned as Joshua stepped out. Kate held her breath. She had forgotten about him being there. As her hand flew to her chest, he cleared his throat, looked from one woman to the other, and nodded.

"Pardon the intrusion, ladies. I overheard that John was shot. Is there anything I can do?"

Kate narrowed her gaze. What could he do? If his Navy wasn't out there, this would never have happened. They could all go away and leave them alone, that's what they could do.

Aunt Sally spoke up. "That's very kind of you to offer, Joshua, but I'm afraid we'll just have to let God do the healing in his time."

Joshua glanced over at Bessie, who sat with her head resting on her hand as she propped herself with a bent elbow, her eyes fighting to stay open.

"I'm sorry, Bessie," he said in a soft voice.

"Mm hmm," Bessie muttered, half-asleep.

The sound of an approaching rider alerted them, and Joshua hurried back inside. Kate started at the sight of Lieutenant Clay Harris as he rode up, and heaviness settled in the pit of her stomach. Clay was the last person she wanted to see at the moment.

Clay dismounted and strode over to the veranda. "Ladies." With a fleeting look at Kate, he turned to address Aunt Sally. "Mrs. McFarlane, I understand your man was shot over on the island today."

Kate's temperature rose at the remark. *Your man?* Aunt Sally stayed calm, so Kate tried to do the same as her aunt answered. "Yes, John was accidentally shot this morning by one of your men."

"I'm sorry to hear that. But he shouldn't have been on the island. Do you know what he was doing there?"

"His boat drifted over while he was fishing, and he got out on the island to take care of business." Aunt Sally recounted John's original story.

Kate didn't dare look at Clay, lest he could read her mind and know the truth.

"You don't think he was planning to signal the Yankee ship, do you, and try to escape?"

"Escape what, Clay? John's not in prison. And he would never leave his wife and unborn child." Aunt Sally's body stiffened as a scowl crept over her face. "Besides, Kate was with him. She wanted to go fishing too."

Clay glanced at Kate, his brows drawing together in a frown. "I see." He looked back at Aunt Sally. "No need to get upset, ma'am. I just have to ask questions. My commanding officer sent me to investigate."

"Well, you have your answer, so you may take your leave and report back to your superior. Good day, Clay."

Kate noticed Aunt Sally failed to use Clay's official title. Angry as she was at him, she stifled a smile as he turned and tramped back to his horse. The women stared after the departing animal in silence. Then they sighed in unison.

"How inconsiderate of him to question John's motives!" Kate crossed her arms and tossed her head.

"I suppose he was just doing his duty. But his attitude didn't set right with me either. It's a good thing he didn't see Joshua. He'd probably arrest all of us for treason."

A chill ran down Kate's body. Joshua. What would happen if Clay knew he was there?

"Now if you'll excuse me, "Aunt Sally said, "I need to go talk with the Lord. My version of the truth ran awfully close to a lie just now, and I don't like having that sort of thing on my conscience."

Chapter Twenty-Eight

In a few days John was able to sit up for short periods. "I'se so useless. Just sittin' here, doin' nothin' all day and you women does all de work."

"You hush now," Bessie said as she walked up on the porch carrying a basket of green beans. "Most de heavy work be done now. We just has to pick what's left fo' cannin'."

"Dem rows needs weedin'." John shook his head in disgust.

Kate smiled at the interchange between the two. Even when they argued they were happy. Bessie sat down next to her and John on the porch to snap beans.

Aunt Sally came up from the well, removing her hat and fanning herself with it. "It's still hot, but I can tell fall's coming. There's a nice little breeze blowing off the water this morning."

"Miz Sally, cain't you give me somethin' to do?"

"He's complainin' 'bout not workin.'" Bessie frowned at her husband. "Been tryin' to tell him he needs to rest up and get well and quit worryin'."

"Here. Snap these beans." Aunt Sally handed him a bowl.

With one arm in a sling, John had to shift the bowl to accommodate his position, so even that job was difficult. But it was obvious he was pleased to be doing something to help.

"Perhaps I can take John's place in the garden for now." Joshua stepped out on the porch, appearing much healthier these days.

"Are you up to it?" Aunt Sally tilted her head and quirked her eyebrows at him.

"I'm feeling pretty good. I think I could handle a hoe." Joshua stretched his arms out to the side slowly, opening and closing his fists.

Kate's stomach fluttered as she watched him. Much as she hated to admit it, she was beginning to enjoy seeing him. His skin color had a healthy glow, and he had put enough weight back on to fill out his frame. Lean but muscular, he cut a fine figure. If he hadn't been on the wrong side of the war, she might be attracted to him—

She shook her head. She must stop thinking about these things. Still, there were times when she let her mind wander . . . . "But what if someone sees you?" Kate asked.

"I've considered that possibility, but I've got a pretty good ear. If I hear someone coming, I'll hide."

"Well, Kate does have a point. And you need to be careful not to work too hard either."

"Yes, ma'am. I'll take it a little at a time. Where's your hoe?"

"Kate, will you take Joshua to the tool shed and show him where we keep things?"

Kate glanced at her aunt, then nodded, set her pan of beans down, and stood up. Kate walked briskly across the yard, hoping to avoid conversation with the man as he followed her to the shed. When they got to the small building, Kate opened the door and pointed out the tools. As she turned to leave, he gently grabbed her arm. She jerked to a stop, eyeing his hand on her.

"Wait, please. I'd like to talk with you in private."

Kate's heart took off like a race after the starting shot. Her breath caught as she looked into his chiseled face.

"What do you want?"

"Kath -- I'm sorry, but may I call you Katherine? We're living under the same roof and it seems like we could be less formal."

Kate studied his face then nodded. Not that they were friends.

"I suppose so. We call you Joshua."

"Well, to be honest, *you* don't call me anything. But I do wish you would call me Joshua." Joshua's soft-spoken tone calmed her.

"Very well." She waited for him to continue.

"Katherine, I know why you and John went to the island."

Alarm struck a chord within her. What did he know?

"Of course you do. Everyone does."

"No, Katherine. I know the real reason you went over there. I overheard you and John talking about it."

Kate arched her eyebrows as her temper started to flare. So he *was* eavesdropping!

"Wait, please don't get angry. It was quite by accident, I assure you. I could hear you talking through the window of the bedroom, and I heard you leave that night."

Horrified he knew their secret, Kate held her breath. Then, feigning ignorance, she crossed her arms. "So tell me why you think we were over on the island."

Joshua looked down at his feet, then out across the yard and back to Kate. "I heard your plans about signaling your father."

"Oh!" Kate gasped. "And what were you going to do with this information? Tell the blockade ship so it could fire on him?"

Joshua placed his hands on her shoulders and held her at arms' length, looking straight into her eyes. "No, no,

Katherine. I would never do that. You must believe me."

"Why, Joshua? Why should I believe you? Aren't you in the Union Navy, the one that's blockading our town?"

Gazing intently at her, he said, "Because I've come to care for your family. For you."

Heat rushed to Kate's face as a flood of emotions flowed through her body – anger, fear, sadness, and others yet identified. Should she, *could* she, believe this stranger, this enemy? She took a deep breath and exhaled. "Well, I suppose you won't have anything to tell anyway, since my plans were for naught, and all I managed to do was get John shot. I can only hope and pray for my father's safety now."

"That you should do. But, Katherine, your plans can still be carried out."

Mouth agape, Kate stared at him. "Whatever do you mean?"

"I can help you send the message."

"You? Help me send a message to my father? Why would you do that? And how do I know you would send the right message and not try to put him in a trap?"

Joshua shook his head slowly. "I don't know how to convince you to trust me and believe I'm not trying to endanger your father. I will only send the message you wish me to send."

"But what do you know about sending messages out at sea? You haven't even seen the lantern I was planning to use."

"From what I heard you say, I believe I'm familiar with the lantern."

Kate continued to give Joshua a puzzled look. "And you know how to use it?"

"Yes, Katherine. I was a signalman on my ship."

~

"This lantern belonged to your great uncle?" Joshua took the lantern from Kate.

"Yes. Aunt Sally's husband, Uncle Duncan. My grandfather was his twin brother, and he also had one. Aunt Sally said they used to send messages to each other."

"Amazing." Joshua examined the lantern, pulling the spring that moved the shutter across the burner. "This must have been one of the first prototypes. We were just beginning to use them onboard, experimenting with various signals. We used Morse code and several other systems for signaling."

"So you're familiar with Morse code?" Kate's pulse quickened as she watched the way Joshua deftly handled the lantern.

"Of course. Signalmen are required to learn it. We used that code, as well as flags, to send signals." He smiled at her and waved his arms to demonstrate flag-signaling. Putting his arms down, he returned his attention to the lantern. "Your father has one of these on his ship?"

"Yes. He inherited it from his father, my grandfather. I saw his lantern the last time I was onboard."

"And you think he'll recognize a signal if we send it?"

"I'm certain the correct wording will assure him it came from me."

"Can you show me the message you'd like to send?"

"Yes. It's 'God go with ye.' That's always been our family's way of saying 'farewell' to our sea-going ship captains, part of our Scottish heritage. I believe he'll recognize the message as a farewell instead of a greeting and understand its meaning to leave and not come here."

Joshua closed his eyes as if contemplating the message. Nodding, he said, "I don't see how another ship could interpret your meaning. If our blockade ship sees the light, they may want to investigate the recipient, but I'm sure your father will have turned back by then."

"His schooner is very swift." She tilted her head up. "He can outrun any ship."

Humor glimmered in Joshua's eyes at Kate's response.

"That so? You know this for a fact?"

Her cheeks warming again, Kate realized she was being teased. "Why, yes! Father has told me how he's outrun many other boats. He had it built just a year ago to replace his older ship. It was especially designed to be fast." Kate shared her father's pride of the beautiful vessel.

"I see. That's a good thing, then, as he may have some boats chasing him these days."

Startled, Kate responded. "Really? There are more blockade ships?"

Again her comment was met with Joshua's twinkle. "Yes, Katherine, there are several ships blockading southern ports now. And there will be more."

Kate fell silent, her eager anticipation beginning to dim. "Oh. So Father may still be in danger when he leaves here."

Putting his hand over hers, Joshua attempted to console her. "Don't let that worry you. I'm certain your father won't place himself in danger by trying to enter other blockaded areas where he'd be at risk. Did you say he's been trading overseas since he left Pensacola?"

"Yes. He goes south to Cuba and the islands and across to England, France, and other countries in Europe."

"Then he'll be all right. We can pray for his safety."

Joshua turned quickly, and the motion caused him to grimace. Kate took notice.

"Are you strong enough to row a boat to the island?"

"I can do it. I'm just a bit sore still, and if you help me wrap my ribs tightly, I'll be fine. I'm getting better every day, so by the time we go over there, I'll be ready. When did you say he's coming?"

"My birthday is September eighteenth, so he'll be coming in the night before, on the seventeenth."

"Two weeks from tomorrow. That's a blessing. I have time to brush up on my Morse code."

Kate stared at Joshua, still stunned he wanted to help. Try as she might to dislike him as the enemy, she had become more relaxed in his company. In fact, in an odd way, it seemed she had known him much longer. How had this happened?

"Joshua, I do appreciate your desire to help me, but I'm reluctant to place another person in danger. I couldn't bear the burden if you were harmed."

Joshua's twinkle returned as he smiled. "You mean, you care about the enemy?"

Irritated by his teasing, she tossed her head, allowing long tendrils of wavy red locks to free themselves. "I just don't want to be responsible for the injury of another human being."

Joshua appeared mesmerized by the tresses now framing her face. He reached out to touch a curl fallen across her eye. "Katherine, you are so enchanting when you're angry. Those emerald eyes light up as much as your fiery hair."

Breathless, Kate grabbed the hair out of her face and tucked it behind her ear.

He was doing it again. Somehow, she was being drawn toward him while she tried frantically to resist. "Please don't tease me like that." She struggled to get the words out, which escaped as a soft whisper.

Joshua withdrew his arm and straightened up. "Don't concern yourself with my safety. I've had military training, so I can handle myself. I intend to take care of both of us and keep us from being discovered. One important thing we can do is be more vigilant in the use of our time."

Kate recovered her breath. "John and I shouldn't have been there at daylight, but we were using the tides to get us there."

"You're right. We have to leave much earlier than you did, allowing for time to get over and back as well as send the signal."

"But won't it be more difficult and take longer if we row against the tide?"

"It would be, but we won't have to."

Kate's eyebrows lifted. "But how is that possible?"

"Before our ship arrived we studied this area, so I know Apalachicola has four tides a day – two low tides and two high tides."

"I never heard of that before. So there's another high tide for us to use?"

"Exactly. There's usually one in the morning and one in the evening. I won't know exactly when they'll be, but I'll monitor them daily until we go so we'll leave at the right time."

Kate considered the undertaking, wondering how he would accomplish it. Fear threatened her resolve as she remembered what had happened before. "Joshua, how do you expect to check the tides? If you're seen going to and from the water, all of us will be in danger."

"You're right." Joshua ran his hand through his sandy brown hair, frowning in contemplation. "Is there another way to see the water's edge? Is there a better view from another room upstairs?"

A smile spread across Kate's face at his question. She couldn't wait to show him her favorite place.

Chapter Twenty-Nine

Joshua followed Kate up the attic stairs, ducking to avoid hitting his head on the small doorframe. He had to take only one step on the ladder to reach the hatch door and push it open. Climbing through first, he reached down and helped Kate up. A hint of fall welcomed them with a cool breeze.

"Ah, how refreshing it is up here!" Joshua lifted his arms out as if to embrace the sky, inhaling deeply.

"It is, especially with the cooler air. This is my favorite place." Why did she tell him that? Somehow sharing this place with him filled her with pleasant warmth.

"I can see why. What a splendid view!"

Kate pointed out their surroundings. "To the east over there is the town. See the church steeple?"

Joshua nodded his reply.

"Around this way to the south you can see the islands and the blockade ship outside the entrance to the bay. Before it got here the water was full of boats carrying cotton and other merchandise back and forth." She cast Joshua a frown, and he grimaced as if struck by her remark.

"And over here on the west side is the marsh. Not much but pine trees and palmetto." Joshua followed the direction her finger pointed.

"And what's to the north of the house?"

Kate paused then shrugged as they turned around. "Beyond those trees is the army camp. Hopefully, no one can see you from there."

Joshua nodded as he spotted the tents. He turned and walked back to the side facing the water. "It's still a bit difficult to see the water's edge from here and how far in the tide is. I wish I had one of the telescopes we had on our ship."

"We have one! There was one in Uncle Duncan's things. I'll go get it."

Kate disappeared through the doorway, leaving him out there. She returned in a few minutes with the telescope.

"This is perfect. I think I may be able to use the marsh as a guide, too."

Kate lifted her eyebrows, and he explained. "See the water in there right now? I can watch to see if it goes down or up. Do you have anything I can write on to keep a record?"

Before Kate could answer Joshua put his finger to his lips, grabbed her arm, and pulled her down to a crouching position.

"I see movement along the bank about a hundred yards down," he whispered.

Kate turned in the direction of his gaze and saw a group of soldiers.

Joshua pointed down and they quietly scampered back inside and down the attic stairs. The two stopped at the second-floor landing to listen. When no sound of approaching men was heard, they both exhaled a sigh of relief.

"You have to be careful, Joshua. You're so tall, you may be easily seen up there."

"I will be. Perhaps I'll just sit behind the railing so I'll be less likely to be noticed."

Kate nodded. "I'll get you something to make notes on." He followed her downstairs to the parlor where she found some paper, pen, and ink in the secretary and handed them over to him. Their hands touched, sending a tremor of warmth up her arm and throughout her body. She jerked her hand away.

Joshua smiled then became serious. "Katherine, we should tell your aunt what our plans are."

Kate looked away, filled with a mixture of regret and apprehension. "I know. After what happened to John, I don't expect her approval. However, it's not fair to her if we don't tell her. " She dropped her gaze before lifting it again as she spoke. "To be honest, I've had to confess my sin of lying—whatever the reason—and ask for God's forgiveness."

His eyes signaled understanding and he nodded. "I'll go with you when you're ready to tell her. I may be able to convince her that I can take better precautions than you and John did the last time."

Kate nodded. "Perhaps after our Bible reading tomorrow morning then."

"An opportune time to speak to her."

~

Since Joshua had joined them, he had shared the Bible reading with Kate. The next morning he selected Psalm 139 and began reading with verse 7. "'Whither shall I go from thy spirit? or whither shall I flee from thy presence?'"

Kate allowed the words to penetrate her mind, listening again when Joshua read verse 9.

"'If I take the wings of the morning, and dwell in the uttermost parts of the sea; Even there shall thy hand lead me.'" Joshua's strong voice comforted her as he reached verse 11 and the scripture promised safety. "'Surely the darkness shall cover me; even the night shall be light about me.'"

Kate remembered how the moonlight brightened the

darkness when she and John had gone to the island. Joshua must have chosen this scripture passage just for them and their mission.

However as he continued with the words in verses 13 and 14, "'thou hast covered me in my mother's womb. I will praise thee; for I am fearfully and wonderfully made,'" Kate glanced at Bessie, reminded of the baby she carried.

Bessie had been unusually despondent since John got shot, but she perked up now, her eyes wide. "What you say? Mr. Joshua, please read dem words again."

"Of course. Which part did you want me to read again?"

"Dat part 'bout de mother's womb. Read dat again, please!" Bessie shifted to the edge of her chair.

Joshua repeated the verse. "'Thou hast covered me in my mother's womb. I will praise thee; for I am fearfully and wonderfully made: marvelous are thy works; and that my soul knoweth right well.'" He stopped and looked at Bessie, who had tears trickling down her face, but at the same time she was smiling.

"Oh, praise de Lawd! John, you hear dat? He be tellin' us our baby be all right. He gonna be healthy – dat what de Lawd say. Oh, thank You, Lawd, thank You fo' dat comfort!"

Bessie leaped up and clapped her hands. John reached out with his good arm and pulled her into an embrace. "How you knows he be a he?" John teased his wife.

"I don't knows and I don't cares. But it gonna be healthy, and dat be good 'nough fo' me."

"Me, too, Bessie. Me, too. Now let's go feed dat chile!"

"May we pray first?" Joshua inquired. All nodded their assent, and he began. "Lord, we thank You for Your word to comfort us and guide us. We ask Your blessings and safety on these, Your humble servants. Amen."

A comforting warmth spread through Kate as she embraced the assurance they'd been given. The baby would be all right. For the first time she truly believed both the child and Bessie would survive the birth. As they were leaving the room, Kate paused and turned to her aunt. "Aunt Sally, after breakfast Joshua and I need to speak with you." Kate looked over at Joshua, who nodded his agreement. Aunt Sally glanced from one to the other and raised an eyebrow.

"So what do you two need to discuss with me? No need to wait until after breakfast." Aunt Sally's smile indicated she expected some news different from what they planned to tell her. They sat back down, as Joshua began explaining their mission. When he finished they waited in silence for Aunt Sally's response. Her expression had become serious while listening to their plans. She glanced from Joshua to Kate and sighed, wiping her hands on her pants.

"Thank you for telling me . . . this time. My heart says not to let you do it, especially after what happened to John, but I've also worried about Andrew's returning during this blockade. He must be aware of the danger. Do you think he'll try to come anyway?" She directed her gaze at Kate.

"He's never missed my birthday. When I was twelve he braved a hurricane to be back in time. And on my sixteenth he was held up in Cuba, due to quarantine. He barely got home before midnight, but he still managed to get there. Nothing has ever stopped him before, so I think he'll try to come anyway."

"Very well then." Aunt Sally pointed her finger at Joshua. "It's only because I believe that you, young man, know what you're doing, that I'd even consider it now. I'm certain you know how risky this undertaking is, and what would happen to you if you got caught. All I can say is, make sure you've thought everything through, and I pray God will protect you and bring you home safely."

Kate sprang to her feet and hurried over to the woman to hug her. "Oh, thank you, Aunt Sally. We'll be careful. Joshua has all the details figured out."

Joshua rose and went to Aunt Sally as well. "I'm grateful for your blessing, ma'am."

"You just take care of my great-niece."

"Yes, ma'am!" Joshua said, saluting Aunt Sally as his commander.

A knock at the front door silenced their conversation. Exchanging anxious glances, they waited. Another knock, then, "Mrs. McFarlane?"

Kate knew that voice – Clay's. Aunt Sally saw her expression and nodded. "I'll go to the door. Stay here."

Kate stayed as instructed, and she listened. Had Clay heard Joshua talking through the open windows?

"Mrs. McFarlane, I owe you an apology for my behavior the other day."

Standing in the doorway of the parlor, Kate craned her neck to hear better.

Clay continued. "I didn't mean to cast dispersions on your household, ma'am. I'm afraid I was a bit rude, and I'm sorry. Please accept my apologies."

Kate was incredulous. He was apologizing?

"You're forgiven, Clay . . . Lieutenant Harris. I can't get used to calling you anything but Clay."

"I understand, Mrs. McFarlane, since you've known me all my life. Might I ask you a favor, though?"

"You may ask. What is the favor?"

"I'd like to speak with Katherine. I know she hasn't been too pleased with me for a while now, and I'd like to try to make amends."

Kate gasped. Now? He wanted to make amends *now*? But why?

Aunt Sally's voice was heard next. "I'll see if she has a moment to speak with you. Please have a seat out on the veranda while I go find her."

As Kate turned back around, she found Joshua still standing in the parlor, gazing intently at her. Her cheeks grew hot and she groped for words. She wiped sweaty palms on her apron as she looked down to avoid his gaze.

Aunt Sally came into the parlor. "Did you hear, Kate? Clay's here and says he wants to speak with you, to make amends. Would you like to speak with him?" Aunt Sally tilted her head as she awaited Kate's response.

Glancing from Joshua to Aunt Sally, Kate felt pulled in two directions. She had lost her interest in Clay, yet she was curious to find out what he had to say. Aunt Sally lifted her arms out and shrugged. "I suppose it can't hurt to hear him out, Kate."

Sighing, Kate said, "Very well. I'll go see what he has to say." Casting a look at Joshua, she added, "I'll not ask him to come inside."

When Kate joined Clay out on the veranda, he tipped his hat and bowed slightly. With a smile she remembered from months past, he waved his arm toward a chair. "Katherine, how nice it is to see you. Please sit with me for a few moments."

Kate nodded and accepted the seat. Clay sat on the edge of the chair nearby and turned to face her. His face appeared older than she recalled. His responsibilities as an officer had surely made an impact on him. He was still handsome, but she noticed tired lines at the corners of his eyes.

"You wished to speak to me?" Kate stated calmly, as she tried to slow the rapid beating of her heart.

"Katherine, I know you've had reason to be displeased with me. I should have explained to you about my role as an escort for the Marquesa."

She raised her eyebrows. So he was going to tell her the truth?

"You see, my father and her father agreed I would accompany her around town since she didn't know anyone here. They felt she needed to be protected from the advances of unsavory suitors. I really had no choice in the matter."

Perhaps he was telling the truth, but why didn't he explain it to her before? Her stomach knotted.

"I'm sure it was quite an imposition for you." Kate bit her lip to stymie more sarcasm.

Clay reared back as if she'd shot him.

"Kate, that was arranged before you came to town. When I met you I preferred to spend time with you. However I still had a commitment to my father and hers."

"And so you continued to escort her without my knowledge?"

Clay's neck turned red, and the color spread over his face. He seemed to be at a loss for words as he slowly turned the hat in his hands, studying it. Finally he looked up at her with a sad expression. "I suppose I should have told you about the arrangement. I just didn't know how. I hope you can forgive me."

Who was this man? How could he change from the cold, stone-faced person she had seen the past few months to this pitiful, pleading soul in front of her? Much as she'd yearned to hear an apology and confession from his lips, now that she'd heard it, the satisfaction she'd expected wasn't there. Too much time had passed for her to care anymore. But could she forgive him? Somewhere deep within she heard, "Be careful of wolves in sheep's clothing."

Kate expelled a sigh. "Yes, Clay, I forgive you. Thank you for taking the trouble to come all the way out here to tell me the truth." She stood and wiped her sweaty hands on her apron, strengthened by her resolve to keep him out of her life. Even though she forgave him, she knew she'd never trust him again.

Clay got to his feet and stepped in front of her to garner her attention. "Kate, I miss you. I hope I can call on you again as my duties and time permits."

Kate's eyes widened at his remark. Did he still believe she was interested in him?

"Good day, Clay."

He stepped down from the veranda and put his cap back on. After taking a few steps, he stopped and turned to face her. "I'll see you again soon, Kate." As he finished speaking, he glanced up at the house, a look of curiosity on his face. Then he tipped his hat to her again and strode away.

What had he seen? And when would he return? Why had he bothered to come see her now? The tightness in her stomach told her something wasn't right about his visit and that she'd just witnessed a scene performed by an experienced actor.

Chapter Thirty

Kate blew out a breath, then returned inside. Where had Joshua gone? With a start, she thought of the widow's walk. Had Clay seen him up there?

When she climbed the stairs to the second floor, she saw the attic door open. Scampering up the steps and the ladder, she poked her head through the opening and saw Joshua sitting outside looking through the telescope.

"How long have you been up here?" she said, trying to catch her breath.

"Long enough to see your gentleman caller leave." He continued to look through the telescope toward the water.

"He's *not* my gentleman caller." Kate climbed through the opening and crawled over next to Joshua.

"Oh? Seemed like he was."

Flustered, Kate tried to explain. "He used to . . . he was . . . Oh, bother. It doesn't matter. He's not."

Joshua lowered the telescope and faced her with his soft hazel eyes. "Good. I don't care for him."

Kate's mouth gaped. "You don't . . . But why not?"

"Just instinct, I guess. He doesn't strike me as an honest fellow."

What did he know that she didn't?

"It doesn't have anything to do with his uniform, does it?"

"Perhaps. But I'm a pretty good judge of character."

Kate put her hands on her hips and cocked her head. "Truly?"

"I think so."

"Aren't you being a bit bold, coming out here now? What if he saw you?"

"He didn't." Turning back to face the water, he nodded in the direction of St. Vincent's Island. "Looks like they're adding to the enforcements on that island. I've seen a few boats carrying supplies over there."

Kate shielded her eyes from the glare to look. Joshua handed her the telescope. True, it looked like there was more activity on the island. She lowered the instrument slowly, her breath held for his next remark, afraid of the answer. But she had to ask.

"So do you think it's too dangerous for us to go now?"

"Not too dangerous, but more dangerous than it was."

~

"We leave at eight tonight. The sun will set around a quarter 'til, so it'll get dark soon after. Are you prepared to go?"

"Yes. I've packed the lantern, a tin of oil, matches, and a hammer and spike to break the chain on the lock. I'll also take a cloth to clean the window so the light will shine through more clearly."

The day had arrived. Kate's birthday was the next day, and if her father kept his promise as usual, he'd be approaching tonight. She tried not to think about what had happened the last time she went to the island, but her stomach churned as the day approached, killing her desire to eat any meals. Since Aunt Sally was aware of their plans now, she had encouraged them to read certain passages from the Bible that morning.

"Read from the book of Joshua, your namesake," she'd

said, her gaze on their Union guest.

Joshua complied. Turning to the first chapter, he began reading God's command to the biblical Joshua as he took over leadership of the Israelites after Moses died. Verse nine resonated through them: "Have not I commanded thee? Be strong and of a good courage; be not afraid, neither be thou dismayed: for the LORD thy God is with thee whithersoever thou goest." Joshua looked up from his reading and said, "Can we believe these words apply to us?"

"Aye, I do believe so. That's just one of the scriptures that tells us not to be afraid because God is with us." Aunt Sally pointed to the Bible resting in Joshua's large hands. "There are several in the Bible, so God must be talking to us too. In fact, that whole chapter says it more than once."

Kate nodded, remembering. "When I was a little girl, I memorized Psalm 56:3: 'What time I am afraid, I will trust in thee.' I used to repeat that every time I was frightened."

"That's a good habit to have. Remember to do that today and tonight," Aunt Sally admonished. "Let's pray now. John, will you please lead us?"

They bowed their heads as John prayed for all of them – for Bessie and the baby, for Aunt Sally, for Joshua and Kate's safety on their undertaking, and for Captain McFarlane's safety as well. Joshua then thanked God for healing him. Peace settled over Kate as Joshua prayed.

Bessie hugged Kate. "You gonna be safe. Don't you worry about nothin'. De good Lawd, He gonna take care of you. I'se prayin' nobody sees you, dat God gonna hide you under His wings, like de Bible say."

"Thank you, Bessie. That means a great deal to me."

John hugged Kate with his good arm, and Aunt Sally put her arms around each of them in turn.

~

At dusk the group stood together on the back porch.

"Take care of her, Joshua, and yourself." Aunt Sally

pointed her finger at the tall man.

Joshua nodded. "I won't let anything happen to Katherine." He gazed at her as he spoke, penetrating Kate with warmth.

He and Kate waited for the sun to drop below the horizon, then checked the watch piece Aunt Sally had given them to use. "Let's go," Joshua said.

Kate grabbed the sack with all the equipment. Joshua had insisted they bring Uncle Duncan's pocket compass as well. Under cover of darkness they climbed into the boat and pushed off. The light of the rising half-moon was brilliant, illuminating everything in muted hues of gray. Kate wore a black cloak of Aunt Sally's, which blended her with the darkness. Joshua had donned a dark jacket and hat Aunt Sally found in the wardrobe as well. Looking like shadows they rowed across, their oars hitting the water in tune with the waves.

Facing him from her seat in the rear, Kate watched Joshua move the boat with skill and determination. He showed no sign of pain from his injuries. Occasionally he rested the oars to relax his arms, allowing the outgoing current to propel them forward. There were a few lights visible on the mainland from residents who hadn't yet retired. Kate saw them grow dimmer as they moved farther away, then disappear from sight. The few clouds in the sky played across the face of the moon, changing shapes and forming mysterious creatures.

Aunt Sally's house shrank in size as Kate observed the dwelling that sat alone, away from town. The splash of fish jumping near the boat surprised her, and she covered her mouth to silence a potential cry. Joshua chuckled quietly and said, "If we had a net, we could catch our breakfast."

Kate smiled at his suggestion, which she might accept under other conditions. A fishing expedition with him might be entertaining. To be honest she enjoyed his company. Gentle, agreeable, considerate, Joshua had many traits she admired. If only things were different; if only he wasn't her enemy. Right now, though, he was her ally, and she was thankful to have him as one.

Gradually, the dark tower of the lighthouse loomed closer. Kate scoured the coastline, looking for signs of anyone on the island, and saw none. Joshua quit rowing to listen. No sound of voices was heard, although there was some muted noise coming from the army camp at St. Vincent's Island to the west. The boat swept onto shore; Joshua jumped out to pull it up on the sand and helped Kate get out. He hid it near a small stand of palmetto, tying it to a slender pine tree nearby.

Staying low they quickly passed the outbuildings. Kate shuddered as she passed the henhouse that evoked the image of John being shot. Joshua must have sensed her fear and grabbed her hand, pulling her alongside him. Brought back to the moment, Kate focused on the door of the lighthouse and the chain around the handle. Once they were in front of it, she tried to catch her breath as Joshua studied the lock. Kate handed him the sack with the mallet. He reached inside the sack, but stopped to look up at the doorway. Stretching his tall body to its fullest, he reached his arm over the transom and felt along the edge. His head turned sideways toward her and he whispered, "Ha! I thought so!"

When he lowered his arm, he held a small ring with two keys. Kate's mouth fell open. He winked and nodded, then taking the smaller key, unlocked the chain and removed it. Next he used the larger key to unlock the door. They glanced around again to make sure no one was near then pushed the heavy door, which creaked as it opened. Stepping inside, they gently closed the door so as not to give away their presence.

Kate grabbed her skirt while Joshua took the bag, and they made their way up the winding stairs as quickly as possible. At the top, they found a ladder leading to a hatch door. Joshua went ahead first and pushed it open, then climbed through, then reached back down and helped pull Kate up. Although she knew they were standing in the lantern room, it was strangely vacant without its lens.

Through the large windows, a panorama of the area spread out around them – the town to the northeast, the army camp to the west, and the blockade boat to the southeast. They quickly removed the signal lantern and the supplies to light it from the sack. They had also brought the telescope box, which Joshua removed and opened, taking out the telescope and extending it to its fullest length. He peered through, scanning the horizon. "There," he said, pointing due south. "There's a ship way out there. It must be your father's."

Kate's heart raced and her hands trembled as she handed Joshua the lantern. After pouring oil into the chamber with the wick, he struck a match on the side of the metal matchbox and lit the lantern, while Kate wiped the glass of the lantern room. Once the fire was steadily glowing, Joshua raised the lantern, holding it near the window. He then used the lever to slide the shutter back and forth, creating a flashing sequence. With a progression of short and long flashes, he spoke the words as he created the message: "God go with ye." When he was finished, they waited, looking through the telescope for a response. After ten minutes passed without a response, Joshua resent the message.

Kate stared out the window, searching for some sign the message was received. She held her breath, praying Father had seen and understood the signal. What if it didn't work? Another ten minutes passed, then Joshua sent it again. This time there was a flash returned. Joshua grabbed the telescope and stared at the flashed reply. Making out the letters, he spoke the words out loud: "A.n.d – w.i.t.h – y.e. - C.a.n.t.y –b.i.r.t.h.d.a.y – R.o.s.e."

Kate shrieked with joy. "And with ye! Canty birthday,

Rose! That's Father! He got the message!"

Without a second thought she leaped into Joshua's arms, exhilarated by the communication. Joshua laughed aloud and wrapped his arms around her, holding her close. They stood holding each other as their hearts celebrated in unison. Slowly and gently Joshua pushed her away enough to search her face. Without another moment of hesitation, he leaned down and kissed her full on the lips. Kate floated along on a current of passion as she allowed herself to be engulfed by the kiss.

Time temporarily vanished as they rested in each other's arms. Stopping to breathe Kate laid her head on Joshua's shoulder as he stroked her hair, which had worked its way loose. "Ah, Katherine, you take my breath away."

She gazed up at him and smiled. "Thank you for sending the message. I can never thank you enough."

"So this is appreciation you're showing?"

Kate could barely make out the twinkle in his eye in the dim light. "Perhaps," she said, her voice barely above a whisper.

"Then thank me some more!" Joshua kissed her again, fervently.

Kate's laugh was smothered by another kiss. What was happening to her? Was this a dream? No, this was real. Joshua was real. Her heart beat wildly, like a caged animal trying to break free. She fought for self-control and sighed relief as he leaned back and gazed into her eyes.

"May I ask you a question?" he asked.

She tilted her head. "Yes?"

"What does 'canty birthday rose' mean?"

She chuckled. "'Canty' is Scottish for happy. Father was saying 'Happy Birthday.'"

"And Rose?"

"Rose is a pet name Father gave me because of my love for roses."

"Ah, now I understand the message. And it was a

definite confirmation it was from your father to you. What assurance!" He pulled her close again, and she was comforted by the rhythm of his thumping heart.

A light to the right caught their attention, and they turned their heads, seeing the shape of a dinghy being pushed away from the nearby St. Vincent's shore. "Kate, we need to go. It looks like a patrol is coming over. Let's gather these things and move quickly back to the boat."

Startled back to reality, Kate threw their supplies back into the bag then climbed down the ladder from the lantern room. They were hurrying down the stairs when they heard the door creak. Joshua stopped, motioning with his hand down behind him for Kate to stop as well. He turned his head, placing his forefinger across his lips. The two listened closely for another sound. Kate's heart was pounding so hard, she could barely hear anything else. They waited motionless for what seemed like hours, but heard nothing more. Joshua moved to see out one of the windows along the stairs. The patrol boat was still in the channel when he pointed it out to Kate. "See there. They've not made it here yet. We must have heard the wind. Let's keep going."

Kate squelched a shudder. *Stay calm.* The words of the Psalm that had comforted her in her childhood came back to her, and she repeated them over and over in her head. "What time I am afraid, I will trust in thee."

When they reached the bottom of the stairs, they glanced around but saw no one else. Slowly Joshua opened the door, stuck his head outside and peered in each direction, then motioned for Kate to come. Slipping outside, they paused for Joshua to relock the door and return the key above the transom. Then Joshua took Kate's hand as she grabbed her skirt with the other, and they ran across the beach in the direction of their boat. When they passed the outbuildings again, she looked behind her and tripped on a piece of driftwood that sent her sprawling across the sand. "Oh!" she cried out as she fell, letting go of Joshua's hand.

He ran back and pulled her up, but when she tried to stand, she winced as pain shot through her. "I'm afraid I've twisted my ankle." Kate fought back tears.

Joshua swept her up in his arms and carried her the rest of the way to the boat's hiding place. He set her down gently on the sand, then pulled the boat out and placed her in it. Joshua then shoved the dinghy into the water and jumped in. As he began to row furiously, the boat rode past the incoming waves and out into the sound. Darkness was their ally as they stayed covered by the shadows. Kate glanced over her shoulder, expecting to find soldiers in pursuit. However none appeared, and she expelled a deep breath of relief. Once they were out a safe distance from the island, Joshua spoke in a low voice.

"Is your ankle hurting?"

Kate nodded then whispered her reply. "Yes. I'm sorry to be so clumsy. I hate to be such a burden."

"A burden?" Joshua chuckled softly. "Dear Katherine, you're light as a feather! Guess you'll learn not to look back again, though."

Kate tilted her head at his comment. "I suppose I shall, in more ways than one."

When they reached the shore at Aunt Sally's, they found the rest of the household clustered on the porch, waiting for them. As Joshua pulled the boat ashore and lifted Kate out, they all ran to the young couple. "Is she hurt? What happened?"

Kate spoke up. "I'm fine. I just fell and turned my ankle."

Aunt Sally gave orders. "Joshua, carry her inside. We'll have to wrap that ankle up and keep her off it a few days."

"Yes, ma'am." Joshua carried Kate up to the house and laid her on the sofa in the parlor. She smiled up at him as he put her down.

"Thank you." Her eyes moistened as she was overcome by gratitude and tenderness. Or was it just relief?

Joshua gave her hand a tender squeeze, smiling as he let it go.

"So tell us what happened," Aunt Sally said. "Were you able to make contact with Andrew? Did you get a response?" Bessie and John followed Aunt Sally into the parlor, watching the young couple expectantly.

Kate and Joshua took turns telling the events of the evening, glancing at one another and nodding in affirmation. Kate was exuberant as she reported her father's message. When they were finished Aunt Sally exclaimed, "Thank the Lord, you returned safely! And thank Him, too, that your father was kept out of danger. We can all rest easy now."

Bessie stood and stretched, patting her growing tummy. "Well, dis one needs to get some rest now. I'se so happy y'all come back safe."

"We could all use some sleep. Joshua, do you think you can carry Kate up the stairs to her room? If you're too tired, we'll just make her a bed here on the sofa."

Joshua was already putting his long arms under Kate to lift her. "Yes, ma'am, I'll take her up there. You need to start feeding this young lady. She doesn't weigh anything at all!"

Kate beamed at his teasing, and with her arms around his neck, looked lovingly into his eyes while he carried her upstairs, Aunt Sally following. "I'll help you get ready for bed," she said.

Joshua set Kate down on the bed and started to leave the room. When he reached the door he turned, grinning. "Oh, by the way, I forgot to tell you something."

Kate returned a puzzled look. "What is it?"

"Happy birthday, Kate."

Kate opened her mouth to reply, but stopped as cannons boomed in the distance.

Chapter Thirty-One

Kate bolted upright on the bed, exchanging startled glances with Aunt Sally and Joshua.

"What was that noise?" Kate looked to Joshua for an answer.

The booming sounded again and appeared to come from the direction of the water.

"Sounds like cannon fire from the blockade ship."

Tears filled Kate's eyes. "Oh, no! Do you think they're firing at Father?"

"I'm sure not. I'll go up and see if I can find out what's happening." Joshua headed to the attic stairs.

"I'll go, too." Kate tried to get out of bed, but when she put her feet on the floor, she cried out in pain and fell back.

"You just wait right here, Kate." Aunt Sally hurried to her side to help her back into the bed. "You can't put any weight on that ankle yet. If anyone can tell what's going on out there, it'll be Joshua."

"Lord, please don't let them be shooting at Father," Kate pleaded.

After what felt an interminable amount of time, Joshua returned. "Looks like they're firing at a boat headed east toward Crooked River. The Navy ship was outside the sandbar in the deeper water."

"Doesn't sound like it would be Father's ship." Kate twisted a lock of hair near her shoulder.

"No, I think not. I couldn't see the boat clearly, but it wouldn't make sense for your father's ship to be in the sound. Besides, didn't you say his was a schooner? The boat I saw didn't look like a schooner. The water in the sound is too shallow for boats of any size."

Kate clapped her hands. "You're right! His ship couldn't get into the shallow water either. He'd leave it out in the deep water on the other side of the island and use the dinghy to cross the sound."

Aunt Sally nodded. "Aye. That's what he did when he brought you here."

"So it couldn't have been your father's ship," Joshua said. "It must have been another ship trying to run past the blockade."

"Thank God!" Kate fell back against her pillow.

"My, what an exciting evening it's been!" Aunt Sally shook her head. "Maybe now we can all get some rest before sunup."

Relief and exhaustion overcame Kate as she tried to stifle a yawn.

"I'll bid you ladies goodnight then," Joshua said as he exited the room.

~

The entire household slept past sunrise the next day, later than their usual wake-up time. Kate managed to get downstairs by leaning on Joshua and trying to keep her weight off her swollen ankle. When they'd all had breakfast, Aunt Sally stood and grabbed her hat.

"We need some things from town. John, why don't you come with me and leave Bessie here with Kate?"

"I cain't tote much yet, Miz Sally, but I'se do what I can."

"We'll manage. I just don't want to leave Kate here by

herself."

"I'm not by myself. Joshua is here," Kate protested.

"But no one else knows that, do they? It would make people wonder if we all left you behind."

Kate started. She was so accustomed to having Joshua around that it felt natural, and she'd forgotten his presence was a secret to the folks in town.

"We'll be back in a couple of hours. Kate, stay off your ankle and keep your foot propped up. If you need anything, Bessie can get it." Aunt Sally motioned to Bessie.

"I'll try to help these ladies while you're gone," Joshua said, one hand resting on the back of Kate's chair.

She glanced up, beaming at him, warmed by the sound of protection in his voice. As John and Aunt Sally walked away, he gazed down at her. "Is there anything I can get for you?"

The charming twinkle in his eyes made her heart flip. She swallowed to still the quaking before speaking. "Well, yes, if you don't mind. Would you please bring me my embroidery from the parlor? I hope to accomplish something if I'm forced to sit all day."

"At your service, ma'am," Joshua replied with a bow.

When Joshua left Bessie turned to Kate, rocking and nodding. "Somethin' done happen 'tween you two out dere, didn't it?"

Kate's cheeks grew hot. "What makes you say so, Bessie?"

The woman continued rocking and nodding. "Oh, I'se can tell. You didn't like him too much befo', but you likes him a whole lot now. Yo' face gots dat look when you sees him – and he gots it too. Um hum."

Kate's mind flew back to the lighthouse. Folded in his embrace as his lips smothered hers. Was it a dream?

"Here you are, my lady." Joshua handed her the embroidery.

Kate jumped at his voice. "Oh! Thank you."

Their gazes locked in silent communication.

"Joshua, what you gonna do today?" Bessie asked.

The two jerked their heads in her direction as if surprised to find her there.

Clearing his throat Joshua said, "I thought I'd remove the dead plants from the garden and clean it out. Looks like that needs to be done before you can plant any winter vegetables."

"Dat be a good thing fo' you to do. John cain't do all he wants to just yet."

Joshua nodded and put on a hat before going to the shed. As the women watched him leave, Bessie grinned at Kate.

"Yes, ma'am. Somethin' done happen."

"I appreciate what he's done to help us, that's all. And he has a pleasant demeanor as well."

"Um hum." More rocking and nodding.

As Joshua started working in the garden, Kate tried not to stare and focused on the needlework in her hands. Each time she glanced up and caught sight of him, her heart skipped a beat. The memory of those strong arms embracing her and the tender kiss that melted her lips sent tremors through her body. Would she ever experience that feeling again? Or had it just been the excitement of the situation, an accidental reaction? She must stop thinking about it.

A sound interrupted her reverie. Joshua heard it too and ran to the shed. As a horse approached from the direction of town, Kate recognized Clay astride the saddle. He rode up to the house and dismounted, removing his hat as he stepped onto the porch.

"Good day, Katherine."

"Clay." Annoyed he failed to acknowledge Bessie, Kate's eyes flashed fire.

"What happened to your foot?" He nodded at Kate's propped-up leg.

Memories of running across the beach at night, falling, then Joshua carrying her raced through her mind.

"I turned my ankle."

Clay studied her clothbound foot. "A lady like you shouldn't have to work outside."

Kate made no reply. All she could think about was Joshua hiding in the shed. What if Clay discovered him?

"Was there something you needed, Clay? I'm afraid Aunt Sally isn't here; she went to town."

"I just wanted to see you, Katherine."

Bessie coughed, and Clay shot her a glare.

Remembering the sounds she heard last night, Kate asked, "Clay, we heard some noise during the night that sounded like cannons being fired. Do you know what happened?"

Clay turned away to look at the water, his voice taking on a more serious tone. "Some of our men from the Perry Artillery took a gunboat on a reconnaissance mission to the East Pass. The Union ship saw them and gave chase, firing on our boat."

Kate put down her needlework and lifted her gaze to him. "Truly? Was anyone hurt?"

"No. The men jumped overboard and swam ashore."

"So the Union ship didn't capture them?" Kate heaved a sigh of relief.

"It couldn't get close enough because the water was too shallow. Fortunately for us they have a deep-draft ship and have to stay outside the entrance to the bay."

"I see."

Clay spun around, his eyes wide as if he'd just thought of something. "Katherine, perhaps you can help us."

Her stomach knotted. "How can I do that?"

"The widow's walk on the roof," he said, pointing up. "I'll bet you have an excellent vantage point from up there."

Panic swelled within her as she anticipated his request.

"Perhaps we can use it to scout the area," he said.

Kate took a deep breath before answering. "You'll have to speak to Aunt Sally about that. It's her house and not my place to answer. Why don't you come back another day and speak with her?" She hoped Aunt Sally would refuse. Clay and Joshua under the same roof? Heaven forbid!

His smile returned. "I'll do that. Will you please mention it to her when she returns?"

She gave a brief nod. "I'll advise her of your request."

"Excellent. Well, I'm afraid I must return to duty." He paused and gazed at her. "It's nice to see you again, Katherine."

The gray eyes softened at his last words, stirring an uneasiness within her.

"Good day, Clay." So she had been right. His interest was not in her, but in gaining access to the widow's walk. Did he truly think she would help him? Her temper flared at the thought.

After he'd been gone awhile, Joshua crept out of the shed. He strode up to the porch with his eyebrows raised.

"Please don't say it," Kate pleaded.

Joshua laughed. "All right. I won't say anything about your caller."

Kate scorched him with her glare. "Did you hear any of the conversation?"

"Not too well. Did he tell you what the shots were last night?"

"Yes. He said one of the Confederate boats was fired on by the Navy ship."

"That's what I figured. I hope no one was hurt."

"No one was. But he asked about something else."

Joshua's brow puckered. "Yes?"

"He asked about using the widow's walk to scout the shoreline."

"I'm not surprised. What did you tell him?"

"I told him I couldn't make that decision, as it's not my

house. He's to return and speak to Aunt Sally about it."

Joshua rubbed his chin. "That could present a problem."

"Aunt Sally can just refuse to let him use it."

"And appear unsympathetic to the cause?" Joshua raised an eyebrow. "That would certainly arouse suspicion."

"Then what will we do?" Kate's breath caught. We? She covered her mouth with her hand.

Joshua's tender smile disarmed her. "*We* will pray about it and speak to your aunt. I'm sorry to put you in such an awkward situation."

~

"'As I went down in de river to pray . . . '" John's voice carried through the air as he and Aunt Sally returned in the afternoon. "'Oh, brother, let's go down, let's go down, come on down.'"

Bessie pushed herself out of the chair to greet him. "It sound so good to hear you singin' agin."

"It feel good too. Just thankful to be movin' around. I been sick and tired o' bein' sick and tired!"

Everyone laughed. Kate was thrilled to see John happy again. It wasn't like him to mope around like he'd been doing since he was shot.

"John, what's that song you're singing? I've never heard it before." Kate tilted her head to look up at him.

"Me neither 'til today. A Negro man in town was singin' it. I asked him to teach me de words. He come down on de ferry from Georgia."

"Well, I likes it," Bessie said. "You needs to teach it to me too."

"Sho will. It's de kinda song make you feel good."

"Then we all need to learn it," Joshua said. "Maybe it'll make Kate's foot feel better."

"Cain't hurt." John grinned.

"Aunt Sally, what's the news in town?" Kate asked.

"Folks talking about running the blockade. In fact,

that's what those shots were about last night. One of our ships tried to run past the Union ship and got fired on."

Kate glanced at Joshua and Bessie. "That's what we heard too."

Aunt Sally lifted her eyebrows. "That so? And who did you hear that from?"

Sighing Kate said, "Clay came by. He told us about it."

"So he came by to tell you?"

"No. Well, he said he came by to see me." Kate's face warmed. "But I really don't think that was the reason."

"Oh? And why not?"

"He had a request. He asked if he could use the widow's walk to scout the area."

"Hmm." Aunt Sally sat down in the rocker next to Kate. "Surely you won't allow him. What if he sees Joshua?"

The rocker started moving as the older woman focused somewhere beyond the trees.

"I don't know how I can refuse him, Kate."

"Yo' could tells him it's dang'rous up dere," Bessie offered, "Maybe tell him he be fallin' through de roof or somethin'."

"Might be real dang'rous up dere if Mr. Joshua and him run into each other." John nodded and crossed his arms.

Kate quivered as an image of the two men fighting each other atop the roof. "We'll just have to find a way to hide Joshua while Clay's in the house."

Joshua studied the floor. "There's really only one solution to this dilemma."

Kate tensed. What could it be?

Exhaling a deep sigh, he said, "I have to leave."

Chapter Thirty-Two

"Leave?" Kate stared at Joshua.

"Yes. I'm well enough now, thanks to you good people, to go back to the Navy. There's no reason for me to remain here any longer."

No reason? Kate looked away, not wanting Joshua to see the hurt on her face. Of course he had to leave. He didn't belong here with them. Why would he want to stay? A pain pricked her heart.

"Joshua, I understand your obligation to duty. But right now is not a good time to try to get over to one of the blockade ships." Aunt Sally glanced at John, who nodded.

"Dat be right, Mr. Joshua. Lots mo' soldiers 'round now."

"When we were in town, we heard a lot of talk about a Colonel Hopkins who's having almost all the cannons and soldiers moved over to St. Vincent's Island, leaving the city unprotected. There's still some militia around town, but most of them are over on the island." Aunt Sally continued rocking. "The townspeople are trying to get support from the governor to bring some of the cannons back. But it seems he and the colonel aren't too fond of one another."

"Perhaps right now isn't the best time to leave. But I do need to make plans to return to service as soon as I can work it out. Being here is putting you people in a precarious situation."

"You didn't put us in this situation. We put ourselves in it when we took you in. We'll just have to put our heads together and figure out a good hiding place for you. But let's talk about it after dinner." With those words Aunt Sally disappeared through the door, and John and Bessie left for their house.

Joshua remained on the porch. Kate didn't dare look at him. A rush of emotions had engulfed her at the notion of his leaving. If she could get up easily, she'd run away from him. Why was she so surprised he would leave? Why did the mere idea of it make her queasy?

Joshua sat down in the chair next to her, and she turned her head away. She could not look at him. Not now. *Pretend he's already gone.*

"Katherine, please look at me," his soft voice implored.

Reaching over, he stroked her cheek.

She turned to face him, fighting back the tears pooling in her eyes.

"Katherine, you understand why I must leave, don't you?"

She nodded her head slowly. Yes, she supposed she understood. But understanding didn't lessen the ache in her heart.

"If I had a choice, I wouldn't. It's not that I want to. But these days we can't always do what we want when duty calls."

Where had she heard these words before? A memory flashed through her mind of a little girl crying for her father to stay. Tears escaped and began streaming down her cheeks.

"Oh, dearest Katherine, please don't cry. I can't bear to think I've caused you pain."

He took her hands and kissed the fingertips. Reaching in his pocket he retrieved a handkerchief and tenderly blotted her tears.

Her heart was breaking in two. She wanted him to put his arms around her and hold her close, tell her he would stay forever. But it wasn't possible. Not now. Not ever. Why had she hoped for the impossible?

"Don't you realize I don't want to leave you? Please believe me."

Kate raised her gaze to study his face. Was he sincere? She felt as if she were seeing straight into his soul, and what she saw reassured her. The hint of a smile lifted the corners of his mouth. Without hesitation, she returned it. How could she be upset with this man, this dear, earnest, genuine man? She nodded.

"It appears you'll have to put up with me a while longer. Let's relish the time we have together. I know I will. Will you?"

Kate sniffed, nodding again. Regaining self-control, she wiped her face and smiled. "Would you mind helping me up?"

"My pleasure, madam." Joshua assisted her to her feet, then taking her arm and placing it within his elbow, he said, "May I escort you to dinner?"

~

As expected, Clay arrived the next day. Aunt Sally greeted him on the veranda. "Lieutenant Harris, I understand you would like to use my widow's walk."

Kate, observing the conversation from her chair, admired the woman's direct manner. Someday she hoped to be so self-assured.

Clay's eyes widened at Aunt Sally's neglect of formalities. "Er . . . yes, ma'am. I wanted to discuss the matter with you."

"Kate told me you want to use my roof for observation."

"Yes, ma'am. Your house is the farthest from town, the closest to the islands, and has the highest perch on your roof. It would make an outstanding site for surveillance."

"When would you want to use it? I like to know when to expect guests in my house."

"We'd like to come once a day for a while, then perhaps sometimes at night."

"And what time can we expect you?"

Clay's brows drew together. "I'm not certain yet. Is that important?"

Aunt Sally assumed her hands-on-hips, no-nonsense stance. "If I agree to having my home used for the military, I should be afforded the respect of knowing when someone will be here. I won't have strange men traipsing through my house at all hours of the day and night."

Taken aback, Clay sputtered, "Y-yes, ma'am. Of course. Would two in the afternoon be agreeable to you then?" He glanced over at Kate, his face reddened.

"Two it is. How long will you stay?"

"Perhaps an hour. Maybe less, if there's little to observe."

"It'll be hot up there, so an hour will be enough, I'm sure. And who will be coming? Just yourself, or others as well?"

"Normally I'll come alone. If I have to bring others, I'll let you know in advance."

"Or they can wait outside for you."

"Yes, ma'am. May I see the walk now?"

"No, sir. You'll have to wait until I clear out the attic so you can get to the hatch door. You may come back at two today, if you wish. We'll get working on it."

Clay nodded, again casting a glance toward Kate. He appeared as though he was about to speak again when Aunt Sally said, "We'll see you this afternoon then."

"Yes, ma'am."

~

277

"So at two I'll be in John and Bessie's cabin." Joshua looked at the couple.

"Soun's like a right good idea to me." John nodded.

"We don' mine he'pin' you, Mr. Joshua," Bessie said, leaning on John.

"How will I know when to come out?"

"I'se gonna start playin' a tune on dis sorry harmonica. Don't sound too good, but I'se not aimin' to please Mr. Lieutenant Harris."

"We can put up with this for the time being," Aunt Sally said. "Perhaps it won't last long."

Kate hoped not. The dread of Clay's daily presence weighed like a rock in the pit of her stomach. How strange it felt to know how things had changed. Whereas once she'd yearned for Clay's company, now she despised it. What she desired now was time with Joshua – uninterrupted time.

The plan worked for a few weeks. Clay arrived every day as the grandfather's clock in the hall chimed twice. One day he brought another soldier with him and begged Aunt Sally to let him take the man up with him. She finally consented but insisted on escorting them herself. She informed Kate later the men were sighting the location for entrenchments and breastworks that were to be built outside the town's perimeter to stave off land attacks.

Kate's ankle improved as she hobbled around on a crutch Joshua had made her from a tree branch. She couldn't move very fast or very well, but it felt good to finally be up and around.

By the end of October, Clay's visits were less frequent, so they didn't know whether to expect him from one day to the next. When he did come, he explained he was involved with moving supplies back to the mainland from St. Vincent's. The number of troops in the area had vastly increased, making it seem impossible for Joshua to ever leave. Although Kate was happy with the delay, she worried about Joshua's anxiety. He had difficulty sitting for any length of time without getting up to pace the floor.

"Joshua, when the time is right, God will let you know," Aunt Sally reassured.

"I've been praying for an answer. It's hard to know when it's my will or His sometimes."

"Aye. We just have to make sure our will agrees with His."

"Yes, ma'am. I believe that's true."

Kate listened to the conversation. Did God care about what she wanted? A future with Joshua. An end to the war. Peace and freedom to live without fear of enemies. Was that God's will or hers? Her mind was a battleground between her feelings and her faith.

Approaching noise interrupted. The three froze, listening. It was only one o'clock, and Joshua was too far away to hide in John and Bessie's cabin.

"Quick! Go upstairs and hide!" Aunt Sally pointed to the doorway.

Joshua raced for the door and sprinted inside. Kate followed, turning to say, "I'll help him."

Entering the back door, she glimpsed Joshua speeding up the stairs. When he reached the top and looked down at her, she pointed to Aunt Sally's bedroom.

"The wardrobe. Hide in there!"

Voices reached her from outside.

"Clay, you're early today."

"I'm afraid that couldn't be helped. I have word about another blockade ship approaching, and I need to confirm it."

"Can't say I understand the hurry, but go ahead if you must. Next time try to come at our agreed-upon hour."

Kate didn't want to face Clay, so she withdrew into the parlor. After she heard him go upstairs, she waited, straining to hear his return. Holding her breath, she prayed for Joshua's safety. Footsteps overheard alerted her.

Expecting them to come down the stairs, she fretted when they didn't. Who was walking around up there? Was it Joshua or Clay? And why?

Slipping quietly out of the parlor, she made her way to the stairwell and peered upward. There. She heard it again. Someone was moving about. Creeping up the stairs, Kate watched the landing for a glimpse of someone. When no one appeared, she continued up the stairs. Just as she reached the top, Clay came slinking out of her bedroom. She gaped at his intrusion. When he saw her, a twisted smile stole across his face.

"Why, hello, Kate." He sauntered toward her.

Her heart racing, she said, "What are you doing? Why were you in my bedroom?"

Clay's smirk distorted the handsome face into something sinister and unwelcome. He continued coming forward, forcing her to back up in the direction of Aunt Sally's room.

"Why, looking for you, of course. So did you come up here looking for me? What a coincidence."

"I . . . I don't know what you mean, Clay. You shouldn't take such liberties in Aunt Sally's house."

His advance forced her into the doorway of Aunt Sally's room. Joshua. He was hiding in the wardrobe. She wanted to steer Clay away, but he persisted in pressing forward, backing her into the room.

"Take liberties? Kate, what happened to us? Don't you remember what a romantic evening we had at the ball? Remember how closely we danced? Surely you enjoyed it. I did. We can still be close like we were. You know, I don't have the advantage of having my wife accompany me to camp like many of the men have. I miss you, Kate. Surely you miss me too."

Kate bumped into end of the bed, staring in disbelief at this stranger in front of her. Did Joshua hear what he was saying? Instead of the romantic evening Clay described, she saw him standing on the dock embracing the Marquesa. Anger began to overtake her fear.

"Clay Harris, you're a scoundrel. Whatever I found attractive in you before was just pretense. You are not an honorable man!"

Clay's smirk widened into a grin. "Is that so? Well, maybe you're right. Maybe I'm not so honorable."

By now Kate was pressing against the footboard trying to keep her balance as Clay leaned toward her. *Oh, God, help me!*

Behind Clay Kate saw the door to the wardrobe slowly open. Joshua had heard everything, and he was about to make his presence known.

Chapter Thirty-Three

Noise from the stairwell caught her attention. A discordant tune being played on a bullet-dented harmonica grew louder. Clay jerked his head toward the sound. Through the doorway Kate watched as John appeared at the top of the stairs, then turned in the direction of Aunt Sally's room. When he reached the doorway, he lowered the harmonica.

"Dere you is, Lieutenant Harris. We been lookin' fo' you. One o' yo' men is downstairs askin' fo' you."

The door to the wardrobe closed quietly behind him as Clay straightened up, tugging down on his jacket, his face radiating heat as he assumed his dignified persona. Leering at Kate, he turned on his heel and strode out of the room.

Kate ran to John and threw her arms around him. "Oh, John, I'm so happy to see you!"

John grinned and patted her on the back. "I'se glad to see you too, Miss Kate. Dat Mr. Lieutenant Clay, was he troublin' you?"

"I don't know what came over him. His behavior was so . . . appalling!"

Joshua stepped out of the wardrobe. "John, you arrived just in time. I was ready to give Lieutenant Harris a lesson in manners."

"He sho do needs it. Glad you didn't have to give yo'self away to teach him, tho'."

Kate and Joshua locked gazes.

John looked from one to the other, smiling. "I thinks I best get back downstairs and check on Bessie. She was mighty worried 'bout what was goin' on up here."

As John descended the stairs, Joshua reached his arms out to Kate and she fell into them. They stood in a silent embrace for a few moments before either one spoke.

Finally Joshua whispered, "Katherine, I'm so sorry you had to endure that ordeal. I wanted to defend your honor."

"I knew you would rescue me."

"Well, now I know one of the reasons you distrust men. You've had a bad experience with an untrustworthy one. I hope you know not all men are like him."

"I know you're not," Kate said softly, her head against his chest.

Joshua lifted her chin, his eyes searching hers. Then he kissed her. Once again they were in the lighthouse, a world apart from everyone else. Too soon the kiss ended, and Joshua stepped back.

"We should go downstairs and join the others."

Kate nodded. She wanted the kiss to continue forever but knew it was inappropriate between an unmarried, un-betrothed couple. She didn't even know for certain how Joshua felt about her. She knew how she felt about him, though, because she had never experienced such feelings for any other man. She loved him. The sheer thought gripped her heart so tightly she feared it might burst. Did he love her too? If his kiss signified his feelings, surely he did. But would she ever know? Would he ever declare his love for her? Or would he just leave?

When they joined the rest of the household, John had informed Aunt Sally of Lieutenant Harris's ill behavior. The woman had fire in her eyes at the news.

"That man will never step foot in this house again!"

Aunt Sally's head jerked as she spoke. "I don't care what he reports to his superiors. I'll have something to say to them too."

"Do you think he'll return?" Kate feared another encounter.

Joshua ran his fingers through his hair. "I doubt he'll risk further embarrassment." He turned to Aunt Sally and grinned. "Especially if you confront him in front of his men, which I don't doubt you would."

John laughed. "Miz Sally gonna scare 'em all off!"

They laughed, and Kate welcomed the levity that allowed her to relax. She sure hoped John was right.

~

By November all the troops on St. Vincent Island had been removed. In addition, after five Confederate schooners were captured either leaving or returning to Apalachicola, Florida's governor ordered that no more shipments should be attempted past the blockade. The result was a scarcity of goods available in the town mercantiles.

Kate heard the news at both church and on her trips to town with Aunt Sally. On one of these trips, Kate was greeted by a somber Cora. "Kate, everything here is just dreadful. We can't get many of the items people need anymore. Except for the few boats that manage to come downriver and an occasional blockade-runner, we seldom get any new supplies. The last ship only had coffee and cigars."

Kate was astounded at the worried lines on Cora's brow. The light had gone out of her usually bright and cheerful face. Were things that bad? Despite her dislike of Cora's brother, she still liked the girl. She doubted Cora really knew what a scoundrel Clay was.

"I'm sorry, Cora. I didn't realize things had gotten so bad."

Cora glanced around. Grabbing Kate by the arm, she

pulled her over to a corner of the store away from the other two customers. Aunt Sally stood at the counter speaking to Mr. Mitchell.

"Kate, we're thinking about leaving," she whispered.

"Leaving? Where would you go?" Kate had heard many of the townspeople had moved farther inland to get away from the coast.

Cora lowered her gaze and pretended to examine a piece of fabric on display. "North. Papa has property in New England, and we have relatives there. With the way things are here, we can hardly make a living, much less feed the family. We're planning to go out to one of the blockade ships and ask them to take us."

Kate's mouth fell open. "Oh, my! Aren't you afraid to do that? What if you get caught?"

"Papa thinks it'd be more dangerous for us to remain here. He knows some men who can get us safely out of the harbor. They've helped others already."

"Oh." She hated to bring up his name but had to ask. "But what about Clay?"

Cora's eyes grew moist. "That's the hardest part. Clay knows where Papa's sympathies lie – with his business and his family -- yet he made his decision to join the Confederate Army despite Papa's loyalties. Looks like we'll be going in two different directions."

Her last remark caught Kate by surprise. "Is Clay going somewhere?"

"Haven't you heard? His company has been ordered to leave. Seems the Confederate Army needs them in Tennessee. There won't be many soldiers left here."

"Will Jacob be leaving too then?"

Cora's gaze shifted from side to side. "His family has connections in the north too. He might be leaving with us."

Kate covered her mouth with her hand. A sense of relief over Clay's leaving fought with the shock of Cora's and Jacob's.

"When will the soldiers leave here?"

"Next week. After that, we'll leave too." Cora grasped Kate's hands. "I'll miss you, Kate. I know we haven't spent much time together, but I really like you and hoped we could become better friends."

Kate felt her own eyes growing moist. Despite her previous anger with the girl, Cora was her only friend in town. "I'll miss you too, Cora. Will you be able to write?"

"I'll try. I promise. I hope things go well for you here if you stay."

Where would she go? Aunt Sally hadn't mentioned the possibility of their leaving. Kate and Cora hugged as they said goodbye, knowing it might be the last time they'd see each other.

A sense of dread loomed over Kate and Aunt Sally as they walked home, discussing the changes in town and the departure of the military.

"Aunt Sally, have you considered leaving?"

"No, I haven't. I never planned to leave here. Figured I'd die here."

Die? Kate shuddered at the thought. "But what will we do for supplies if everyone in town leaves?"

"That could pose a problem. I'm not sure where we'd go. I'm not even sure if I still have any relatives alive up in Connecticut where my sister lived before she passed away."

"We have food we canned. Surely it will last us a long time."

"Yes, it will. And if this war ends soon, we have nothing to worry about."

"But I heard that the governor wanted everyone to leave the coast."

"Well, the governor will have to come get me then. I'm not leaving until I'm good and ready."

A smile came to Kate's face as she envisioned the governor coming to the house, begging Aunt Sally to leave.

"I almost forgot!" Aunt Sally retrieved an envelope from her pocket. "Mr. Harris told me this came for you last week. You and Cora were engaged in conversation, so I just tucked it in my pocket to give you later."

Kate eagerly accepted the letter, noting her father's handwriting and the postmark from Alabama. Her hands shook with excitement as she peeled off the seal and pulled out the letter, unable to wait until they reached home. She read aloud.

Dearest Katie Rose,

I pray your birthday was a happy one, even though I was unable to attend. Thank you for your brilliant message. I see you've familiarized yourself with Uncle Duncan's lantern. I'm very proud of you.

The shipping business is more precarious these days, but I am still able to work in other countries and make occasional visits to Mobile. Do not worry about me – I will stay away from dangerous situations.

I trust John is taking care of you and Aunt Sally. I hope and pray the circumstances in Apalachicola are still safe for you all.

Until we see each other again.

All my love,

Father.

Kate blotted the tears on her face when she finished reading. He really had received the message. Thank God, he was still safe.

"Oh, what wonderful news!" Aunt Sally squeezed Kate's arm. "You see, your efforts to protect him were not in vain. And what you did took a lot of courage."

Startled by the comment Kate glanced at Aunt Sally. "I didn't do anything, Aunt Sally. I couldn't have done it without Joshua's help. He's the brave one."

"Oh, I'm not saying he isn't, but it was your idea and your courage in the first place that made it possible. Don't you know that?"

"Well, I never thought of it that way. It was just a something I knew I had to do. I don't even know where the idea came from."

Aunt Sally smiled and pointed up. "I think I know. God gave you the idea, and you followed through with it."

"He gave me the courage too, Aunt Sally."

"Kate, you're a stronger person than you were when you first came here. Stronger physically and stronger in your character. You used to think only of yourself, but you've become a very caring and considerate person, looking out for others."

"I don't feel any stronger, Aunt Sally. I still needed someone else to help me. In fact, I couldn't have sent the signal to Father without help."

"And God gave you Joshua, someone you could trust, and the perfect person to help."

So was that why Joshua came into her life? To help her signal her father? If that were true, then why did she have to fall in love with him?

When Kate and Aunt Sally returned home, they informed the rest of the household about the news in town. John and Bessie shook their heads in unison. "We knowed some folks done gone over to de Union boats," John said.

Kate decided it was all right to tell them about Cora's family. As expected, the others were also shocked by the news.

"Who would've guessed it?" Aunt Sally said. "Especially with Clay on the Confederate side."

"When dey be leavin'?" Bessie asked.

"Next week, after the military is gone."

Joshua stood by, silently observing the conversation. Kate watched him, trying to read his reaction to the news. What was he thinking? Did hearing about Cora's plans give him a way to leave as well? He gazed at Kate with a somber smile on his face.

"Joshua, you're awfully quiet. What do you make of all

the news?" Aunt Sally asked, cocking her head as she awaited his answer.

"I think I want to go up to the widow's walk and take a look for myself. Kate, would you like to come with me?"

Surprised, but eager to talk with him, she leapt to her feet. He took her hand as they went inside and made their way up to the walk. The brisk November air swept across the rooftop as they stood together, viewing the panorama before them. Although Joshua had grabbed the telescope from the attic on the way out, it was evident to the naked eye how different everything looked.

There were fewer tents in the camp outside of town, a sign some of the troops had already departed. The islands were empty, void of people and activity. The lighthouse stood alone and deserted. Out in the Gulf two Union ships sat, one outside of the East Pass and the other just beyond the West Pass, near the lighthouse.

"Kate, it's time for me to go. I think you know that, don't you?"

Kate nodded, struggling to hold back the tears. She had known this day would come and had tried to prepare herself for it. However, she couldn't prevent her heart from sinking to her feet.

He pulled her into his arms. "Kate, I love you. With my whole heart. It pains me to leave you. I hope you love me too."

The tears released. "Yes. I love you too, Joshua," she whispered.

With his thumb, he brushed the tears from her eyes. "Kate, let me look at those lovely green eyes."

She sniffed and smiled up at him, feeling the love in his touch.

He reached into his pocket and pulled out a small package. Handing it to her, he said, "A parting gift."

She gingerly unwrapped it. "Oh!" In her hands lay a delicately carved heart-shaped cameo, suspended on a satin ribbon. "It's beautiful! Where did . . . ? How did . . . ? You made this?" she sputtered.

Joshua chuckled. "Yes, I made it. I needed something to busy myself with while hiding out in the cabin. John showed me how to carve things out of oyster shells. I'm glad you like it."

"I love it! You are quite talented." Kate beamed at him.

"Kate, it's more than a gift. It's a token of my love for you. Every moment I worked on it, I thought of you and how I've treasured our time together. I want us to spend our lives together, as husband and wife. Someday, Kate, will you marry me?"

"Oh, yes! Yes!" She threw her arms around him.

He kissed her fervently, and this time it left no doubt in her mind about his feelings. When they parted to catch their breath, he took the cameo and tied it around her neck. Taking her hand he kissed the back of it and said, "I know I should ask your father for permission, but I couldn't wait until I met him."

"We can send him a letter. I'm sure he'll agree to the marriage."

"Let's go down and share our news with the others."

Reluctant to leave but eager to tell everyone else, she agreed, and they returned downstairs.

~

Soon after the rest of the soldiers left town, Joshua stood at the water's edge telling them goodbye. "I'll have the captain make sure your boat is returned."

The sight of her handsome fiancé in his navy uniform, which she and Aunt Sally had mended since his shipwreck, mesmerized Kate. She had never seen him in it until now. It looked good as new, and so did he. She was so proud of him, despite the pain of his leaving.

"Thank you, Joshua. We'll pray for your safe trip over and hope you'll receive a welcome reception," Aunt Sally said.

"Mr. Joshua, it be a real pleasure gettin' to know you." John extended his hand to Joshua, who shook it firmly.

"You take care of Bessie and that baby," Joshua said. "Looks like it'll be here any minute." He nodded at Bessie's round belly and leaned over to kiss her on the cheek.

Her eyes filled with tears, Bessie said, "Mr. Joshua, we gonna miss you. I wish dis here baby could get to know you."

"Maybe he will," Joshua said with a wink.

"Or *she* will!" Aunt Sally added.

Joshua walked over to Kate, who stood apart from the scene as she took it all in. He grasped her hands and pulled her to him. "Dear, dear Kate. I do love you so."

"I love you, too, Joshua." Kate squeezed the words out through a constricted chest.

"I will come back for you, I promise. I don't know when, but I will." Joshua's earnest gaze caressed her face.

Kate nodded. "I know you will. I trust you, and I trust God to take care of us both."

"Just don't go anywhere. Please don't leave here yet."

"I won't. We'll stay right here. It's too close to Bessie's time for us to go anywhere now anyway."

His passionate kiss consumed her one more time. Releasing her gently, he turned and climbed into the boat before John pushed him out. Joshua lifted his hand in a final wave goodbye before facing away and rowing the little boat out to sea.

EPILOGUE

A small group huddled together on the deck of the *Sagamore* against the chilly January wind. Kate and Joshua stood arm-in-arm before Lieutenant Drake, the captain of the Union ship.

Kate addressed the captain. "Thank you so much for taking my family onboard. The situation in town has become so desperate."

Lieutenant Drake smiled and nodded at Joshua. "Mr. Jones here has made a good case for you people. We're grateful to you for taking care of him after the shipwreck. I was in need of a good signal officer."

Kate beamed at Joshua. The captain didn't know how good a signal officer Joshua was. Joshua winked at her, sending heat racing to her cheeks.

The captain turned to Aunt Sally. "I'm sure it must be difficult to leave your home behind."

"Aye, sir, it is. I've been there fifty years. My neighbor, Mr. Richardson, plans to stay in town and look after the house for me. After this war is over, I can come back home."

"When the next supply ship arrives, we'll put you folks on it for transport to Key West. From there you'll take a ship up north, where arrangements have been made to get you to Ohio."

Ohio. Joshua had told Kate all about his large family spread out on adjacent farms. Even with his assurance that his close-knit family would welcome her, would they really like her? She hoped so. But thank God she'd have the company of Aunt Sally, John, and Bessie. Joshua had contacted his parents, who were excited to meet them, according to their letter. She'd be living on a farm after all, but the idea wasn't as unappealing as it used to be. Living at Aunt Sally's had taught her a lot about working the land, as well as working with others.

The captain cleared his throat. "Well, are we ready to start the ceremony?"

Joshua gazed through twinkling eyes at Kate in her simple ivory wedding dress, Aunt Sally's own bridal gown altered with added length to fit. Her titian curls were pulled back at the nape of her neck with an ivory satin ribbon and covered by a lace-brimmed hat. On her lace collar rested the cameo Joshua had made.

"You're the most beautiful woman in the world," he whispered in her ear.

Kate had never been happier. If only Father could see her get married. Had he received her letter? The mail was so unpredictable now. She exhaled a deep sigh.

Joshua seemed to sense her longing. "I'm sorry your father isn't here, Kate. I'd hoped to meet him and ask him in person for your hand, rather than in a letter. Are you ready?"

She nodded and her smile returned. How could she not smile when looking at her future husband?

Joshua turned to the captain. "Yes, sir. We're ready."

"Captain!" A sailor's voice rang out from the lookout. "Sir, there's a ship approaching."

Everyone on board turned to look in the direction the sailor pointed. A schooner approached from the south.

"Can you tell whose ship it is? What flag are they flying?"

The sailor leaned out with his telescope. "Looks like a flag of truce, sir."

"I'm sorry for this interruption, but you understand this takes precedence. Hopefully the truce flag is not a ruse. Be prepared to take cover. Joshua, see to our guests' safety."

"Aye, aye, sir." Joshua saluted. He tried to pull Kate away, but she stood transfixed as she watched the schooner approach.

Could it be? Kate clasped her hands. *Oh Lord, please let it be!*

"Joshua, I believe that's Father's ship!"

Joshua called out. "Captain! Sir! We believe we know this ship."

Kate and Joshua rushed to the bow to get a better look. Soon they could see someone waving. When the ship got within earshot of the *Sagamore*, a voice was heard. "Permission to come alongside!"

The captain looked at Joshua with raised brows. "You know this ship?"

Joshua exchanged glances with Kate, whose head was bobbing up and down.

"Yes, sir. That is my fiancé's father's ship. Will you allow him to come aboard for his daughter's wedding, sir?"

A look of surprise crossed the captain's face then a broad smile emerged. "Well, certainly! We must have the father to give away the bride."

Kate could hardly wait until the ship was next to them, jumping up and down while waving at her father. She watched with breath held as his dinghy was lowered and he climbed in, then approached the Navy ship. When he clambered onboard, she leapt into his arms, almost knocking him off his feet.

"Oh, Father! I'm so happy to see you! I've missed you terribly."

"I've missed you too, Katie Rose. My, what a beautiful young woman you've become in a year."

He turned to Joshua and asked, "Is this the young man who will be my son-in-law?"

Kate replied, "Oh, yes, Father. This is Joshua Jones. Joshua, this is my father, Captain Andrew McFarlane."

The men shook hands as Joshua said, "Captain McFarlane, sir, I'm very pleased to make your acquaintance. Do I have your permission to marry your daughter?"

"Absolutely! When I received Katie's letter, I was thrilled to know she'd found her true love. And from what she wrote about you, I'm pleased to have you for a son-in-law."

Captain McFarlane's attention shifted to the group behind the couple. "Aunt Sally, you're looking well. Thank you for taking care of my daughter." He enveloped the little woman in a hug.

"Andrew, she took care of me. Kate feels like my daughter now."

Captain McFarlane smiled and turned to John. "John. So good to see you again. And looking so healthy and happy. I believe I've met this lovely lady beside you."

"Cap'n, dis here's my wife, Bessie. And dis be our baby girl, Sally Rose. Ain't she purty?"

Bessie peeled back a corner of the blanket covering the bundle in her arms. A tiny caramel-colored face stretched into a wide yawn.

"She's beautiful. Congratulations to you both."

Behind them the ship captain spoke. "Excuse me, but can we proceed with the ceremony?"

"Yes, sir!" answered a symphony of voices.

Captain McFarlane took his daughter by the arm and faced the captain with Joshua on the other side. Her father then kissed her before handing her over to Joshua.

"Do you, Joshua Jones, take Katherine Mary McFarlane

to be your wife?"

"I do."

"Do you, Katherine Mary McFarlane, take Joshua Jones to be your husband?"

"I do."

"Is there a ring?"

Aunt Sally, clothed in her best church dress, started to give Joshua the ring off her finger, but Kate's father stepped in and retrieved a pearl ring from his pocket to hand over instead. "Saw this in the islands and thought it would make a lovely wedding ring."

A look of profound gratitude crossed Joshua's face as the men exchanged smiles.

Joshua placed the ring on Kate's finger, and the captain pronounced them husband and wife. As Joshua kissed his bride, a cheer went up from the crowd of sailors witnessing the ceremony.

The couple then turned to the wedding party and hugged each one. A little cry came from the bundle in Bessie's arms.

Pulling back the blanket to peek into the tiny face, Bessie said, "Sally Rose want to 'gratulate you too!"

Kate and Joshua each kissed the infant, who emitted a "coo" in return.

Laughing, Joshua put his arm around Kate and faced the others. "So how do you folks think you'll like living in Ohio?"

Kate smiled. No matter where she lived, she knew she could trust God to take care of her.

The End

Don't miss Revealing Light or Redeeming Light

About the Author

Marilyn Turk loves learning about history, especially that of the coastal United States and lighthouses in general. She is the author of A Gilded Curse, a romantic historical suspense novel set in 1942, and Shadowed by a Spy, its sequel. She has also published Lighthouse Devotions – 52 Inspiring Lighthouse Stories, based on her popular lighthouse blog: http://pathwayheart.com.

A graduate of LSU's School of Journalism, Marilyn's work has also appeared in a number of other publications including Guideposts Magazine and Guideposts Books including Daily Guideposts.

Marilyn and her husband live in Florida where they enjoy boating, fishing, tennis and gardening when they're not climbing lighthouses are playing with their grandsons.

Acknowledgements

There's no way a historical book, whether fiction or nonfiction, can be written without knowing the history of the era and place where the book is set. To discover this information requires a multitude of sources to recreate the world of the past for the reader.

To that end, the aid of historical societies is priceless. I was fortunate to work with two, the Pensacola Historical Society, and the Apalachicola Historical Society, both of whom were extremely cooperative.

However, there is one person who helped me more than any other and that is Mark Curenton, then president of the Apalachicola Historical Society. Mark was a treasure to work with, providing me not only with answers to my countless questions, but directing me to other sources and books helpful to my research. I can't express how much I appreciate Mark's time, effort, and congenial attitude to get me the information I needed about Apalachicola during the Civil War.

Others who helped me were Neil Hurley of the Florida Lighthouse Association and author of Florida's Lighthouses of the Civil War, the St. George Island Lighthouse Association, the volunteer who gave me a personal historical tour of the Pensacola Lighthouse, Evelyn Ogilvie of Trinity Episcopal Church in Apalachicola, and Mike Kinnett, entertaining Park Ranger at the Orman House.

I want to thank the late William Roberts, author of Lighthouses and Living Along the Florida Gulf Coast, whose family were lighthouse keepers at both the Cape St. George Lighthouse and the Pensacola Lighthouse.

Thanks to all my readers who took the time to read my story and offer suggestions.

And finally, I'd like to thank God for nudging me along and helping me find the information I needed to connect the dots in the story which He wanted me to tell.

Discussion Questions for Rebel light

1. The only men Kate trusts are her father and John. After Clay betrays her, she'd determined not to trust any more. Have you ever experienced betrayal or an event which made you afraid to trust others again?

2. Speaking of trust, sometimes Kate is afraid to tell Aunt Sally the truth. Why do you think that's the case?

3. Kate sees John as a surrogate father, since he's always been there for her. Do you have someone outside your family that has been like a parent to you?

4. Who was your favorite character in the story? Why?

5. Who did you relate to in the story and why?

6. Do you think Kate should have gone to Alabama like she was supposed to?

7. Kate didn't want to like Joshua because he was the enemy. Do you sometimes have mistaken impressions about people like she did?

8. What event in the story surprised you?

9. If you could change something in the story, what would it be?

10. Did you find the characters in the story believable?

11. Everyone is the household finds comfort in their daily Bible reading. Why do you think that is?

12. Did you learn something about Civil War history that you didn't know before?

Revealing Light

Sally Rose McFarlane follows her dream of being a teacher when she accepts a position as governess in post-Reconstruction, Florida. A misunderstanding of her previous experience in Ohio forces her to keep a secret to retain her job. When she learns about the recent Jim Crow laws, she realizes she also has to hide her bi-racial ancestry.

When Bryce Hernandez, former Pinkerton agent, becomes a law partner to Sally Rose's employer, he and Sally Rose become involved with each other to stop a smuggling operation involving their employer's dishonest business partner.

What will happen when the family Sally Rose works for learns the truth of her work experience and her parents? How will Bryce react when he finds out? And will anyone find her when she's captured by smugglers, or will it be too late?

Redeeming Light

Cora Miller, a recent widow, moves to St. Augustine in 1875 with her young daughter Emily to start life over as a single mother. She opens a fine millinery shop to court the tastes of the wealthy and become part of the town's social elite. She succeeds in gaining the hat business of tourists Pamela Worthington and her daughter Judith, as well as, the attention of their family friend, extravagant Sterling Cunningham. But aloof Daniel Worthington, Pamela's son, is more interested in the Indian captives recently brought to the fort.

Daniel Worthington has escorted his mother and sister to St. Augustine. Their trip has coincided with the arrival of Plains Indians being brought to Fort Marion as prisoners. He is sympathetic to the plight of the Indians and seeks to help them learn to communicate through art. Daniel believes Cora Miller is only concerned with unimportant frivolities, but when he sees her with a benevolence group at the fort, his opinion begins to change.

Just when Cora's business is picking up, jewelry from her wealthy customers begins to disappear and then mysteriously reappear in Cora's shop. What will happen to her when she is accused of theft? Will her reputation and future be ruined? Or will someone else step up in her defense?